CW01082285

When young sailor Feli
his estranged uncle beg;
Blackrabbit Island for the first time in ten years. There he
discovers his uncle missing and his aunt positioning herself
as the new head of the notorious Diamond family. With
nowhere else to turn, Felix must enlist the help of former
crime lord and current Watch Commander, Vince
Knight—a man he trusts less than anyone alive. He'll also
have to contend with his opium-addicted cousin and a
handsome apprentice horologist with secrets of his own.

With time running out, Felix must race to uncover the
truth behind his uncle's disappearance while keeping his
delinquent family's claws off his childhood home—the run-
down playhouse named The Star We Sail By.

For Colin

THE STAR WE SAIL BY

THE KNIGHTS OF BLACKRABBIT,

BOOK TWO

GLENN QUIGLEY

Thank you. Glenn Quigley

A NineStar Press Publication

www.ninestarpress.com

The Star We Sail By

First Edition, February 2024

ISBN: 978-1-64890-741-8

Also available in eBook, ISBN: 978-1-64890-742-5

CONTENT WARNING:
This book contains sexual content, which may only be suitable for mature readers. Depictions of graphic violence, murder, death of secondary characters, mention of past trauma, kidnapping, and murder.

For my husband, Mark.

Author's Note

Though this story begins in December 1781, this is not the world as it was, but rather the world as it might have been. An event named The Illumination coincided with the fall of the Roman Empire and ultimately led to the abandonment of religious practices across the world. Then, in England in the year 1141, Queen Matilda passed a law declaring women equal to men, with no restrictions placed on their education or the roles they could hold within society. These events led to those who experienced life outside of the traditional to blossom and become accepted as simply another part of life. Prejudice based on gender, race, or sexuality became almost unheard of.

In These Young Wolves: The Knights of Blackrabbit, Book One, we saw Vince Knight take his first uncertain steps as Watch Commander for the rough-and-tumble harbour town of Port Knot and, by extension, the whole of Blackrabbit Island. Now, a month later, he's settling into his new role in life, but the misdeeds of his past continue to haunt him.

This is a world of sailing ships and clockwork marvels. A world of second chances and new beginnings. A world where a former crime lord can become a force for good.

Or try to, at least.

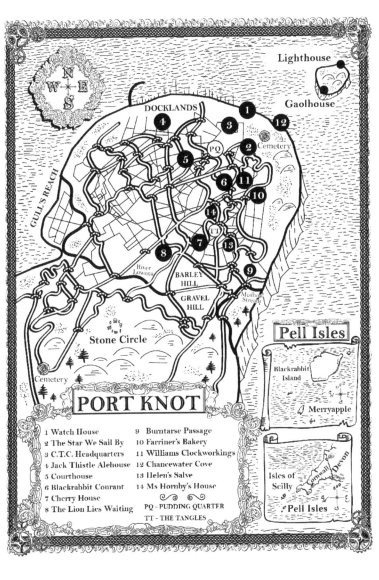

Lighthouse

Gaolhouse

DOCKLANDS

Cemetery

PQ

GULL'S REACH

River Lowena

BARLEY HILL

GRAVEL HILL

Medham Stream

Stone Circle

Cemetery

PORT KNOT

1 Watch House
2 The Star We Sail By
3 C.T.C. Headquarters
4 Jack Thistle Alehouse
5 Courthouse
6 Blackrabbit Courant
7 Cherry House
8 The Lion Lies Waiting

9 Burntarse Passage
10 Farriner's Bakery
11 Williams Clockworkings
12 Chancewater Cove
13 Helen's Salve
14 Ms Hornby's House

PQ – PUDDING QUARTER
TT – THE TANGLES

Pell Isles

Blackrabbit Island

Merryapple

Isles of Scilly

Cornwall

Devon

Pell Isles

CHAPTER ONE

"*IT IS THE waves which break—not I.*" Felix Diamond repeated this refrain to himself over and over again as he picked his way through the hustle and bustle of the Port Knot docklands. His personal maxim acted as a lifeline, leading him through any given storm and safely back to shore.

The ship on which he served had arrived at dawn to an already cluttered harbour. Without a word to his crew-mates, Felix had stepped off and made straight for town. On that early December morning in 1781, the air was soft and wet, and the light thin. With his breath clouding about him, he pushed through the market, ignoring the stench of fish guts. Bundles of fresh flowers hung next to rows of empty birdcages. Furs from several kinds of animals sat in high piles on salt-rotten tables. Books and pamphlets on all manner of topics—from rumours about revolution in France to condemnations of the town's new street lamps—cluttered several stalls. Cranes creaked as they unloaded goods from all four corners of the world. At the roofless court house nearby, hammers struck nails and men shouted obscenities and instructions in equal measure.

Felix had not long turned twenty-four and had the pinkish skin of a man who worked at sea in all weathers. He wore a short beard the colour of strong coffee, and a single curl dropped from beneath his woollen cap, coming to rest on his brow. The small gap between his front teeth whistled as he shouted away a mangy dog sniffing about his legs.

On the corner of Bibbler's Brook, a man in a white frock coat embellished with seafoam-green oak leaves stood under a five-sided street lamp, working a long, knobbly, metal pole into its head. The light within the lamp dimmed first, then disappeared entirely. Two more dogs chased one other along the narrow, cobbled road and ran straight past the lamplighter. He jumped away and shouted at the young boys who, hooting and chattering, chased at full pelt after the dogs. Farther along, someone flapped a sheet out of a high window to give it an airing while a woman with a bony horse and slender cart collected odds and sods she found on the road.

The Star We Sail By stood on a bend in Bibbler's Brook, not far from the harbour, on the north-eastern side of town. Its slim front doors nestled neatly between two jutting bay windows. Felix lingered at the locked front doors and tilted his head. Above the entrance, the prow of a sailing boat jutted out as a balcony for the first floor. Its masthead, called Atlas by the townsfolk, had seen better days. Shaped like a rotund and entirely naked gentleman whose modesty was halfheartedly covered with only a single, sheer ribbon, its paintwork curled like pages from an old book. Atlas held a murky stained glass star in its outstretched hands as if catching it or perhaps offering it to the weary traveller who stopped by.

Felix hesitated before taking two keys from his pocket. He found the first too small for the lock. The second fitted snugly. He turned it. Several bolts clicked and clanked. He readied himself and pushed the doors open. Inside, cracks of light pierced the rickety shutters. A shiny beetle scurried across the dusty bar. The tables held sticky pools of dried beer and gin. Tankards and glasses lay on their sides, some smashed on the wooden floor. Ashes sat undisturbed in the fireplace, and at the rear of the room, a little stage with tatty purple curtains stood primed but empty, like a broken promise.

"About time you opened." A scruffy, unshaven man with a grog blossom nose had slipped in through the door unnoticed. He threw open the rest of the shutters in the windows, flooding the room with light, then coughed at the cloud of dust they released.

"I'm not open," Felix said. "Please get out."

"I've been here every morning for days. Days, I tell you!" the man said. "I've been practically homeless without this place."

"I said get out." His duffel bag slumped to the floor, and he readied himself to kick the man out if he had to. He hoped the man wouldn't notice his rapid breathing.

"Don't get all worked up," the man said. He held his hands up and sat on a stool by the bar. "I don't mean any harm. It's nice to be home again." He squinted at the sailor. "You're the nephew, aren't you? The one that ran away? The seaman. Fenton?"

"Felix." He relaxed his hands and opened the other shutters. Clearly, this man wasn't going anywhere.

"I'm Tassiter, since you didn't ask," the man said. "Dick Tassiter." He had beady eyes and straggly hair, and a face like a crumpled shirt abandoned at the bottom of the wardrobe. He eyed the bottles of gin lining a shelf behind the bar. "I'm your uncle's best customer. Or I was."

Felix peeked around a corner to the stairs. "He hasn't been open for a while?"

"It's been three days since those doors last opened. Three long, dry, thirsty days," Tassiter said. "I thought I was cursed to wander the world forevermore without a drop to drink." He pointed to one of the bottles. "Do you mind if I...?"

"Help yourself," Felix said. He climbed the stairs.

The ground floor of the Star We Sail By held the bar and stage, the next floor had little round tables and a handful of booths with their own privacy curtains. Felix opened the glass doors to the sailboat balcony and stepped out to the briny air. A gull landed on the gunwale of the sailboat for a moment before Felix shooed it away. He leaned on the balcony and surveyed Bibbler's Brook. The little road had changed quite a lot since he'd last been there. Tall, thin buildings, likely home to dozens of people, had replaced the little cottages which used to stand across from the Star. The road also now held a handful of street lamps, and one of the Entries—the network of crisscrossing alleyways which acted like arteries for the town—now held a clamorous and well-stocked cooperage.

He finished his little tour of the Star in his old bedroom on the third and topmost floor. The furniture was different, the smell was different, but the room's only window still overlooked a small graveyard and beyond it—across a short stretch of water—the little island which was home to the gaolhouse and lighthouse. He'd grown up in that room though he could tell from the wear and tear it hadn't stood fallow in his absence. He trod on a loose floorboard by the bed. It squeaked. Some things would never change.

He stepped into his uncle's room, finding the bed unmade and some clothes strewn about. Nothing unusual about it at all. His uncle had never been what one might call houseproud.

Muffled voices from downstairs caught his ear and he arrived back at the bar to find out who had been keeping

Dick Tassiter company. A pair of arms circled Felix's waist from behind, and he staggered forward with a shout.

"Don't move a muscle."

He broke free of the grip and spun on his heels to find a laughing woman his own age, maybe a few years older. She had short, blonde hair, shadowy eyes, and wore a military jacket from the Chase Trading Company, but dyed black instead of the traditional emerald green. In his shock, it took him a moment to recognise who she was and who she had been when he last lived here.

She slunk off and slouched onto the bench that ran across the longest wall. She produced from her jacket pocket a thin pipe. She tipped some tobacco in and flicked open a clockwork striker. Sparks leapt from it, igniting the tobacco. She snapped the striker closed and drew on the end of the pipe. Smoke curled from her nose. "Cousin Felix," she said. "Or are you still going by Lucky?"

"I never did. You're the only one who called me that. Well, you and Tenner."

"He won't be happy to see you back. How long has it been since you've been home? Five years?"

"Ten," he said. "Give or take." He sat facing her. He realised he was clenching his fists. "You've changed since

I've been away."

She laughed and dragged on her pipe again. "We're supposed to change," she said. "That's sort of the whole point, isn't it? Though I prefer to think of it as outgrowing my old sex, as a blossom does a bud."

"I take it I can't use your old name so what do I call you now?"

"Dahlia," she said, her voice husky but melodic, rusted from too much tobacco and whiskey. "What brings you back our way?"

"Uncle Gregory wrote to me, asking me to come home."

Dahlia frowned, just for a moment. "When?"

"A couple of days ago."

Her eyes blazed. " *When?*"

Felix clenched his fists harder. "I received a letter from him on the thirtieth. I came back as soon as I could."

Dahlia studied Felix's face intently. He had the distinct impression she was checking to see if he was lying.

"Where is Uncle Gregory?" Felix asked.

Dahlia inhaled her pipe again. "Rather a good question," she said, leaning back. "It seems you received your letter just before dear old Uncle Gregory disappeared."

CHAPTER TWO

FELIX NOTICED DICK Tassiter was already halfway through polishing off a bottle of cheap gin. A short stack of coins rested on the bar by his elbow.

"Who let you in?" Dahlia swiped the bottle from his hand and swigged from it.

Dick Tassiter held his little glass up. "Your cousin was kind enough to grant me access. Which is more than you've ever done for me."

"I told you before, Mr Tassiter, we're closed," Felix said. "Permanently."

Mr Tassiter's face dropped. "No, no, no, don't say

that. The Star can't close; it's a second home to me."

"It's a first home to you from what I can see," Dahlia said.

Felix whistled in air through the gap between his front teeth. "You'll have to go and drink somewhere else, I'm afraid."

"He can't," Dahlia said. "Nowhere else will have him."

The doors to the Star banged open and a cocksure young man swaggered in, unshaven and affecting an aggressive demeanour. He swung his shoulders and held his hands away from his sinewy body as though trying to take up as much room as possible.

"Tenner," Felix said.

"Lucky." Tenderling Diamond—known as Tenner by the family—led an assortment of boorish men and women into the bar. They spread out, checking around corners before nodding to Tenner.

Last of all came a woman, older than the rest. "Felix!" she said. "Well, at long last."

"Aunt Alma," Felix said. "And the whole Diamond clan. What a surprise."

"Whole? Oh, no, not even half." Aunt Alma

narrowed her eyes.

Cruel as a shark's, Felix thought. But no, not a shark; on his travels he had once seen a crumbling statue of a vicious Roman emperor which had eyes like hers, sculpted from pitiless, cold marble. Much like her brother Gregory, she had cheekbones sharp enough to cut glass. Her eyebrows arched like arrowheads, and she sat as though attending dinner at a palace. She wore fuchsia, as she had always done when Felix was a boy. Fuchsia ruffles hung on fuchsia sleeves, and fuchsia velvet hugged her fuchsia waist. She'd gathered her dark hair at the back of her head without much thought to appearance. Goosebumps gathered on Felix's flesh as she bade him to sit. "Tenner, bring some chairs over."

The cocksure Tenner did as he was told, and soon Felix found himself encircling a table with the family he hadn't spoken to for a decade. Tenner didn't join them and instead hurried upstairs and out of sight.

"Clarity, Slate." He nodded in turn to each of the cousins who now flanked him. "Are you here to stop me running?" He meant it as a joke but Slate set his hand on Felix's shoulder and pressed down. The angled looking glass on the longest wall revealed some other cousins standing at the bar, keeping a close eye on Dick Tassiter.

"It's so good to have you back home," Aunt Alma said. "Back where you belong."

Felix squinted at her. "Uncle Gregory always had a strict policy against Diamond family gatherings on his premises. Usually because of all the drinking, and the gambling, and the fighting..."

Aunt Alma laughed without warmth. "Gregory is no longer here."

Felix scanned around the filthy room. "And yet you didn't seize the opportunity to take over running the Star. The door was locked up tight when I arrived."

"We've been too busy to bother with all that," Aunt Alma said. "Ever since the Watch did away with all the gangs, there's been something of a vacuum just begging to be filled."

"The Watch?"

"You've been gone too long," Dahlia said. "You missed quite a bit."

"Uncle Gregory always had a soft spot for you," Felix said to Dahlia, "why haven't you kept the bar open for him, at least?"

"I am not a taverner." She hopped up onto the bar. "I

am a performer. My place is on the stage." She pointed a cracked nail to the rear of the room. She took another drink from the bottle and winced. "This'll make you go blind."

Dick Tassiter waved his hand in front of his own face. "So far, so good."

"What happened to Uncle Gregory?" Felix asked. "Where did he go?"

Dahlia shrugged. "No one knows. He just vanished," she said with a click of her fingers.

"And you didn't think to look for him?"

"Of course I looked," she said. "But he never went anywhere else, not really. This place was his whole life. I asked the regulars; no one knew anything."

"What about the rest of you?" Felix asked.

The Diamonds looked to one another. Clarity crossed her arms. Slate shrugged. One man spat on the floor.

"I told you," Aunt Alma said, "we've been busy."

"So that's it, then? He's just gone."

Aunt Alma smiled her cold smile and fussed with the sleeves of her floral jacket. "He's a grown man, and a Diamond. He can take care of himself. He'll show up eventually. I'm certain."

Dahlia stared at the floor and said nothing. The circle of Diamonds drew closer around Felix.

Tenner returned and stood behind Aunt Alma. He stared at Felix, desperately trying to appear threatening but looking more like someone who was in dire need of the privy. "I didn't find anything in his room."

"You went through my belongings?" Felix's mouth ran dry, and his stomach twisted itself into knots. Every sound came to him louder than ever—the drip from a jug on the bar, horses hooves on the road outside—his eyes stung from the sunlight gleaming in through the bay windows.

Tenner's eyes widened and he jutted his head like a chicken at feed, begging for Felix to start a fight. At sea, Felix had known plenty of men to behave that way and been dismayed at how often it provoked a violent response.

"Gregory sent you more than just a letter," Aunt Alma said. "I want it."

"You want what, exactly?"

"Please don't play stupid." She sharpened her gaze without blinking.

"I'm not," Felix said. "Here." He emptied his pocket onto the table in front of her. "Here is the letter, here is the key to the front door. There is nothing else, I have nothing else."

Aunt Alma snatched the letter from the table and read it aloud. "*Dearest Felix, The Star We Sail By is yours. Come and find me. Gregory.*"

Dahlia leaned over Aunt Alma's shoulder to read the letter, over and over.

Felix sighed and raised his voice as much as he could without it cracking. "You. Mr Tassiter. What do you think happened?"

Dick Tassiter pouted and shrugged. "He was a good man, your uncle. I don't know anyone who'd want to do him any harm."

"That's a lie," Dahlia said with a snort. "Listen, I owe him a lot, but he was a Diamond. We make enemies like other people make hot meals."

"Anyone in particular?" Felix asked.

Dahlia's gaze darted from Felix to Aunt Alma. "Why do you think someone is responsible? Why couldn't he have just had enough and decided to walk out? Leave it all behind him?"

"Because of this," he said, pointing to the letter. "He knew something was going to happen to him and he was desperate enough to reach out to me because of it."

Dick Tassiter retrieved the gin bottle and drained the last of it into his glass. "Why don't you go to the Knights?"

"The who?" Felix asked.

"The Knights of Blackrabbit," Mr Tassiter said. "The Watch, lad, the Watch."

"How can they help? Bunch of skullkickers and decrepit old soldiers."

"You've been away for too long," Aunt Alma said. "But some things never change. Diamonds don't ask for help, certainly not from the Watch."

"You mean you haven't even spoken to them?"

"There are more Diamonds than there are Watchfolk," Dahlia said. "What can they do that we can't?"

Felix sat back and huffed. "They can actually try to find him, for one thing."

Aunt Alma leaned in so closely the tobacco on her breath stung his nose. "Don't get the Watch involved, Felix," she said. "I'm warning you. Now, run along. And leave the front door key here."

Felix's mind raced. "I don't understand. You were just

waiting for me to come and unlock the door?"

"It's called respect," Aunt Alma said.

Felix knew what she really meant. Aunt Alma was afraid of her brother, Uncle Gregory. She always had been. All the Diamonds were, to a certain extent. Uncle Gregory had been the de facto head of the Diamond family since the passing of some grandfather or other around the time Felix had been born. Uncle Gregory gave them advice when they needed it and a sound thrashing when they didn't heed it. Aunt Alma and the rest of the family hadn't broken into the Star because they knew if Gregory ever found out, he'd be livid.

"The Star is the only home I've ever known on Blackrabbit," Felix said. "Where am I supposed to go?"

Aunt Alma pushed the letter across the table. "You can read, can't you? Your uncle wants you to find him. And you don't want to let him down."

CHAPTER THREE

WATCH COMMANDER VINCE Knight sat with his feet up on his desk in his cramped, white-walled office. His bulldog, Crabmeat, lay nearby in a little bed, snoring. Vince usually kept the door to his office open but that morning he needed some peace and quiet, and a chance to shut his eyes for ten minutes. He rubbed the skin under his eyepatch, then pulled his tricorne cap low over his coarse white-bearded face, intending to doze peacefully while a little fire crackled in the hearth.

He had been up all night keeping a close eye on some newly docked sailors who were causing trouble in the Jack

Thistle tavern, farther along the waterfront. He'd been asked by the landlord to help keep them in line. A couple of minor fights had broken out, but Vince had quickly put an end to them. As soon as dawn had broken, he'd escorted the sailors back to their ship and watched them sail off.

It had been less than a month since he'd taken over as commander of the Watch. Back then, he hadn't been wholly sure what his daily duties would involve. His first act had been to expand the Watch not just in numbers but in responsibilities. No longer confined to the hours between sunset and sunrise, the Watch would now operate around the clock. Something the townsfolk had yet to approve of. As far as Vince was concerned, though, the main threat to the town had been the gangs, and since he'd resolutely crushed them, what the people needed now was an organisation ready to step in and help when asked but would otherwise leave people to get on with their day-to-day lives.

"Can we help you?" Sorcha Fontaine's muffled voice came from the other side of Vince's door.

"I, uh, I needed to talk to someone." Vince didn't recognise the other person's voice.

"Well, I'm someone," Sorcha said.

"It's about my uncle. He needs help. I think."

"And what's your name, then?" Sorcha asked.

"Felix," he said. "Felix Diamond."

Vince rushed to the door of his office and flung it open. "Diamond?" His voice boomed. "*Diamond?*" He filled the door frame with his bulk and squinted at the man.

Felix Diamond flinched and stepped back. "Is that...Vince?"

"Get in here," Vince said.

Sorcha followed them into Vince's office and gently closed the door.

Vince sat behind his desk and leaned his powerful forearms on it. He frowned, deepening the wrinkles in his forehead. "Diamond comes in here asking for help? Must be serious."

Felix's throat had apparently run dry, and he coughed a little as he sat fidgeting with the button loops of his striped shirt. He looked quickly around the room, stopping at the charcoal portrait of Captain James Godgrave hanging above Crabmeat's bed. Felix frowned, his mouth slightly agape, but he quickly recovered. He licked his own lips. "My uncle Gregory is missing."

"Landlord of the Star We Sail By?" Vince asked. "Since when?"

"A couple of days, according to my cousin. Uncle Gregory wrote to me, asked me to come home because he thought something bad was going to happen to him."

"Astute of him," Vince said. "Enemies?"

"Well," he said, adjusting his positing in the chair. "You, for one."

Vince rubbed his hand across his own scruffy, snowy white beard. "Not these days," he said. "Turned over a new leaf. On the side of law and order now."

Felix's eyebrows climbed so high Vince thought they were trying to escape his head entirely.

"Know your family," Vince said. "Everyone does. Diamonds are troublemakers. Usually only a matter of time before you lot meet a bad end."

Felix crossed his arms. "Are you saying you won't help me?"

IT IS THE *waves which break—not I*. Felix repeated his refrain over and over again. He kept stealing glances at Vince as he led both him and Sorcha Fontaine out of the Watch House. Felix couldn't believe it. Vince Knight, the king of Blackrabbit's criminal underbelly, was the Watch Commander. Vince Knight, the criminal other criminals told stories about, was going to help him to find his uncle. Felix wasn't looking forward to seeing Aunt Alma's face when he walked in with Vince. She was going to have kittens.

The Watchfolk wore a uniform, which Felix hadn't expected. In his day, they showed up for their shifts in whatever clothes they'd been wearing all day. This new Watch wore long scarlet overcoats trimmed with black, tight breeches, and dark tricornes. Felix couldn't help but notice the scowling faces of the townsfolk they passed by.

"Have you been away for long?" Sorcha asked. A woman around his own age with straight, dark hair and an Irish accent, she smiled readily and all but skipped along the road.

Felix wondered if she was the pleasant face of the organisation. "About ten years," he said. "It feels like a lifetime."

The Watch house sat at the edge of the harbour and the walk away from it, back towards town, brought them past the court house. Its tympanum held a relief of muscular, naked fishermen hauling in catch from the sea on one side and athletic, naked women doing the same on the other. The roof was nothing but an exposed ribcage of wooden beams. "What happened to that?"

"Some gang trouble a month ago," Sorcha said. "They set a few places on fire. The court house was one of the first casualties. It's all sorted now though."

Felix eyed Vince. "I bet it is. I heard the gangs had been broken up. Not hard to guess who's responsible."

Vince said nothing. He stood a head taller than Felix, at least, and had the bearing of a shire horse. He exuded an air of menace, yes, but also a faint aroma of sweet tobacco. He remembered Gregory and the family talking about Vince in hushed whispers. When they got up to no good, it wasn't the Watch or the magistrates they feared catching them—it was Vince. Felix had hoped never to meet him face to face and as they approached the Star, he began to wonder if he was doing the right thing.

Dick Tassiter still propped up the bar, having reached the end of the gin bottle. He blanched when Vince entered, tucking his head low and keeping his gaze firmly on the countertop in front of him.

Vince ran his hand across a table, touching some sticky residue. "Clean as ever."

Aunt Alma all but jumped out of her chair. She squinted at the Watchfolk. "I asked you not to get them involved, Felix. And I didn't for one second think you'd be stupid enough to bring them here."

"They said they wanted to check the place," Felix said. "And since you and the family have done nothing to find Uncle Gregory, I didn't see the harm."

Vince marched up to Aunt Alma. He was at least a head or two taller than her. "Alma," he said, his voice rolling like distant thunder. "Keeping out of trouble?"

"Of course, Commander," she said. "And may I just take this opportunity to thank you for sweeping away the gangs which had plagued this town since...well, since you first organised them, I suppose."

Years ago, Vince had taken a bunch of rival criminals and banded them together into a network of gangs which had terrorised not just the town of Port Knot, but the entire island of Blackrabbit. That he had turned on them came as no great surprise to Felix. That he had taken them to the gaolhouse and not to some shallow graves in the woods very much had.

"What's the point of this?" Dahlia asked. "Don't you think we'd have noticed any pools of blood or screams coming from the cellar?"

Vince turned to stare at her with his single, icy blue eye. The leather strap of his eyepatch cut into the heavy pale skin of his forehead.

Dahlia licked her lips and laughed. "Uncle Gregory never liked you coming in here," she said. "Trouble has a tendency to follow you about."

Vince clamped his meaty hand on Mr Tassiter's shoulder. "Had such good times here though," he said, squeezing. "Dick. Seen anything we should know about?"

Mr Tassiter spluttered into his glass. "Not a thing, Vince. Honest."

Vince leaned around to look him right in the eye. "Not much happens here that you don't see," he said. "Expect me to believe you don't know anything?"

Mr Tassiter whined, just a little. "I didn't see anything this time, I swear."

Vince waved his hand at the Diamond clan who sat tensely, ready to spring into action. Or to bolt out the door.

"Always heard Gregory didn't like family operating from his bar."

"He doesn't," Mr Tassiter said.

Aunt Alma shot him a look, and his head sank into his shoulders.

"I knew it," Felix said, his lip trembling. "Out, all of you. Now, come on, Uncle Gregory doesn't want you here and neither do I."

"This was—is—my brother's alehouse," Aunt Alma said. "If he—"

"Playhouse," Felix said quickly.

"If he is dead, then it's only right for it to pass to me. What makes you think you get to have any say in this whatsoever?"

Felix held up the letter and the key. "These," he said. "He didn't send them to you—to any of you. He sent them to me. He wanted me to look after the Star. He wanted me to help him because...because he knows you lot can't be trusted." He tried to stop his hand from shaking as Vince took the letter.

Tenner and some of the other cousins took exception to Felix's remarks and began shouting their objections.

"Would you like to have someone read it to you?"

Aunt Alma asked.

Vince ignored her. "Seems clear to me. Rightful owner passed the Star on to Felix."

Felix thought he might vomit. "And as such, I'm demanding you all leave. Now. Please."

Alma stared at him. "I could take that letter and burn it."

"You could but you'd always know what it said. And so would everyone else in here. And if it came to it, I'd testify in front of the magistrates."

"You're determined to live up to your black sheep reputation, aren't you?"

"I'd hate to disappoint you at this late stage, Auntie."

Aunt Alma held her ground until Vince lifted a glass tumbler and hurled it against a wall, bellowing at the top of his lungs as he did so. "Out! *Now!*" The tumbler shattered and the Diamonds froze, wide-eyed, until Vince roared at them again. Felix's cousins almost fell over one another as they darted out of the Star. Last to leave was Aunt Alma, who glared at Vince as she passed by.

"Don't come back," Vince said to her. "Mean it."

"This isn't Watch business," Aunt Alma said. "It's family." She stared at Felix, making his blood run a little colder.

"Landlord has evicted you," Vince said. "Landlord has enlisted help from the Watch. Watch will remove you by force if we have to."

"The widow Knight. How far you've fallen." She tutted and left, not even bothering to close the front doors behind her.

Felix hurriedly locked them again, aware he was locking himself in with Vince Knight. The heavy, elaborate bolts turned and clicked into place. "Why did she call you that?"

"Because it's true," Vince said. "Happened a long time ago. Time was she wouldn't have dared say it to my face."

Sorcha stared out the window, making sure the Diamonds had left. "It's a barb crafted to sting. To undermine."

Vince snorted. "Will take more than that. Someone mentioned a cellar?"

"It's back here." Felix pulled on a metal ring set into the floorboards behind the bar. A hatch opened. He took a striker-lantern, ignited it, and carefully climbed down the short flight of stone steps.

Vince stood at the hatch and grunted. "Never going to fit down there."

He wasn't wrong. There was no way his enormous bulk would squeeze through the opening.

"Stand back," Sorcha said. She hopped down the steps.

The cellar had a low, domed ceiling frosted with cobwebs, and contained a dozen or so empty ale barrels. A stack of crates filled one corner, next to some pewter jugs and glass bottles.

Vince lay with his head poking through the hatch. "Anything?"

"Nothing," Sorcha called up to him. "I don't...wait." She pointed to some marks on the ground. "What're these?"

Felix swallowed hard. "Nothing," he said. "Just wear and tear from moving barrels about, I expect."

Sorcha grabbed the lantern from his hand and bent down for a closer look. She followed the marks to an old bookcase filled with rusted tankards, busted bellows, and other bric-a-brac, all covered in a thick layer of dust, save for one dented cannonball, the size of an apple. She grabbed it and pushed. It didn't budge. So she pulled. The bookcase clicked and swung open. She turned to Felix and raised her eyebrow. "Well?"

"Smuggler's tunnels," Felix said with a sigh.

"Don't mention the bleddy tunnels in front of the Watch, you fool!" Dick Tassiter shouted from the bar.

"Don't care," Vince said, his head still poking down from the hatch. "Taxes are the custom house's business. Watch is here to help people, not to enforce every little rule. Leads to the harbour, does it?"

Felix shook his head. "No, not the harbour."

CHAPTER FOUR

WITH RAINDROPS BEADING on his woollen cap, Felix led Vince and Sorcha to the cemetery behind the Star We Sail By. A piece of land surrounded by a rotting wooden fence, at its core stood a single yew tree. They picked their way among the spherical gravestones. The wealthier the grave's occupant, the larger the sphere. Family members' gravestones orbited the older, moss-covered orbs of distant ancestors, like little planets around their own sun.

The cemetery stopped a few paces from the edge of a steep, chalk-white cliff and Felix pointed down to some rocks. "There's an inlet just there," he said. "No beach, no place to land but you can sail right in." He kept back, worried the incessant drizzle of the morning had made the grassy verge slippery.

Vince had no such concerns. He marched right to the edge and peered down. "Chancewater," he said. "Didn't think anyone was still using it."

Sorcha rolled her eyes. "Of course you know about it."

Felix stood behind Vince, behind the vast bulk of him, and wondered what would happen if he were to put his hands on Vince's back and shove with all his might. In normal circumstances, Felix likely wouldn't stand a chance of budging him an inch but with the wet grass and the pull of the cliff's edge...surely they would do most of the work for him? This might be his only chance to rid Port Knot of its ruin.

"Star We Sail By isn't the only place to use it," Vince said, snapping Felix from his daydream. "Used to be a few other alehouses connected to those tunnels."

"Playhouse," Felix said.

Vince ignored him. "Dangerous. Small. Been a few cave-ins, as I recall."

"Uncle Gregory used to make me meet smugglers in those tunnels." The moment had passed, and Vince had walked back a few yards. Felix had missed his chance. "He used to get salt from Brittany, before the customs house got wise to other people using the tunnels. I can't imagine he'd given up the practice entirely, though where he's been hiding the goods nowadays, I couldn't say. The cellar at the Star is crowded enough as it is."

"Will have to check the tunnels," Vince said. "Sorcha, first thing tomorrow, get some Watchfolk in there."

"You think my uncle is down there?" Felix asked. "I suppose he could have had an accident..."

"More likely he's dead," Vince said. "Meeting with a supplier turned violent. Seen more than one person meet a sticky end in there."

Felix exhaled loudly, whistling a little through the gap between his teeth. He shivered, but not from the rainfall. He found Vince's stilted manner of speech most off-putting. The way he missed the start of every sentence blunted his words so they hit like hammers.

Sorcha shot Vince a look. "Tactful as ever, aul man." She put her hand on Felix's arm. "It's only been a couple of days. We'll find him. I promise."

LIKE MOST BUILDINGS in the town, the Star We Sail By was tan-hued and half-timbered. Its double doors were sunk between two bay windows and upon entering, one found oneself in a long, high-ceilinged room, cleanly split down the middle. To the left, a long row of benches broken only by a small hearth ran the length of the wood-panelled walls beneath tilted looking glasses, grubby and wearing at the edges. To the immediate right, a clockwork lift granted access to the upper floors and next to it, the bar proper stood in front of yet another looking glass and shelves of liquor. In the middle of the room could be found table after table with chairs and stools. Finally, at the far end of the room, heavy purple curtains adorned a small stage.

"It's barely a quarter of the size it had been in the Star's heyday," Felix said of the stage.

"As the town's interest in theatre dwindled and its interest in gin rose," Mr Tassiter said, "the stage shrank, losing prominence, an aging beauty fading and shrinking against the shiny new baubles come to tempt its admirers away."

Felix trudged across the sticky floor and sat at a grimy table by an unwashed window. Above him, the chessboard pattern of the ceiling he so clearly remembered from his youth had become stained a grimy mustard colour.

"The Star may not be what she once was," Mr Tassiter said, "but there's hardly an actor in town who didn't tread her boards and cut their teeth here."

Felix had been unable to convince Dick Tassiter to leave so resigned himself to having him permanently in-stalled at the corner of the bar closest to the front doors.

"It used to be a rite of passage, you know," Mr Tassiter said. "Every young performer—youthful in experience if not in age—would go through the same rituals. Singing in front of a rowdy crowd, monologuing in front of an indif-ferent crowd, dodging rotten vegetables from a belligerent crowd."

"Going to open up again?" Vince asked. "People need alehouses. Keeps them off the streets." He flicked rainwa-ter from his tricorne and slumped onto a bench.

"Stop calling it an alehouse," Felix said. "It's not an alehouse; it's never been an alehouse. At least, it was never meant to be one." He glanced towards the stage. "This was supposed to be a theatre."

Vince snorted a laugh. "Hate to break it to you but this place has never been much more than a cherry house. Know many theatres with topless boys and girls hanging off the balcony, beckoning punters inside? Don't know what memories you have of the nights here, but I bet mine are a damn sight clearer. Want a theatre, go over on Quarrier's Run. See an opera, some Shakespeare. Want to hear a bawdy song from the tropics? See a puppet show about the council's dalliances behind closed doors? Want to watch a man try to lick himself? Come to the Star."

Sorcha threw her hands in the air and stared at him. "Tact. *Tact.*"

Felix knew the place had a reputation, of course. For every actor, there was the temptation to join the bedworkers plying their trade from the Star's notorious sailboat balcony. It was good money, better than a young actor could hope to earn, and if one was the kind to enjoy the pleasures of the flesh, why not make some extra money at the same time? It did no harm to one's reputation, and indeed, knowing about an actor's past added—in the eyes of the audience—a certain frisson to their performance. The skilled actor, upon embarking on a chaste and innocent role, would learn when to wink knowingly to a crowd well-versed in their history. Blackrabbiters found brazenness endearing. The sailboat balcony was infamous even in his day. He remembered well the sailors who docked had a rite of passage involving their partner of choice and a very intimate act performed on the balcony to the cheers of onlookers.

But he remembered the other nights. The nights when singers with voices of honey and gold sang their hearts out on stage. When actors moved him to tears with their soliloquies. That was how he chose to remember the Star We Sail By.

The Star had been a constant fixture in the life of the Diamond family since Gregory had first opened it, just shy of thirty years prior. While Gregory absolutely forbade any of the family from conducting business within its walls, he did initially allow them to drink there, provided they behaved themselves, which they seldom did. Something about being allowed in drove them giddy with excitement, and they would soon lose the run of themselves. Before long, Gregory closed the Star to Diamond trade.

That said, more than a dozen Diamond children had been sheltered there by Gregory in the years Felix had lived in the place, and he was certain there had been plenty more since. Uncle Gregory had never turned his back on a Diamond in need, and it had been a great source of comfort to the family to know that no matter how far they fell, their children would always have a home to go to. Provided they obeyed Uncle Gregory's rules.

"Anyone special in Gregory's life?" Vince asked. "Liked women, didn't he?"

"There was someone," Mr Tassiter said. "I saw them groping one another on the stairs a couple of times. Big woman. What's her name?" He frowned, and squinted, and dredged his gin-soaked memory. "Underhay," he said. "Briony Underhay. Gregory talked about her a little. I saw them together over Samhain. I teased him about proposing, and he got this funny, watery look in his eye. I didn't think he'd ever wed again. I thought they were just screwing."

"Know her. Works on the docks. Will have a word." Vince slapped his own meaty thighs as he stood up. "Last time Gregory was here? Last time anyone saw him?"

"I came by around sunset," Dick Tassiter said. "He'd already gone and locked the Star up tight. I met the barmaid on the road outside, and she said he'd rushed out in a hurry but didn't say where he was going."

"Barmaid?" Vince asked.

FELIX HURRIED ALONG the road after Vince. For a big man, Vince moved surprisingly quickly. He dodged and weaved through the crowds, and ducked down tiny alleyways Felix didn't even know existed.

"Probably weren't built when you were last here," Vince said. "Port Knot doesn't sit still."

They arrived at the address Dick Tassiter had given them, amongst a square mile packed tightly with skinny, run-down houses, no two exactly alike, but each punctured with clanging and steaming copper pipes. Washing hung from lines overhead and clockwork mangles rattled and popped as children ran wet clothes through them. Voices came from within the house—adult voices, singing and shouting, some laughing.

Vince knocked on the door. Then he thumped on it with his fist.

"Give them a chance," Felix said.

"Want to find your uncle or not?" Vince asked. "Longer he's missing, harder it'll be."

"You already think he's...gone," Felix said.

The door opened a crack, and a woman with a pleasant, plump face peered out. "Yes?"

"Hannah Hornby? Need to talk," Vince said, pushing the door open. He stopped just short of barging in.

Ms Hornby flinched and stood frozen to the spot, staring up at Vince's scowling countenance. Behind her, some men and women sat at a table playing cards. Others passed through on their way to another room.

"Work at the Star We Sail By?" Vince asked.

"I do," Ms Hornby said. "I'm a dash. A barmaid. Or I was until it closed. I don't know if it's ever going to open again, I had to take on extra lodgers just to make ends meet." She smiled and wiped her palms on the front of her skirt. Vince's comportment made her nervous.

Vince leaned in, just a touch. "Need to know what happened last time you saw Gregory Diamond."

Ms Hornby took a moment to gather her thoughts. Or her courage. "I was clearing tables, as usual, just before sunset this was. Gregory was behind the bar when all of a sudden his face dropped. He kicked everyone out—me included—and bolted the doors. I've not seen him since."

"And you actually saw him leave the Star?" Felix asked.

Ms Hornby crossed her arms. "Well, not exactly. He must have left by the back door because I hung around the front for ages, waiting to talk to him."

"Anything happen just before?" Vince asked. "Customer come in? Someone speak to him?"

"No, nothing," she said. "It was quiet, only a handful of people in."

"Know their names?" Vince asked.

"Sorry, I don't. But they were so soused they probably wouldn't have noticed anything."

Vince stared at her silently for a moment before nodding curtly and walking away.

Felix tried to keep up. "You didn't need to shove her door open like that, you know."

On a tiny, damp road, barely wide enough for two people, Vince stopped in his tracks and stared down at him. "Known people to hide weapons behind doors. Cudgels. Knives. Pistols. All sorts. Had to be careful."

"You scared her," Felix said.

Vince scowled at him. "Worth it."

CHAPTER FIVE

"THIS IS A waste of time." Iron Huxham threw his screw-driver onto his desk. It hit some loose cogwheels, knocking them to the floor. He closed his eyes and pinched the bridge of his nose. He'd been working all day and knew that when his eyes stung and he started talking to himself, it was time to take a break.

The old master cogsmith would be along presently to pick over Iron's work and point out where he'd gone wrong. Iron was approaching the end of his apprenticeship and had taken on more and more responsibility of late. Still, Mr Williams worried about his good name being tarnished and checked everything Iron made.

Mr Williams had found success late in life, when he recently invented a type of striker-lantern which had quickly became popular with sailors. Horological devices were by their very nature delicate and prone to wear, especially when used in salty sea air. Mr Williams had not only developed a method of sealing away the vulnerable workings of a striker-lantern, but by sliding a bar in the cap, his lantern would become sealed up tight to prevent being extinguished should it fall overboard or become splashed.

It had been Iron who rightly pointed out the candle could only burn so long as there was air inside, and suggested making the candle small and the casing larger than usual striker-lanterns to compensate. Mr Williams had incorporated this idea into his design. Along with the addition of crafty prisms to boost the brightness, Iron also suggested adding hidden air holes in the cap which would automatically slide open every few minutes to replenish the air supply inside. Of course, this mechanism required calm weather when there was no chance of an errant wave dousing the lantern.

These lanterns were a huge success and were quickly adopted by the Chase Trading Company on all of their vessels. Sailors dubbed them Davy lights because they claimed the lanterns burned underwater long enough to reach Davy Jones's Locker.

Despite his involvement in the design, Iron had received little recognition. Owing to the competitive nature of his trade, Iron knew no other horologists. Not socially, at least. He tried not to hold Mr Williams to account for hogging all the glory around the Davy lights but it hadn't gone unnoticed how Mr Williams had written to every horologist in town, telling them of his success and omitting Iron's name entirely.

Aside from Mr Williams, Iron had no one to talk to about his days, no one who knew or cared about the complexities of his work. Mr Williams's mind had started to wander of late, and he made for an unreliable conversationalist.

Iron rubbed his hand along his neat stiletto beard, took his jacket from the hook by the door, and locked up the workshop. Let Mr Williams come and inspect whatever he liked. Iron needed a break.

It would still be an hour before sunset and the weather had cleared, though shimmering puddles remained between almost every cobblestone. Iron strolled along the winding road, passing a point so narrow the roofs of the leaning buildings on either side almost touched. He liked to walk this way because of the abundance of clockworks in use.

High above his head, a skinny man leaned out a window and flicked a lever to move his washing along a line. Hot water pipes—an offshoot of horological advances—weaved through every wall like thread, and rattled when used. Above a scrubby bookshop, a sign shaped like a weighty tome had its metal pages turned by an unseen hand. In the window of a chandler, a candle dipped into a vat, over and over again, demonstrating the techniques used by the business.

He entered through the sage-green door of Farriner's Bakery. It was much too late in the day to find any fresh bread, but the bakery was known for its selection of buns and cakes. Iron picked one out and told the woman behind the counter not to bother wrapping it. He planned to eat it on the way home.

He always found Mrs Farriner very pleasant, and she was one of the few other Black residents of the town. He had offered to work with her to create a sign to hang above the bakery door and even offered her as much discount as he thought he could sneak under Mr Williams's nose. While she had yet to take him up on his offer, she always knocked a little off the price for his cakes, and often kept something special aside for him.

"You really shouldn't," he would always say, patting his belly. "I should be cutting down."

"A growing lad needs his food," she would say back to him.

Sometimes he wished she had been his mother. She was just about old enough, he thought, though would never dream of asking her age.

He ate his buttered fruit scone as he walked back towards home—a little set of rooms above the workshop. He had a meeting with Ms Sorcha Fontaine of the town Watch that evening; apparently they needed to discuss some issues raised by townspeople who felt put out by the street lamps. Iron had heaped a good deal of his self-worth into those lamps. Despite the time pressures involved, he had agonised over their design, aesthetically as well as functionally. He saw in them a chance not only to make his name as a horologist but to leave a mark on the landscape of the town itself.

He found a card waiting for him at home. Ms

Fontaine wanted to move their meeting from the Watch house to the Jack Thistle tavern. He finished his scone, splashed some water on his face, and headed back outside.

He hurried along the twisting roads of Pudding Quarter, cutting through a handful of Entries, until he emerged in the docklands, at the rear of the well-lit and spacious Jack Thistle. He found Ms Fontaine waiting at a table.

She struggled to be heard over the sound of enthusiastic bagatelle players nearby. "I hope you don't mind meeting here," she said. "I couldn't bear the Watch house any longer today."

A group of grey-haired men all had wagers on the game and were jostling amongst themselves, trying to egg each other on and put rival players off.

She shot daggers at them. "I'll arrest the lot of them if they don't keep the noise down."

Iron sat opposite her. "I don't think you can arrest people for enjoying themselves, can you?"

Sorcha shot the group a wicked side-eye. "Vince would."

The bagatelle players hooted and hollered as one game came to an end. Next came the slapping of backs and the begrudging exchanging of lost wagers.

"Bad day?" he asked.

Ms Fontaine sank back in her chair and blew air from her lips like a horse.

Iron laughed. "Ah, one of those days."

"If I have to listen to one more amadán telling me these lamps are...stopping...I don't know...fish from breeding or some such nonsense, I'll scream. I will. I'll scream right in their face."

Sorcha Fontaine had an open, honest appearance and a friendly way about her that Iron found comforting. She was one of the few people his own age that he spoke to on a regular basis. They sat and ordered two bowls of beef-shin soup while discussing complaints about the glare caused by the lamps.

"Ah, Iron, what are we going to do about them?" she asked. "We can't make them any dimmer or there won't be any point in having them at all."

Iron finished chewing a chunk of bread and swallowed. "Well, I suggest we do what I always do in cases like this."

"Which is?"

"I let someone see me tinker with the lamp without actually changing anything and then tell them the problem is solved."

Ms Fontaine just blinked at him. "That cannot possibly work."

Iron laughed again and took another spoonful of soup. "You'd be surprised how often it does, Ms Fontaine. People will trust you if you look like you know what you're doing."

She laughed with him. "Listen, we've been working together for long enough. You can call me Sorcha, if you want to."

"Thank you, Sorcha."

"And I still can't get over the fact your name is *Iron*. I mean, no offence, but Blackrabbit names will always make me giggle. Just a bit." She held two fingers close together and raised her voice. "Just a teeny, tiny bit."

Iron did take offence, just a teeny, tiny bit, but he didn't let on. "The town orphanage said it was the name my mother called me when she left me with them," he said. "She said she thought it would make me strong. Help me to weather life."

"Oh, no," Sorcha said. "Oh, I've been rude. I have. I do that. I'm after making a hames of things, I'm so sorry. I don't think sometimes. My mouth just makes these noises, and I can't control it."

"Don't worry," Iron said. "Think no more of it." He clamped his lips together and smiled but they turned inwards. He knew he'd done it, and he knew it wasn't a proper smile, but it was the best he could muster just then.

"You know Vince grew up in the same orphanage as you?" Sorcha asked. "This was well before either of us were born, of course. What age were you when you were sent there?"

"About a year, so I'm told," Iron said. "They didn't know when I was actually born so the day I arrived became my official birthday. I spent my entire childhood there until I was thirteen. Then they turfed me out onto the streets."

Sorcha sat back in her chair. "How awful. What did you do?"

"I, ah... I spent a few years sleeping rough, taking work when I could find it, and...um...stealing what I needed when I couldn't. Please don't arrest me!" He faked a laugh.

Sorcha dipped some bread into her soup, letting the meat juices soak into it. "Hah, no, don't worry. Sure I had a similar beginning here myself. When me and my sister arrived, we slept under bridges and stole food." She sucked the wet bread.

"I didn't know that," he said. "I've never met anyone who was, well, who was the same as me."

"And look at us now," she said. "You a fancy horologist and me a fancy Watchwoman! Sure, who would have thought it?"

CHAPTER SIX

LOST IN HIS thoughts, Felix returned to the Star alone. Before unlocking the double doors, he checked the road for any sign of his family. He didn't trust them not to rush in the second he opened up. He expected Mr Tassiter to be lingering nearby. He'd had to get Vince to intimidate Mr Tassiter out of the Star before they'd gone to Ms Hornby's house.

He undid the bolts and stood in the empty bar, inhaling decades' worth of the stale tobacco and spilt ale. He stepped into the horological lift and flicked the lever. Nothing. He tried again. He opened a casing and wound the mechanism. It crunched, and clicked, and stuttered. Somewhere deep inside, some unseen component sprang and popped.

"It hasn't worked in years," Dahlia said.

Felix jolted. He hadn't noticed her sitting on one of the benches. "How did you get in?"

"The back door," she said. "It's easy enough to pick the lock."

Felix closed the lift door behind him. He stood and leaned one arm on the bar. "So why doesn't the rest of the family do it? Why wait for me to unlock the front doors?"

"You'd have to ask them," she said.

"I'm asking you."

She drew on her long, thin pipe. "If I had to guess, I'd say it's because they're all useless layabouts who are terrified of both Gregory and Alma. Gregory doesn't want them here, and Alma has drilled into them how Gregory's word is law."

"But she wants this place," Felix said.

"But Auntie Alma is no lock picker," Dahlia said.

Felix drew up a chair and sat facing her. "I don't know what to make of this new you," he said. "When we were growing up, you were always so...obedient."

"I didn't know who I was back then," she said. "I was just a little goody two shoes who didn't want to cause waves. Thankfully I grew out of it." She blew a pillow of smoke directly at Felix.

He knew she did it to make him flinch, or cough, but he did neither. "What are you doing here, Dahlia?"

"I need someplace to stay," she said. "Just for a couple of days."

Felix shook his head. "Gregory wouldn't—"

She shot forward and snapped at him. "How on earth would you know what Gregory would do? You still think of yourself as the favourite, don't you? Just because you never got caught up in the family business. Just because you went to sea and made something of your life, whatever that means." She settled back onto the bench, satisfied with her outburst.

Felix had spent years cooped up with sailors spoiling for a fight. He'd long ago learned how to avoid rising to the bait. "Fine," he said. "Stay here if you want to. But just you. And no family gatherings."

"It's not given to you to decide these things."

He took the letter from this pocket and held it up. "I think you'll find it is. Until Uncle Gregory returns, at least.

Did no one think to have the lift repaired?"

"It wasn't really a priority," she said with a shrug.

"How fortunate for you all."

He stood and toured the bar, noting the occasional squeaking floorboard and cracked looking glass. The stage was in the worst condition of all. Unwaxed, poorly lit, and generally unloved.

"I remember when the stage took up this whole part of the room," he said, holding his arms out. "Now look at it."

"People stopped coming to the performances," Dahlia said. "They wanted ale. Then they wanted gin. Then they *really* wanted gin. You can't blame Gregory for giving the people what they want. We all do what we have to do to keep the candles lit."

The light in the bar was different to the rest of the building. Despite the two large bay windows at the front of the room, the air itself had a yellowish tinge to it.

He made for the door.

"Where are you going now?" Dahlia asked.

"If I'm going to stay here," Felix said, "there's going to have to be some changes."

FELIX FOUND THE nearest horologist on the next road. Above the door hung a sign—an elaborate clock face with exaggerated hands which moved about in an unpredictable pattern. Behind the hands, on the face itself, lively copper animals darted amid bushes while tall trees waved in an absent wind. The sign read:

WILLIAMS CLOCKWORKINGS

A bell above the door tinkled as Felix entered. He stood and shook the rain from his cap. The shop held a number of clockwork devices—including the ubiquitous striker-lanterns—most of which ticked incessantly and out of time with one another. In the centre of the room, a table held the five-sided head of one of the new street lamps. From the road, it had been difficult to make out the delicate patterns embossed onto the rainshield. Sculpted rabbits—alert for trouble—kept watch from the canopy. Felix leaned in for a closer look.

A man approached him with his hand extended. Felix

hesitated before shaking it. Not for any reason other than a momentary fluttering of both his heart and his nether regions. The sturdy man before him was close to his own age, had dark skin, an easy smile, and wore a stiletto beard and pointed moustache. He had at some point, Felix felt certain, discarded his ruff and velvet jerkin, and escaped from a painting by one of the great masters.

"Hullo, yes, I'm sorry," Felix said, regaining his composure. "Those lamp heads appear far larger up close than they do at the top of...of a pole. Mr Williams? I wish to solicit your skills in some repairs." It took a herculean act of will for Felix to prize his gaze from the finest pair of thighs he had ever seen.

"I'm sure I can help you," the bearded man said. He blinked excessively when he spoke, as though the words tickled his eyelashes. "But I'm not Mr Williams. He is the Master Cogsmith. My name is Iron Huxham. I'm his apprentice."

"Do I need to speak with Mr Williams, or can you help me?"

"Let's find out," Mr Huxham said. "What do you need?"

"It's a lift," Felix said. "I'm afraid it's quite stuck in

place."

An old man with a tired carnation in his lapel appeared in the doorway leading to the back of the shop. "A lift that cannot lift is nought but a cupboard, wouldn't you agree?"

"Mr Williams, I take it?" Felix asked.

Mr Williams nodded. He was an unshaven, white-haired man with a long beard, small eyes, and well into his seventies, if he were a day. "Where is this non-lifting lift to be found?" He spoke more loudly than necessary, likely due to his ears not being quite what they used to be.

"At the Star We Sail By," Felix said. "On Bibbler's Brook. I have just taken over the place from my uncle. My name is Felix Diamond."

"Ah, I see." Mr Williams took a step back. "I believe we are quite busy at the moment." He flicked through a book on his counter. "We are engaged with the task of providing street lamps for the town, you see." His voice cracked like ice.

"Yes, I couldn't help but admire your handiwork," Felix said. "When might you be free?"

"It could be months, I'm afraid," Mr Williams said.

"Months?" The *S* whistled out of his mouth.

"Or longer." He never once looked at Felix; he just kept running a wonky finger down the pages of his book.

"A pity," Felix said. "I suppose I shall have to look elsewhere."

"Yes," old Mr Williams said. "Yes, I believe it's for the best."

Mr Huxham hovered by the lamp head, his fingers stuffed into the pockets of his forest-green waistcoat. He frowned and tapped his thumbs against his belly. "Wait one moment, please." He darted to the counter. "Might I have a quick word in private, Mr Williams?" He flashed an unconvincing smile to Felix.

He and Mr Williams removed themselves to a room at the back of the shop but neglected to close the door tightly.

"I can work on the lift." Mr Huxham kept his voice quiet but not quiet enough. "I can nip out now; it shouldn't take long."

"We don't have time," Mr Williams said in his raspy voice. "And you have enough on your plate with these street lamps you insist on working on. Do not take on more work than you are capable of completing, Mr Huxham. If you promise the whole entire sun and deliver but a candle, the customer will not return. And I will not tolerate you producing work that is any less than your absolute best. This business will be yours soon enough, but it is my reputation upon which you trade. Besides, the man out there is a Diamond, and the Diamonds are not known for paying their bills on time. Or at all. Let him find someone else to take advantage of."

Felix moved his damp cap about in his hands, his ears burning and cheeks reddening. He didn't wait for them to emerge. With a tinkling of the bell, he flung open the shop door and hurried out onto the slippery cobbled road. He tugged his woollen cap onto his head and hastily paced away from Williams Clockworkings and wondered how far he would have to go to find another horologist. Surely there must be more than one in the town. As it would happen, he hadn't gone very far at all before he heard his name being shouted.

Mr Huxham cantered along the road to him. "Please, Mr Diamond, do wait a moment."

Felix tapped his own pockets. "I didn't steal anything, if you're—"

"No, no, nothing of the sort," Mr Huxham said, gasping for breath. "No, I wanted to say I am available, after all."

Felix's eyebrows shot up. "Oh, you are? Come, step in out of the rain, you seem to have forgotten your coat and hat." He led them both under an awning dripping with rain. They stood quite close together.

"Yes...um...yes," Mr Huxham said. "I had forgotten we had a...um...a cancellation earlier today. I quite forgot to write it in our book, so I can come to the, ah, to the Star this afternoon if that's suitable?" His kind, brown eyes held within them a world of comfort.

Felix couldn't help but be a tad transfixed. "Perfectly suitable, Mr Huxham. I shall see you then." He nodded politely and set off towards the Star, occasionally glancing back over his shoulder.

CHAPTER SEVEN

FELIX HUNG HIS damp coat on the rack by the lift. He had braced himself for an argument with Mr Tassiter but found the bar unoccupied. He twitched at the muffled voices coming from the next floor and climbed the stairs to find Dahlia sitting with a man, in one of the curtained booths, engaged in serious conversation.

"Lucky, this is Mr Marwood," Dahlia said. Her black military jacket hung off her bare shoulders, and she held herself tightly. "He's come to make a very generous offer."

"What sort of offer?"

"On the Star," said Mr Marwood, a man of slight build

with protruding ears, a balding head, and hugger-mugger eyes he never once opened fully. "It's a shame how your uncle has let the place fall to ruin over the last few years. I offered to buy it from him, but he turned me down. I thought perhaps the new landlord might be more amenable." He turned back to Dahlia.

"I tried to tell him," Dahlia said, "but dear old Gregory was never much of a listener."

Felix's face flushed, and he clasped his fists. "Dahlia is not the landlord. I am. Get out."

Mr Marwood's eyes grew smaller still, and he slid out of the booth, taking a step closer to Felix. "I'm dreadfully sorry; it appears I was misinformed. I had thought Ms Diamond here said she was the new owner. As a matter of fact, I'm absolutely certain she did." He shot Dahlia with a most peculiar look. "Still, there's no reason you and I cannot do business. The offer stands with whichever of you is the rightful owner. But perhaps we can discuss this some other time." He held the baggy sleeve of Felix's shirt. "You're a touch too damp to negotiate. I'll leave you to think about it. Good to meet you, Mr Diamond. I'll see myself out."

When he had gone, Felix slammed his palms on the

table, startling Dahlia.

"So this is why you broke in," he said. "You had to be in here to have your little meeting. You can't sell the Star because despite what you've obviously been telling people, it isn't yours." His whole body quivered.

Dahlia recovered quickly. "I'm the closest thing Gregory has to a daughter," she said, teeth bared. "I've worked here my whole life. Did you know that? Did you even think to ask? I tread those boards; I mop up spilt ale and vomit every night; I deal with the wandering hands of drunken customers."

Felix studied her face to see if she was lying. She wasn't, of course. It would have been a stupid lie, easily disproved. He hadn't considered that Dahlia might still have a connection to the Star.

"Gregory is dead, Lucky. He's dead, and he's not coming back. He was going to leave the place to me, so I will decide what's to be done with it."

Felix's legs turned cold, and his stomach heaved. "How do you know? How do you know he was going to leave it to you?"

"He said as much, plenty of times. Ask Dick Tassiter. You didn't really think he was going to give it to you, did

you? I don't know why you think this is any of your concern; you haven't set foot in this place for ten years. You're
going to disappear back to the sea soon, aren't you? So
what does it matter? I'm selling it, Lucky. I'm selling it before it collapses around our ears."

"I won't let you."

Dahlia spat out a curt, sharp laugh. "*Let* me?"

"Uncle Gregory sent for me," Felix said. "He must
have had a reason."

"He probably did, but I don't see how it's relevant
now."

"Maybe he sent for me to stop you from doing anything foolish." Felix immediately regretted saying it.

"Ah, there we have it." She narrowed her smokey
eyes. "Big, brave Lucky come to save his poor cousin from
self-inflicted ruin." She gathered her dark jacket closer
about her gaunt, pale frame. "Do whatever you think is
best, cousin dear. When your sailor's pennies run dry and
you're left without a souse, let Mr Marwood tell you his
offer and we'll see how quick you are to reject it then." She
stomped off downstairs and out of the Star, slamming the
front doors as she left.

Felix walked out onto the sailboat balcony and

watched her go until she disappeared around a corner. He gripped the edge of the sailboat and took some deep breaths of the briny air. *It is the waves which break—not I.*

This was the reason he'd stayed away for so long. Not Dahlia, specifically, but this weight, this tension that always came with family interactions. Nothing he ever did was right; nothing he ever said was suitable; no move he made was ever the correct one. Feelings lay scattered about like eggshells on the floor; one wrong step would crush them. For a family so steeped in criminality, so keen on fighting, collectively the Diamond clan had surprising thin skin. Though perhaps such was the way with all families. *We are all born with weapons capable of piercing armour otherwise unbreakable to those not of our blood.*

In the kitchen, Felix took a bucket and filled it with hot water. The pipes rattled and clanged as the bucket filled. He found soap and an old scrubbing brush and set them at the front door of the bar. Then he knelt down, dipped the brush into the water, rubbed it fiercely with soap, and set about scrubbing the floor for, he suspected, the first time in quite some years.

PROGRESS WAS SLOW but steady. After some time—he didn't know how long—he became aware of the sound of a brush behind him. Dahlia swept under tables, making a neat pile in the centre of the room. He assumed she'd come in through the back door again. He caught her gaze, just for a moment, and then they both returned to their work. The argument would be swept away, the harsh words forgotten. Such was the way with family.

One of the front doors of the Star creaked open slowly.

"Get out, Mr Tassiter!" Felix shouted. "We're not open yet!"

A puzzled head poked around the door. "It's not Mr Tassiter; it's Iron Huxham. I've come about the repairs?" He blinked hard, over and over.

Felix leaned back on his ankles. "Oh, my apologies, I thought you were someone else. Do come in, please."

Mr Huxham entered, removed his cap, and nodded to Dahlia. Then he looked at the wet floor and lifted his boots. "I've trodden on your nice clean floor..."

"Don't worry," Felix said, rising to his feet. "I could scrub this floor for a hundred years, and it would never be what one would call *clean*."

He showed Mr Huxham, who now stepped like a cat to avoid the wettest parts of the wooden floor, to the broken lift. Mr Huxham had brought with him a case which he set on the floor. It opened to reveal many levered trays filled with the delicate tools and instruments of the horological trade. From his overcoat pocket, he drew a long pole with flat edges. He stepped inside the lift, opening panels and generally poking about, muttering to himself all the while. "This old thing always sticks."

"Oh, you've been here before?" Felix asked.

"Um, no," Mr Huxham said. "I've worked on these types of lifts before. I installed one in the Blackrabbit Courant offices. And this particular one is somewhat...infamous. I have heard many a person with a sore—or missing—leg complain about it. Lots of people who work near me drink here. It's the closest alehouse."

"Playhouse," Felix said without thinking.

"Forgive me," Mr Huxham said, smiling. He removed his coat and rolled up his sleeves to reveal smooth, bulky forearms. He lay on the floor of the lift and thrust his hands into the guts of the machinery. He grunted as he worked, his eyes focusing on nothing in particular as he funnelled all his concentration into the unseen parts deep within the lift. He turned onto his side, tugging his shirttail free from his breeches and exposing the underside of his belly. "Can you pass me the long screwdriver, please?"

"The what?" Felix asked, trying not to stare.

Mr Huxham pointed to a heavy, flat-edged pole. When he had it in his wide hands, he twisted the end and a thin chiselled head popped out of the tip. He worked it into the gap, feeling around for the correct spot. "Perfect," he said. "Would you mind terribly holding this just as it is? That's it, try not to move it at all. I had to make this tool specially because whoever designed these things didn't think to make a hatch for the mechanism. This saves me from having to dismantle the entire frame."

Felix knelt down and did as he was asked. Mr Huxham took another instrument from his bag—a sort of spring with some weights on either end—and pushed it in through the gap. He nudged closer to Felix for a better angle, pressing the bare flesh of their forearms together. The warmth of Mr Huxham's skin flowed through Felix's arm. He tried not to notice but wondered if Mr Huxham had.

"No, it's no good," Mr Huxham said. He withdrew his oily hands from the mechanism and wiped them on a rag he took from his case. "The whole section will have to come out."

Felix pulled out the screwdriver and handed it to him. "How long will it take?"

"I should have enough parts to build a replacement," he said. "It shouldn't take more than a couple of days."

"That sounds expensive," Felix said. "I don't know if we have the funds to pay for all the work just now."

Mr Huxham pursed his lips together and looked to one side.

"I can pay you in drink," Felix said. "At least some of it? Or hot meals, maybe? I'm a cook, and I have to make meals for myself anyway. You could...come by of an evening?"

Mr Huxham smiled and nodded. "I would like that very much, Mr Diamond."

"Felix. Call me Felix," he said as he handed the long screwdriver over.

Mr Huxham turned the handle, retracting the tip. "Iron," he said with a smile.

VINCE REACHED INTO his pocket for his pipe and found the tip had snapped clean off. A common hazard with clay pipes which is why he always kept spares dotted about his house. As part of his role in the Watch, Vince had been given a little cottage next to the Watch house. He found the rooms wholly too small and the beamed ceilings far too low, and thus spent much of his time hunched over so as not to bang his head. The world didn't build houses with men like him in mind. Still, he had no better options just then.

His tiny bedroom window looked out across the sea and he found the sound of the waves soothing. Regardless, he'd had another restless night, and it had nothing to do with the narrow bed.

He stomped into his kitchen and prepared himself a breakfast of four eggs, four sausages, and a hunk of bread with lashings of butter. Sorcha had taken it upon herself to ensure his larder was always stocked with food from the market. She must have feared he'd waste away without her supervision.

He caught his reflection in the kitchen window and turned to the side, holding in his round, hard belly. He had lost some weight, he noticed. Though it would be some ways before he was anything less than the hulking brute he'd always been.

His nose wrinkled from the sizzling sausages, and he wasn't alone in that. By his feet, Crabmeat sat patient as could be, mouth drooling and paw raised in courteous pleading.

Vince remembered the day one of his men, Penhallow, won Crabmeat by cheating in a game of dice. He'd only been a week old then, sired by a notorious fighting dog. Penhallow spent a few months training him to become a ferocious attack animal. Vince had taken a shine to Crabmeat but never let on to anyone. He secretly fed Crabmeat when no one was around and trained him to obey his commands. Partially out of fondness but also as a precaution. Penhallow had always been an ambitious wretch, and Vince knew one day he risked being on the receiving end of Crabmeat's slobbery jaws. He never did learn how the dog had ended up with such an odd name. He resolved to one day visit the gaolhouse and ask

Penhallow about it.

Vince picked a sausage from the pan and blew on it. "Don't want you burning yourself." He dropped it to the floor. Crabmeat leapt on it, picking it up in his mouth and dropping it over and over again as it was still too hot to eat. Vince laughed and rubbed him behind his ear, making the dog's back leg wobble. "Good boy." After washing and dressing in his uniform, Vince left his cottage for the Watch House.

At that time of the morning, the night shift were just preparing to leave for home. As he scraped dirt from the brass casing of his clockwork lower leg, Clive Hext caught Vince up on the goings-on. Apart from a tussle outside the town hall, and a few disgruntled spectators at a boxing match, it had been a quiet night.

Sorcha sauntered into his office through the open door. "We're back." She rubbed a green apple on her sleeve.

"Didn't take long," Vince said.

Sorcha sat on the edge of his desk. "There wasn't much to look at," she said. "We sailed right inside the cave. There's a little post to moor at and a tunnel leading up to the door in the Star's cellar." She took a bite of the apple and wiped juice from her chin.

"Find anything useful?"

Sorcha shook her head. "Not a thing. No blood, no clothes, nothing at all. Whatever happened to Gregory Diamond, it didn't happen in the caves."

Vince slumped into his chair. It creaked. He grunted a little under his breath. "Shouldn't speak with your mouth full."

She set the half-eaten apple on his desk. "Never mind me, you look like you woke up in a hedge. Have you no looking glass at home? Come here to me." She licked her hand and smoothed down the top of Vince's hair.

"Give over," he said ducking out of her way.

She tutted loudly and went back to her apple. "You're making me wish Captain Godgrave was still here. You made more of an effort when he was about."

Without another word, he grabbed his tricorne cap from a hook on the wall and marched out of the Watch House alone. Crabmeat used to follow him around everywhere, but since Vince started working from the new Watch House, Crabmeat was content to remain near his warm bed. Vince missed his company, not that he'd ever admit it to anyone. Of course, no one would ever think to ask, except maybe for Sorcha. He stopped outside a shop window and checked his reflection. He ran his fingers through his snowy white hair and smoothed some strays in his short beard.

He marched deeper into the docklands. The sun had burst through the grey clouds long enough to dry the roads. He passed through the market where some of the stall-holders stared at him and some did their very best not to. He knew some of the merchants by name and those were the ones who were quickest to hide their wares. It wasn't uncommon for stolen goods to make their way through market stalls and into the hands of an unsuspecting public.

He wondered how angry the proximity of the new Watch House had made those unscrupulous traders. He would certainly have hated it, back when he was concerned with such matters and likely would have set fire to it long before now. In fact, he'd briefed the Watch on his pre-ferred arson methods so they could be on the lookout for any attempts to attack the Watch House.

A packet ship bobbed in the water, laden with sacks and parcels. The C.T.C. ran an efficient postal service. It had to. The C.T.C. had many outposts spread across places as far-flung as the Province of Quebec and the East

Indies and thus required a vast amount of administrating. It also asked a lot of its sailors, deploying them to far corners of the globe, often for months or years on end. The least the company could do was provide a reliable lifeline to their families back home.

Vince marched along the nearest pier and sure enough, that's where he found his target, standing halfway along it and pulling on one of a number of wet ropes. Seaweed hung from it like garlands at Midwinter.

"Need to talk," he said.

Briony Underhay ignored him and kept pulling, her strong arms bulging from the short sleeves of her shirt.

"About Gregory Diamond," he said.

"Have you lot found him yet?" She worked hand over hand, pulling and pulling on the rough rope. It coiled by her feet, soaking the knotted wood of the wide pier.

"Not yet," Vince said. "Thought you might have some idea where he might have gone."

She stopped and pushed a strand of reddish blonde hair from her large, dark eyes. Vince knew of her, though they'd never met. She wasn't the sort to take kindly to any underhanded dealings and had run off any of his gang members who had tried to recruit her. "Why? I don't really know him. I just drink in the Star sometimes. And not very often, as it happens."

"Heard you two were close is all," Vince said.

She started pulling again and an empty lobster pot broke the surface. Miniature waterfalls poured out from its mesh walls. "And who told you that? That niece of his?"

Vince didn't correct her.

She wrinkled her sharp nose at the mention of Dahlia. "She's useless, that one. Spends her days in bed and her nights in the opium den."

"Expensive pastime," Vince said.

"Very." She finally pulled the last of the lobster pots free. She dropped the heavy rope and wiped her hands on the legs of her coarse trousers. "You know she has debts? Dahlia? She begged Gregory to help her pay them off. He wouldn't. He told her she had to make her own way in the world." A gull landed nearby, and she kicked at it, sending it on its way.

Vince squinted at her. "Close enough with Gregory to talk about his family problems, then?"

She stood stony-faced, then laughed. "Well, you've got me there, I suppose. Look, I don't know Gregory very well. We had some fun at Samhain and had a little pillow talk. There's nothing more to it. He's a nice man, for a Diamond, and a good lover. Gifted in certain ways, if you follow me. But too scrawny for my liking. I prefer a man who's wider in the boughs." She eyed Vince from the sole of his boots to the tip of his tricorne.

"That so?" There was a time when Vince would have considered taking her up on her not-so-subtle offer but the older he got, the more he preferred the company of men in his bedchamber. "Mentioned Dahila has debts?"

"Are you not even going to buy me a drink? Butter me up before you ask for sensitive information?"

Vince didn't move; didn't speak.

"She's quite fond of her opium is Dahlia Diamond. She's been promising to pay her bills for quite a while now. I can't imagine the den owner will wait too much longer."

Vince nodded and left Briony Underhay to her work.

She stood with her hands on her hips and called after him. "Come by any time, big man."

CHAPTER EIGHT

AS VINCE APPROACHED the Star We Sail By, he became aware of raised voices coming from within. He hesitated and leaned against the wall, listening intently.

"I don't know who you think you are, swanning in here after all this time and throwing your weight around."

"Shut your mouth, Tenner," Felix said. "Uncle Gregory wouldn't let you set one foot over that door if he were here."

"Ah, but he's not here, is he?" Tenner asked. "He's gone. Dahlia, talk some sense into him, will you?"

"He's right, Lucky," Dahlia said. "He's a mouth and

a proper rusty guts, but he's right. Gregory isn't coming back."

"You don't know that," Felix said.

"Why don't you piss off back to sea, you meddling git?" Tenner said. "You turned your back on this family years ago; it's got nothing to do with you."

"Then why did Uncle Gregory write to me for help, hmm?" Felix asked. "Why didn't he ask you? Or Aunt Alma? Or Aunt Gayle? Or any of the rest of you? Because he knew you'd all be worse than useless. Get out. Go on, get out."

Tenner fell backwards through the doors of the Star as though shoved and landed on his arse in the road. He winced and held his side. His nose had a cut, barely healed, and red welts decorated his forearms. Felix stormed out after him, red-faced and brandishing a sopping wet mop which he held out like a battering ram.

A wet-bellied Tenner jumped up quickly and raised his grazed fists but spotted Vince leaning against the wall. "I see you've got your pet watchman with you." He dismissed Felix with a wave of his hand and walked away. "Diamonds don't work with his kind," he shouted over his shoulder. "Diamonds work alone! As a family!"

"That's not what alone means, you halfwit!" Felix shouted back at him. "And you," he said, turning to Vince. "Heard enough, have you?" He barged back inside. Vince followed him, smiling.

"What are you grinning at?" He paced the clean floor, stabbing at it with his mop.

"Had you pegged as a bit of a milksop," Vince said. "But you've got some fire in your belly, after all, Lucky."

Felix stopped dead in his tracks. "Don't call me that. That's not my name."

"It is, in a way." Dahlia hopped up onto the bar counter and swung her slender legs. "It's what Tenner and I used to call him, as a joke. Gregory looked up Felix's name once, at the library. Apparently it's Latin for lucky, so we started using it."

"It was mean," Felix said. "You told me that being left at the Star by my parents wasn't very lucky at all. You and Tenner thought you were being funny."

Dahlia stopped swinging her legs and slinked off behind the bar.

Vince cocked his head towards the front doors. "Tenner going to be a problem, is he?"

"No," Felix said, "he's just a simpleton. He always has

been. I remember watching him pick flecks of paint off a wall and eat them. He was about fifteen at the time. He lived here for a spell. We were friends in the way cousins of similar ages so often are. Me, him, and Dahlia had the run of this place. He's a bully. You can't let him get under your skin or he'll never leave you be."

"Not had many dealings with him," Vince said. "Know his face, mind. Hard to forget it. Looks like an angry potato. Talks a good game but about as much use as bubbies on a fish. Conversation sounded heated. Looks as though you gave him a beating."

Dahlia stood behind the bar and leaned forward, resting her elbows on it as if waiting to hear what Felix would say.

"He already had those marks on him," Felix said. "He's always been on the receiving end of one beating or another. He thinks we should sell the Star. He just wants a piece of the profit. He lived here for a while so he thinks he's entitled so some of the cash."

"Tenner been out looking for Gregory?" Vince asked.

"As far I know he hasn't even done so much as ask around. None of the cousins have."

"Not much of a family," Vince said.

Felix sucked in his own bottom lip. "Most people would be too polite to say that to my face."

Vince shrugged a little. "Someone looking to buy the Star then?"

Felix's gaze darted to Dahlia and back. "Not yet, but once word gets round about Gregory, it probably won't be too long."

Felix climbed the three steps to the stage and started swabbing.

"Changed your mind about keeping the Star closed?" Vince asked.

"The doors weren't stopping people from coming in," Felix said. "No sense fighting it. Why are you here?" He flinched then, as if struck. "I'm sorry, I didn't..." He took a deep breath. "What can I do for you, Commander?"

Vince held his tricorne in his hands. "Vince will do. Came to talk to Dahlia."

"What have I done now?" She wore a man's topshirt with the sleeves rolled up and shiny black boots. She carried a bucket of soapy water from behind the bar to the stage.

"Working here?" Vince asked.

Felix shrugged and nodded. Clearly, he wasn't very

happy about it. Vince almost said something but all he could hear in his mind was Sorcha shouting *tact* at him, over and over again. "Spoke to Briony Underhay. Ever see her and Gregory together?"

Dahlia struggled to focus on him. The theatrical paint smudged around her tired eyes made them appear even heavier.

Vince raised his eyebrows and stared at her. "Seen her since Gregory disappeared?"

"Not even once," Dahlia said. "Can I get back to work now? These heavy buckets won't carry themselves."

Vince balled his fists on his wide hips. "Don't seem too concerned about your uncle."

Dahlia shrugged and pulled up a fallen sleeve, shooting a sideways look to Felix. "It seems Gregory wasn't too concerned about me, I'm just returning the favour." She marched off downstairs, her boot heels striking on the bare steps.

Vince settled himself into a chair in front of the stage. Sconces on either side of the purple curtains held blazing candles and made shadows dance like performers in a silent routine. "Odd way to behave," he said. "Thought Gregory as good as raised her?"

"He raised both of us, more or less." Felix didn't lift his head to look at Vince and kept on swabbing the stage. "Dahlia's parents were not very reliable at the best of times. They left her on Gregory's doorstep when she was about eight years old so they could have their little adventures together. Stealing from ships in the harbour and getting drunk off the proceeds, mostly. It's a Diamond family tradition: when things get too hard, just send your child off to Gregory. He'll look after them. He'll feed them and he'll shelter them. He'll give them work do to. We're all just jetsam, washing up on the shore of the Star."

Something happened to Felix's eyes when he spoke. They hardened.

"Same thing happened to you?" Vince asked.

Felix stopped swabbing and fixed him with a serious glare. "I came here when I was about nine or ten years old. My parents upset the wrong people and had to go on the run. They couldn't risk taking me with them, so they left me here and never returned. Uncle Gregory showed me how to change an ale barrel and shortchange a customer. He showed me how to cook a meal. He was good to me, all things considered." His thick eyebrows fluttered. "I feel like...like I'm letting him down."

Vince's brow knitted. "Going to find out what happened to him. Swear to you." He glanced towards the stairwell. "Want to ask you something about Dahlia."

Felix stopped swabbing and leaned the mop handle against a wall. He landed heavily onto a chair. The redness in his cheeks had subsided. He pulled off his cap and locks of chestnut brown hair fell over his eyes.

He had a sweet face, Vince thought. Innocent, in a way. Unmarked and soft at the edges. "Assume Dahlia thinks you should sell the Star too?"

Felix's eyes darted about again; then he nodded. "She thinks it makes sense to do so while we can. The Star needs some repairs and we can't afford to do it. I've got a horologist to fix the lift, but I don't think there are many carpenters, or tilers, or glaziers who'll take payment in hot meals. The worse the place gets, the cheaper it'll be." He ran his hand through his hair, pushing it away from his nut-brown eyes. "I don't know; maybe we should sell it."

"Gregory won't be pleased if he were to come back and find himself homeless."

Felix fixed him with the pleading eyes of a puppy. "Do you think there's any chance he's still alive? Truthfully?"

Vince rubbed his own thigh and sighed. "Could still

go either way."

Felix sucked in his own bottom lip again and chewed it. "But in your experience? I know who you are. Who you were. You used to run all the gangs in Port Knot. You've seen more crime and criminals than anyone."

Vince glared at him and considered his response. Felix was, what, in his early twenties? Same as Dahlia? Same as Sorcha? Felix had been to sea—he was a man of the world—but he was still a nephew worried about his uncle, worried about the man who raised him. He hid it well, but Felix was desperately looking for some shred of hope to cling to.

"No," Vince said. "Don't think your uncle is still alive. Been gone too long and too suddenly. No ransom note, no word of any kind."

Felix exhaled loudly, as if suddenly struck by an unseen fist. He gripped the armrests of his chair so tightly his knuckles turned white. He hung his head for a moment, then shook it. "No, I can't... I can't give up on him, not yet."

Vince wanted to set him right, but he knew Sorcha would give him a bollocking if she found out. He gave Felix a moment to calm down. "Heard of a man named Lyton

Marwood?"

Felix avoided looking at him. "I can't say I have."

Vince lowered his head, casting his face in shadow. He deepened the gravelly rumble in his voice. "Second time you've lied to me since I walked in here. Want to keep doing it, you're going to have get better at it."

Felix swallowed hard. "I've met him. Only once, mind you. He...he tried to buy the Star from Gregory at some point. He made me an offer, too, just yesterday."

Vince clenched his fist. "Didn't need to lie to me about there being a buyer."

Felix rubbed his hands over his own face. "I know, I just... I didn't know if I should say anything."

"Marwood owns the opium den in the Tangles," Vince said. "Dahlia has debts there. Serious ones. Selling this place would pay them off, I'm sure."

Felix looked at him, his eyebrows knotted. His eyes held firm. "What are you saying?"

"Gregory didn't want to sell. Maybe Dahlia did," Vince said. "People can do surprising things for money. Maybe you need to be careful."

Felix stood and climbed the stage to retrieve his mop. "I think it's time you left," he said quietly.

His face cold as the grave, Vince stood and walked out.

CHAPTER NINE

FELIX THRUST A short poker into the fireplace, hoping to stir up some more life from the embers. "I'm sick and tired of being cold." He'd spent too long shivering below deck in the middle of the ocean to find anything bracing about a chill in the air or the first fluttering of snowflakes.

In the tiny bathing room on the top floor of the Star, he leaned into the tin bath and turned a wheel. Pipes along the wall clattered as though filled with hungry rats before spitting out piping hot water from the spout. He stepped back until the temperature settled into something more bearable.

When the tub had filled, he stripped off his clothes and left them in a heap on the floor. He dipped a toe into the water before stepping fully inside. The water stung his legs, then his hirsute bum as he settled in. Hot, running water. How he'd missed it. This was to be the first proper bath he'd had in years. Or at least, the first one in a long time that came without crowds of sailors waiting for their turn.

Plumbing of this kind had been common enough in the Pell Isles for years and was catching on elsewhere, albeit slowly. Other places were unwilling to deface their towns and cities with ugly pipes and brackets, not so Port Knot. A place in constant upheaval, constant renovation, it clutched the pipes to its bosom and gleefully thrust them over and through whatever wall they required until they became coppery veins on the skin of the town. Convenience above all.

He took a bar of purple soap and sniffed it. Cloves and something else. Rose, maybe? He worked it into a lather in his hands, then applied the bar first to his armpits and then over the rest of his body. He found it all a far cry from jumping into cold seawater or using a damp rag over a barrel.

When the water cooled, he slipped into a pair of striped corduroy trousers, a cream topshirt, and a thickly knit jumper he'd found in Uncle Gregory's room. With his woollen cap pulled over the tops of his ears, he finally felt warm and ready to face the rest of his day.

Windowless apart from the bays at the front, a series of striker-lantern chandeliers hanging from the chessboard ceiling saved the Star from lamentable gloom. Felix had always needed to stand on a chair to tend to them when he'd last lived here. Now, he found he could simply reach up and turn their keys. The walls—covered in blood-red paper with fine, gold damask detailing—held framed play-bills from the earliest days of the Star, featuring the names of performers either long forgotten or moved on to bigger and better things. He took a cloth, stood on the bench, and wiped the frames in a vain attempt to stop himself from moping, as he'd been doing all afternoon.

He'd never felt so powerless in all his life. He knew Vince and the Watch were working to find Gregory but he felt as though he should be doing more.

As the sun began to set, he spotted the lamplighter, clad in his white greatcoat, working at the street light on the corner of Bibbler's Brook. He thought the lamps were a fine idea and remembered walking the streets of Port Knot in darkness many times as a lad. They were especially risky in winter, when the nights drew in ever earlier. He'd hurried home many a time, fearful of running into the sort of people his own family turned out to be.

Back then, he was starting to understand who the Diamonds really were, and he'd already grown to dislike it. While his Uncle Gregory and Aunt Alma revelled in getting one over on the average person, Felix just saw it as the kind of life that led one to abandoning their child or ending up in the gaolhouse.

Dahlia finally reappeared from the kitchen. She wore her black military jacket buttoned up tight, and she hugged herself as she walked towards the door. Her eyes were red.

"Is it true?" Felix asked her. "You've been taking opium?"

Dahlia hesitated by the front doors. "It helps."

He hopped down from the bench and toyed with the rag in his hands. "Helps with what?"

Dahlia withdrew a clay pipe from her pocket. She wouldn't look at him. "In the Odyssey, Helen of Troy is so moved by the suffering of the people who lost loved ones in the Trojan War that she used a potion to help them forget their pain. The potion, so I'm told, contained opium." She laughed a dry laugh. "Now, it may well be that ignoring pain isn't the best solution but it is still a solution. And right now it's the only one I have."

Felix slung the rag across his shoulder, as he'd seen his uncle do a thousand times. "What do you need to forget?"

She threw her hands in the air. "I don't know, Lucky, maybe the fact of losing my parents to the sea when they tried to steal from a greencoat ship? Maybe the fact I'll never have a proper home of my own? Maybe the fact I'll only ever be shunted from pillar to post on the whims of Aunt Alma, or Aunt Gayle, Uncle Basil, or any of the other great and powerful family elders who view us as nothing more than cogs in the Diamond family machine? As mere...bait in the water." The clay pipe snapped in her hand. She threw it on the floor. "We didn't all get the chance to escape, Lucky." She placed her hand on her breast and drew her jacket tighter still. With her other hand, she flung open one of the doors and hurried outside.

Dick Tassiter stood aside to let her pass.

"We're still not open," Felix said, but he knew he should have saved his breath.

Mr Tassiter parked himself in his favourite spot on the corner of the bar. "I would have thought you'd be glad of some custom," he said. "How else are you going to afford to feed yourself?"

Felix reluctantly agreed and after retrieving the broken pipe, he gave Mr Tassiter his usual cup of ale. Though the more he thought about the lack of money coming in, the more he worried.

Mr Tassiter tasted his drink and winced. "Flat as my arse. Might be time for a new barrel, my lad."

Felix huffed as he opened the hatch to the cellar. He would have been worried about leaving anyone else alone in the bar with all those bottles of gin just begging to be stolen, but he knew Dick Tassiter wouldn't do anything to get himself barred from the Star.

Felix climbed down the steep steps into the cellar. He took a strap and tied it round a barrel, ready to pull it up to the bar and cursing Uncle Gregory for not having the lift come down this far. He brushed away some old cobwebs from the low ceiling and wiped his hands on his striped trousers.

In one corner sat a chipped chamber pot with a broken handle. Off-white in colour and painted with cavorting nude women, Uncle Gregory had always insisted it remain in the cellar. The cold air below the Star played havoc with his kidneys, he said, and so whenever he had to go down here he'd invariably need a pee. When Felix, or Dahlia, or Tenner misbehaved, Uncle Gregory would make them empty the pot for him. The smell could be overpowering and Felix avoided looking inside in case reflex compelled him to empty it.

He hesitated by the door to the smuggler's tunnels. He tried to piece together what had happened the night Uncle Gregory vanished. Had he climbed down here and run through those tunnels? Or had the kidnapper come in that way, sneaked up the steps and grabbed Uncle Gregory unawares? Felix didn't know how it happened, and as the hours ticked by he started to think he might never know. And what if, for whatever reason, the kidnapper came back? Should Felix seal up the tunnels or might they be his only chance of escape? Should he check them to familiarise himself with the route? What if there was a cave-in while he was still there? He put both hands on a dusty barrel and lowered his head, breathing heavily. The cellar started to spin about him, and his legs wobbled.

Dahlia knew the Star better than anyone. She could

have picked the lock to the back door in the middle of the night and hidden down here, waiting for her chance to strike. She needed money. Vince had said so. What if she and Lyton Marwood had planned it together? She could have attacked Uncle Gregory and passed him to Lyton Marwood in the tunnels. Felix had lied to Vince. He'd lied about knowing who Marwood was and he'd lied about there not being a buyer for the Star. Felix had heard the stories, he knew what Vince was capable of. He should have been honest; he should have told Vince what he knew straight away. The next time Vince came looking for information, he might not ask so politely.

He rummaged in his pocket and withdrew a key. Not the front door key but a much smaller one, clumsily etched with a star—a second key which his uncle had included with his letter. What would Vince do when he found out about it? When he found out Felix had kept it from him? What would Aunt Alma do when she found out?

He clutched the key to his chest. Sweat pooled in his armpits, on his brow, between his legs, he dropped to his knees, no longer able to support his own weight. "It is the waves which break—not I." Felix whispered the refrain to himself, over and over again. "It is the waves which break—

not I." His breathing slowed. "It is the waves which break—not I." The quivering of his heart steadied and, in time, the room stopped its dizzying dance. Composing himself, he pocketed the key, climbed the steps, and used the strap to haul up the last barrel of ale in the cellar. No one else need know about the key. Not yet. Not until he knew where it fit.

CHAPTER TEN

THE BUILDINGS OF Port Knot stood stacked like books on an overstuffed shelf, each a different height, a different width, but all sewn together by rattling and clanging copper pipes. Vince stomped along Bibbler's Brook to the corner of White Horse Way, heading for the area of town known as the Tangles.

He cursed himself for not finding a gentler way of approaching the subject of Dahlia's debts. He had wanted to gauge Felix's reaction to the idea, to see if perhaps Felix thought Dahlia might have been desperate enough to do away with her uncle. Instead, all he'd accomplished was annoying a decent lad and probably making yet another enemy.

He pushed his way past a throng of sour-faced people gathering outside a house. He almost shouted at them to move but caught himself in time to stand aside and let them carry a coffin out through the door.

The roads of Port Knot were too narrow for standard carts so the people used longer, thinner ones than were found in other towns. They bred their horses to be smaller than average, too, though they were no less powerful for it. The mourners loaded the coffin onto the cart and followed it out of the laneway, presumably headed for the large graveyard to the south of the town, over the river.

He hurried on his way and ducked under little Gallynan Bridge. When he emerged from the other side, his head suddenly turned cold. He looked up to find a gang of young boys sitting on the parapet, holding his cap and laughing. "Oi! Little rats!"

The boys stood to run, but Vince darted up a set of stone steps and caught one of them by the collar. He grabbed his tricorne cap back. "Don't let me catch you again." He let the boy go, who quickly scampered off after his friends, his heels scraping on the cobbles as he went.

Cap-snatching was a popular pastime for boys that age, and with so many bridges to choose from, there was no way to stop it from happening. Still, Vince thought, they could be getting up to far worse, like he did when he was their age. For one thing, on the rare occasions when he and the other boys were let out from the orphanage, a favourite game of theirs had been to line a bridge and see who could piss into the most carts passing underneath. He'd often been the winner.

From the outside, the opium den was the most unassuming of places. A single teal-coloured door, always closed, and a single window covered with bars. The name painted above the door read *Helen's Salve*. Inside, however, was as different as night is from day. A plush red carpet led one straight through to the giant metal squid at the rear of the den. Three stories tall, formed from sheets of battered copper, and fed opium from below by three bare-breasted women, its fires were stoked by three men clad only in boots, leather aprons, and gloves. The squid's eyes were fiercely burning lanterns, and its tentacles wound along the mezzanines of the den, feeding intoxicating smoke to the stalls thereupon.

Ignoring the woman on the door who usually greeted

people, Vince stormed along the carpet, past stall after stall of smoke-stung patrons lying on divans, past the sweat-dewed squid attendants, and straight into the office at the back of the premises, flinging the door open upon entering. "Marwood," he said in his lowest growl. "Want to talk."

Lyton Marwood didn't so much as glance up from his bookkeeping, much to Vince's annoyance. He didn't barge into offices for the good of his health; he did it to put his quarry on edge. Marwood's office was gaudily decorated in reddish maple wood with gold-painted bas-relief poppies. The ceiling held three long, opaque glass panes painted with leaves. The chairs, of which there were many, each held entirely too many cushions, and on the wall behind Marwood himself hung an insipid painting of some imagined landscape—a copse beside a lake, under a brassy sky. The frame, thick as his forearm, held more artistic merit, being carved with realistic ivy leaves and vines.

Marwood, still not looking at him, held up a finger until he finished writing some numbers into his ledger. When he was done, he returned the quill to its pot. "Now then, Mr Knight, what can I...? Sorry. I can see you are in uniform. What can I do for you, *Commander* Knight?"

Vince didn't care for the inflection Marwood put on Commander. It spoke more of mockery than respect. "Place is a disgrace." He pointed back through the door. "People out there who look like they've been here for days. Thought the whole point of this place was to be safe for opium fiends? Not somewhere for them to be left to wallow in their addiction."

"I must object, I simply do not care for the use of the word 'fiend'." The lace cuffs of Marwood's purple coat billowed as he gestured. "I find it somewhat disrespectful." His sharp voice cut like a goldsmith's blade.

"Enthusiast, then," Vince said. "Deserve a better environment than this."

"Have you really burst in here to complain about my stewardship?"

Vince snorted. "Hear you're in the market for some real estate."

Marwood templed his fingers under his nose. "And what might that have to do with you? Must every purchase go through the approval of the Watch? Has your organisation infected society to such an extent already?"

Vince balled his fists on his hips and puffed out his barrel chest. "Suppose you've heard about Gregory

Diamond's disappearance?"

"I suppose I have, yes."

"Suppose you know how it looks to me. Gregory rejects your offer to buy the Star We Sail By. Goes missing soon after. Should Felix reject your offer, might he go missing too?"

"Well, Commander Knight, I certainly don't care for these insinuations. As if I could have possibly had anything to do with poor Gregory's disappearance!" He held his hand splayed open on his chest as though mortally offended.

"Star is a playhouse," Vince said. "Getting into the theatre business, are you?"

Marwood stifled a laugh and flashed a toothy grin. "I have always liked the Star. I find its current state a sorrowful one. Gregory had let it become quite run down in recent years. Can you remember the last time you saw Atlas's star spin? My business is going well and I find myself in a position to expand my holdings. Surely there can be no law against it? Nothing for the Watch to object to?"

"Star will be overrun with opium fiends by Midwinter if you get your hands on it." Vince leaned down and slammed his palms on the desk.

Marwood flinched. Good. It meant Vince was getting under his skin.

"Watch gets wind of you being involved in Gregory's disappearance? Will have to look into it," Vince said. "Bound to be evidence around here somewhere. Watch will tear your den apart to find it if need be."

"I don't like threats, Commander Knight."

"Might not like what I say next, then. Plenty more where that came from." He held Marwood's gaze, refusing to blink. He could hold it all day long.

Marwood swallowed, hard. "I made Dahlia Diamond a very generous offer for the Star."

"Dahlia?"

"I thought she was the new owner because, well, she said as much. The offer has been extended to her cousin, Felix. Should he refuse, so be it. I shall walk away, knowing I am defeated. I have no particular horse in this race. Port Knot has no shortage of properties for me to invest in. You're barking up the wrong tree here, Commander."

Vince's brow furrowed. Felix lied to him. Again. "Dahlia was going to accept your offer, wasn't she?"

Marwood templed his fingers again. "You'd have to ask her."

Vince shoved himself away from the desk and marched out of the office and out of the den. Every instinct he had told him Marwood wasn't lying. Which meant he was no closer to finding the real culprit.

CHAPTER ELEVEN

AFTER SUNSET, IRON dashed through the rainy streets and down Bibbler's Brook, not far from the Star We Sail By. Water gathered in the gutters and gushed ahead of him. He thought it would be easier to sail down the road than run. The wheels of passing carriages splashed through puddles of reflected street lamps, scattering glowing drops as they went.

He kept as close as he could to the walls, hoping for shelter and paused beneath the awning of a glazier to catch his breath. Wet, slippery cobblestones and lateness made for a dangerous combination. The last thing he wanted was to show up at Felix's door with scuffed breeches or a broken bone.

He knocked on the back door to the Star and was enthusiastically welcomed in by a smiling Felix who wore an olive shirt open at the throat to reveal a bush of chest hair and his pinkish skin beneath.

"Filthy weather." Iron shook the water from his leather tricorne cap.

Felix took his coat and turned to hang it on a hook in the little laundry. More hair peeked from the collar of his shirt. Iron's heart beat faster. Open around his neck, Felix wore an indigo handkerchief. Indigo with a white pattern Iron couldn't quite discern without staring a little more than politeness would allow.

Deep sinks lined two walls, with linens soaking in them. "Sorry about the washing," Felix said. "Has to be done, though. I haven't quite finished preparing dinner."

Felix led them downstairs to the kitchens beneath the Star. Iron marvelled at the height of the ceiling. It curved slightly and the bevelled edges of the shiny moss-green tiles caught the candlelight. The tiles continued down onto the walls where battered copper pots hung from hooks beneath cupboards the colour of fresh straw. A long, heavy table filled the centre of the room, upon which two great horological mixing bowls sat lifelessly. On the stove, a pot bubbled and steamed, filling the air with the scent of ginger and onions.

Felix fussed about with the pot, stirring with a ladle. He hooked out one great potato and stuck a knife in to see if it had cooked through, then he threw in some thyme, parsley, and pepper.

Every second sconce held a lit candle. Just enough to work by, and no more. Just enough to highlight Felix's pert bottom in his linen sailor's trousers.

"Don't worry, we're not eating down here," Felix said. "We can bring the food up to the top floor."

"I think it's perfectly charming," Iron said. "One might almost say romantic." He regretted saying it, but Felix's smiling response set him at ease. Iron's breeches had yet to dry out, and he stood by the fireplace to warm them. "I hope you've locked the front doors up tight or else you might get a river streaming in."

"We won't get flooded," Felix said. "That's what those steps out the front are for. Didn't you know?"

Iron shook his head.

"All the buildings on this half of the road have raised

doorways. To avoid the Bibbler's flood."

"I want to be polite," Iron said, "but I have no idea what you're talking about."

Felix took a bottle of wine and uncorked it. "When this road was first built—years ago, this was—there were a bunch of alehouses at the top of the hill. After closing time, all the drunks—bibblers, they used to be called—would spill out of the bars and head into the alleyways to relieve themselves before staggering home. Sometimes there were so many of them doing it that their piss would run down the road like a stream."

"Or like a brook," Iron said.

"Hence the name Bibbler's Brook," Felix said. "I'm surprised you've never heard the story before."

"Mr Williams would never speak of such things," Iron said. "He's much too polite."

"Whereas I am nothing but an uncouth sailor."

Iron's stomach clenched tight as a mainspring. "Oh, no, I didn't mean... It's not at all what I..."

Felix winked at him. "I'm just teasing you."

Iron held the sides of his own face. "You had me worried." He was wholly unable to stop a nervous titter from escaping his lips, so he quickly changed the subject. "I had no idea this was even here." He craned his neck to examine the high ceiling again.

"There's no reason why you would, is there?" Felix said.

Iron cleared his throat and settled himself on a tall stool at one end of the long table. "I meant I didn't know anywhere on this road had kitchens as big as this."

Felix set out two bowls and placed slices of bread on two plates. With a cloth wrapped around the handle, he carried the pot from the stove and dished out prawn soup for both of them. No great lover of prawns, Iron's heart sank a little as they splashed into his bowl.

Felix returned the pot to the stove and, having set out some bread and burnt butter, he pulled up another stool to the corner of the table and poured them both some red wine. "To your health."

"And to new friends," Iron said as they clinked glasses. "Although, I must admit to some trepidation on my part. Mr Williams spent most of the day bending my ear about the exploits of your family."

Felix set his glass down. "I hope you won't hold their deeds against me."

"Mr Williams has impressed upon me the importance

of reputation. He plans to pass his business to me any day now and should I end up with a..."

"Reputation."

Iron licked his own lips. "Should I end up with a mark against my name, it may impact upon the business he worked so hard to build."

Felix turned the glass of wine back and forth in his fingertips. "My family are my family, and I am myself. I hope you will judge me upon my own merits."

Iron lowered his head to hide a smile. "I shall endeavour to."

"I hoped you saved some for me." Dahlia glided into the room. "I only came down for an apple, but I'll take some soup, if there's any left over?"

Felix set his glass down. "There isn't, as it happens." He glared at her.

Iron's head sank into his shoulders.

Dahlia lifted the ladle from the pot. "There's enough left for me, I'm only little, you know." She put a hand on her bony hip. "I'm sure you won't mind, will you, Felix? And who is your— Oh, it's Mr Huxham, isn't it? The horologist?"

"Yes, um, hello, Ms Diamond." Iron waved his hand.

He tried not to but he physically could not stop himself from doing so.

Dahlia filled a bowl and dug a spoon in. "I didn't know you boys were so close." She tasted the soup.

"We're not," Felix said. "Not yet, anyway."

Iron tugged at his own shirt collar. He could swear it tightened around his throat.

"Oh, I see," Dahlia said. "Well, in that case, I shall take my food upstairs and leave you both to it. I won't make a sound, honest." She crept out of the room on tip-toe in the most exaggerated way possible, holding a finger to her lips the entire time. "This needs more mace next time, Felix. Just so you know."

Felix hadn't stopped glowering and Iron felt bad for laughing at her antics.

"Don't encourage her," Felix said. "She loves an audi-ence."

"Most performers do."

Felix's brow wrinkled as he dipped some bread into his soup and took a big bite.

Iron slid his spoon into his own bowl and blew on the broth before tasting it. "Oh, my."

"Is something the matter?" Felix asked.

Iron took another spoonful—with a prawn, this time. "This is..." He ate the spoonful. "This is wonderful."

"You don't have to sound so surprised," Felix said, laughing. "I am a cook, you know."

"You are?"

"I'm a ship's cook. I thought you knew that? I'm aware food on board ship doesn't have a very good reputation, but I know the way to keep a crew happy, and it's called seasoning. More mace, indeed."

Iron laughed and tried more prawns. "This is very good of you. It's nice to have a meal cooked for me. It doesn't happen very often."

"You don't have anyone special in your life, then?" Felix asked.

"Ah, no, no I don't. As a matter of fact, there has never been anyone...anyone special."

"Oh, I see," Felix said. His spoon stopped moving.

"I don't mean... I'm no virgin if that's what you're thinking."

"I wasn't," Felix said. "I am now, though."

Iron laughed. His neck grew hotter. "I just mean I've never been... I haven't ever met anyone who...well, anyone who I felt particularly close to. And you?"

Felix took a drink of wine. "Once," he said. "The feeling was not reciprocated."

"I find that difficult to imagine."

Felix's brow furrowed and the ends of his moustache lifted, just a little. "How very kind of you to say. But it was for the best, honestly. I suppose there's many a young sailor who falls in love with his captain. Or perhaps I simply suffered from an infatuation. Whatever the case, it has long since passed." He took another sip of his wine, holding Iron's gaze the entire time.

Iron's heart beat faster. "It can't be cheap to serve food such as this."

Felix wiped the corners of his mouth. "We don't have much of it, but I know how to make it last. So to speak." The twinkle in his eye made Iron laugh again. "But honestly, it's the least I can do to repay you for working on the lift. Especially considering the fact you are doing so on your own time and against the master's wishes."

Iron spluttered some broth. "What, ah, what do you... What makes you think so?"

"I heard you and Mr Williams talking. He does not speak quietly, that one. He didn't want you working here. And he was right, in a way. I cannot actually pay you. But

I can assure you I would, were I able."

"What are you doing for money?" Iron swallowed a limp piece of carrot. "If you don't mind me asking? Which of course you do. Who wouldn't? What a rude thing to ask. Forget I said it." His ears burned and he hoped the ground would open up and swallow him.

Felix reached out and touched his forearm, ever so lightly. "Iron, calm down, it's fine. It's a perfectly valid question and my answer is—nothing. I don't know what to do. Aside from Mr Tassiter, we've had no customers and I don't even know if I want any. When I received Uncle Gregory's letter, I imagined I would come home and be here for a day or two, at most. But until I know what's happened to him, I can't leave."

Iron held his hands open. "Why don't you open this place? The Star, I mean. Not the kitchen. Well, also the kitchen, actually. People need ale and they need food. Especially when it's this good."

Felix pushed some potato around in his bowl. "I'm no taverner and besides, I don't like the idea of people using the Star just to drink in. She was supposed to be a place for people to come and see a show, be entertained, be educated. She's not an alehouse, she's a playhouse."

"So?" Iron asked. "Why don't you put on a play? Or a show of some kind, at least? You have everything you need to do it. If you think the Star should be a playhouse once again, if you think it's something the people of the town want and need, then prove it to them. Give them a taste of what they've been missing out on."

Felix looked at him and frowned. "I can't do that."

"Because?"

Felix snorted a laugh and shrugged. "Well, because... I... Huh."

CHAPTER TWELVE

"I'M SORRY TO send you out in this terrible weather." Felix led Iron back upstairs to the laundry. He spotted his drawers hanging up to dry and, red-faced, swiftly pulled them from the line and dropped them into a sink, hoping Iron hadn't noticed.

Iron took his overcoat from the hook. "It looks to be easing up now."

Felix stood on a finely patterned rug, worn at the edges where the sun had touched it, and held the back door open for him. Across the Star's yard and over a piece of wet grassland, the cemetery yew tree stood silhouetted against a bright, half moon.

"I used to lie in bed and watch the glow-worms in the grass around the graveyard," Felix said. "Uncle Gregory told me they were ghosts dancing with happiness because somebody, somewhere, remembered them and spoke their name, spoke kindly of them. Silly, I know."

"He wasn't all bad, then, your uncle?"

Felix licked his own lips. "I suppose no one is all bad. He took good care of me. I hope...I hope I get the chance to thank him."

"You will. I'm sure of it." Iron flicked up his coat collar and hesitated on the step. "This has been...this was... Thank you, Felix."

"You'd better take this with you." Felix retrieved a small brass striker-lantern from a shelf and turned its key. The candle came to life, bathing them both in its warming light. Felix smiled and held on to Iron's elbow. Iron leaned in, just a shade, just to test the water. Felix met him halfway. Their eyes closed and their lips touched, lightly. How soft Iron's lips were. How warm.

Iron held the corner of the indigo handkerchief around Felix's neck and ran his thumb across it. "Seahorses," he said of the white pattern upon it. Then he took the lantern and donned his tricorne cap. "Well, I will, um, I will see you tomorrow."

"Tomorrow?"

"The lift repairs," Iron said. "I haven't—"

"Of course, of course!" Felix said. "Tomorrow, then."

Iron tipped his cap and with the lantern firmly in his grasp, he hurried out into the night. Felix closed the door slowly behind him and hesitated.

"You'll have to dry those drawers all over again."

Felix turned to find Dahlia sitting halfway up the stairs licking the last of the soup from her spoon.

Around her shoulders she wore a heavy, lime-coloured blanket, frayed at the edges. "He seems nice. Too nice for you, don't you think?"

Felix didn't rise to the bait. Instead, he just smiled.

"You're looking in much better form," Dahlia said. "Should I be worried? Have you changed your mind about selling?"

"I have not," Felix said. "I know you need money but that's not the way to get it."

She set the bowl down beside her and leaned back, resting her elbows on the step behind. "What do you mean?"

"I've heard some talk about your financial woes."

Dahlia rapped the spoon on her knee. "The bleddy cousins can't keep their traps shut about anything."

Felix didn't see any need to correct her. He stood at the bottom of the stairs and leaned on the newel post. "Tell me truly—do you think Aunt Alma could have anything to do with Uncle Gregory's disappearance?"

Dahlia thought about it for a moment. "I don't know if she's that ruthless."

"Could she have had Tenner do it? He is covered in fresh cuts and bruises..."

Dahlia scoffed at the notion. "Tenner's all talk. He was far too afraid of Gregory to dare cross him. Besides, if Alma is responsible then why didn't she take over the Star before you arrived?"

"Because I had the key for the front doors."

"She could have broken in through the back door. It doesn't take much skill to break a window. As a matter of fact, even if she didn't have anything to do with what happened to Gregory, she could have still taken advantage of the situation. She could still have broken in and taken over."

Felix drummed his fingers on the post. "Maybe she

was worried about what Uncle Gregory would do when he returned?"

"But if she did away with him, she'd have nothing to worry about."

"A bluff, then," Felix said. "To hide it from you and the rest of the family. Or from the Watch."

Dahlia stuck out her bottom lip and nodded her head. "She is a gambler."

Felix's hand hung limply on the newel. "If you'd sold the Star, you'd have burned through the money quickly and then what? No home and no income. It would have been a short term solution to a long term problem."

"What do you suggest I do instead?"

"We need to open," Felix said.

"We?" Dahlia asked, raising her eyebrow.

"Yes, we. You and I. I take it your little tantrum yesterday was an excuse to go and fetch your belongings?"

She shrugged theatrically. "You did say I could stay for a week. And I needed to get away from Alma for a while. She's become unbearable. More so, I mean. You should have seen the glint in her eye when news got round about Gregory."

"I seem to remember you asked to stay for a couple

of days. But I really don't have the time or energy to argue," Felix said. "If you're going to stay here you're going to pull your weight."

"How are we going to manage to open the Star with just the two of us?"

"A fine question. I need money coming in soon or I'm going to be in real trouble," Felix said. "I wonder if Uncle Gregory left enough money to pay staff..."

"There's some in his safe," Dahlia said. "I think."

Felix squinted at her. "How long did it take you to find it?"

"Oh please, we've both known where he hides his money since we were ten years old."

The first place Felix had tried to use the little key etched with a star had been Uncle Gregory's safe. It didn't fit and besides the safe had been left open.

Dahlia crossed her arms. "There should be enough to pay Ms Hornby for a couple of nights. But if we pay for staff and no customers turn up, we'll be in worse state than before. People have been talking about the Star, talking about what might have happened to Gregory. I've heard lurid tales about his body being stuffed in the lift shaft, or buried under the stage. We can't be sure people will come just because we open."

"We can encourage them to come along."

"How?" Dahlia asked.

"By doing what the Star does best. By putting on a show." Felix slapped his hands on the post. "We were never meant to just sell ale to dead-eyed drunks."

"Don't let Dick Tassiter hear you calling him that. What will you be doing while this show of yours is going on?"

Felix refused to acknowledge the gnawing in his stomach. "I can make a cheap stew to sell, which should bring in a few extra coins. It's a shame they're out of season, I make a lovely gooseberry tart..."

Dahlia rubbed her hand on the faded and peeling green wallpaper. "It'll be nice to see some life in the place again."

"The Star We Sail By was born a playhouse and it'll die a playhouse," Felix said. "But hopefully not for a while yet. And every show needs a star." He held out his hand.

Dahlia dropped the spoon into the bowl, rose to her feet, threw her lime blanket about her shoulders, and took his hand. "You always were my favourite cousin." She gave him a sloppy wet kiss on the cheek.

CHAPTER THIRTEEN

IRON HARDLY SLEPT a wink all night but when he did, he found himself having the most delightful and evocative dreams, full of soft lips and warm embraces. When morning came, he had all but leapt out of bed, eager to get to his workshop and finish up his day's tasks early so he could hurry back to the Star.

He had spent the morning humming to himself while he worked, to the point where Mr Williams had dispatched him to fetch some bread, ostensibly to have with his evening meal but in reality, Iron later realised, to give himself a rest. Though quite how Mr Williams could hear

Iron's humming when he couldn't hear someone addressing him from three feet away remained something of a
mystery.

Iron left Farriner's Bakery with his basket of loaves.
He thought about heading directly back to the workshop
but feared Mr Williams would have cooked up more work
for him in his absence, so he turned left and walked uphill.
The air in town was particularly pungent, as it often was
when southerly winds picked up scents from the harbour
and blew them inland. Iron had often heard visitors to the
island complain about it though he had never minded it
very much. He found it simply part and parcel of living in
a harbour town.

He cut through Burntarse Passage, an Entry leading
from the back of one of the town's forges to Medhow
stream and said to be named for a poor blacksmith who
stood too close to the fire and had to dash to the stream to
put out his flaming breeches.

At the far end of the Entry, he spotted a familiar face.
Felix's cousin, Dahlia, in the company of three men. One
was of slighter build, wore heavy stubble, and was clearly
giving the orders. The other two were clean-shaven and
wore the slops and leather jerkins of the dockworker.

Their voices echoed in the high, brick walls of the narrow passageway. Iron thought about turning back as there was no room to squeeze past but something in the men's bearing got his hackles up. All at once, the stubbled man grabbed Dahlia's shoulder. She shouted and kicked at his shins, forcing him backwards.

Iron hurried along, still clutching his basket of bread. "You there! Ruffians! Stop!"

The man with sore shins held up his hand to stop his associates from attacking Iron. The tallest of them—a rogue with pockmarked skin—protested but backed down after a withering look from his companion, and so instead, all three walked away.

"Are you well?" Iron asked. "Did they hurt you?"

"They couldn't if they tried." Dahlia brushed herself down. "I thought my sticking close to Felix would deter them, thought they'd be concerned about arousing attention from the Knights." She looked to the basket clutched in Iron's hands. "What were you going to do, throw your loaves at them?" She brushed past him on her way along the Entry.

IRON SET HIS basket of bread on the counter. Mr Williams shuffled around in the storeroom, mumbling about something or other. Iron ran his hand over the clockwork mangle he'd been working on.

"Ah, you're back, splendid. There's something I wanted to speak to you about." Mr Williams said. Crumbs from his luncheon held fast to his jumper and a little wet dot on the front of his breeches told of his recent trip to the privy. "I've been thinking about the business. It doesn't appear as if the council is going to approve your proposals for the street lamps."

Iron sank further into his chair. "What...who...how do you know?"

"I've been speaking to some people in the know, as they say, and I'm told it doesn't look good. The citizens of Barley Hill and Gravel Hill have quite a lot of clout with the council and they strenuously object to their privacy being invaded by the lamps."

Iron threw his hands in the air. "That's ridiculous!"

"Before you say something untoward, you should know I find myself agreeing with them." Mr Williams raised his bushy eyebrows and peered over the top of his half-moon spectacles. "I passed along Bibbler's Brook the other night and witnessed such sights! People behaving in all manner of ways best left to the cover of darkness. I imagined the lights outside my home and wondered about all those ne'er-do-wells watching me coming and going from my own home. No, I think the whole endeavour was a misstep and, to be frank, speaks ill of your judgement, Iron. So I think, for the foreseeable future, I shall postpone my retirement and remain here. Now, Mrs Maunder is expecting to collect her mangle tomorrow morning, so let's get going, shall we?"

FELIX OPENED THE front doors of the Star to find two women standing with a cart of ale barrels. They wore coarse woollen trousers and billowing soiled topshirts.

"Gregory about?"

Felix swallowed hard. "Ah, no, he's... No, he's not.

Can I help? I'm his nephew."

The women exchanged a glance. "It's his weekly ale delivery." One of them thumbed to the cart.

"Oh! I see. Yes, of course, please, bring it inside." He opened the doors as wide as possible.

The women hesitated, peering around the empty bar. "Will Gregory be back soon, do you think?"

"I honestly couldn't say," Felix said. "Is there a problem?"

"Not if you can pay us."

Felix's heart sank. "Pay you? Oh. Does he pay every week?"

"Like clockwork. He never lets us down. He can't. If he did, he wouldn't have any ale to sell." She laughed.

Felix did not. "The Star hasn't been open for a few days and I don't think I have enough to cover, well, all of this." He gestured to the barrels.

The women exchanged another glance. "In which case, we shall bid you good day."

Felix's heart pounded faster and faster. "Wait, wait! I need ale if I'm going to open."

"Then you need to pay for it."

"I can't pay for it until I open!"

"Quite the bind," the woman said. She climbed up on her cart. "But we haven't got all day to talk to penniless landlords. There's plenty of other alehouses who'll buy our wares."

"Playhouse," Felix mumbled under his breath. Despite the chilly December air, sweat beaded on his brow.

The other woman hesitated. "Oh, now, don't pout your pretty lips. Look, you seem like a nice lad. We'll be in town until noon. If you can get any money, you can take whatever we have left. But it may not be much, mind. And we won't be back this way until next week."

Felix stood in the road as the cart heaving with ale barrels trundled up the cobbled road. He put his hands on his hips and exhaled, loudly.

"It appears as though I came just in time."

Felix turned and dropped his hands. "Mr Marwood."

Mr Marwood smiled and walked into the Star. "Coming?" He sat at a small table near the doors.

Felix followed him, slowly.

"I was wondering if you've given any more thought to my offer?" Mr Marwood smiled when he talked but, like Aunt Alma, there was no warmth in it. His little eyes focused on Felix as a rat's might on a piece of cheese.

"I never officially received your offer," Felix said.

Mr Marwood reached into the pocket of his waistcoat. "Oh, I assumed Dahlia would have told you. Here." He handed a slip of paper to Felix. "I think you'll find it more than adequate."

Felix folded the paper. "I think you'll find it's wholly inadequate and borderline insulting."

"Come now, Mr Diamond, look around you! The old girl is falling to pieces. The roof leaks, the floorboards creak, I wouldn't be surprised to find mice in every corner. And let's be honest, you've no intention of becoming a taverner, have you?" A tiny beetle—shiny and green—crawled over the edge of the table. Mr Marwood flicked it across the room.

"If we're being honest, " Felix said, "I think you're taking advantage."

Mr Marwood laughed. "I'm making the most of an opportunity. Something all good businessmen do. I'll tell you what. You need money for ale. Let me lend it to you. Stock up, open up, do whatever it is you need to do to give running this place a fair crack of the whip and then, when you come to your senses and realise it's not the life for you, you can sell it to me. What do you say?"

Felix flopped into a chair. What if Mr Marwood was right? What if Felix decided he didn't want the life offered by the Star, after all? He could just sell it and there would be no harm done. And where else was he going to get the money he needed? He held out his hand.

Mr Marwood shook it.

CHAPTER FOURTEEN

FELIX HAD FORCED himself to sit still at his uncle's desk and come up with a list of things he needed to do but he found it hard to concentrate. His mind kept dancing between thoughts of Iron and last night's dinner, and the show he now had to put on. His stomach twisted itself into knots whenever he thought about trying to find acts willing to perform, the amount of cooking he'd need to do, whether or not people would actually come, and, most of all, what Aunt Alma would do when she found out. The last thing he wanted was the Star full of Diamonds, getting drunk and causing a ruckus. Because then he'd have to ask the Watch to step in, which would cause more problems, and then... No. He caught himself in a looking glass and gave himself his sternest look. "It is the waves which break—not I."

He took a quill and a slip of paper. Lists always helped. Lists made one big problem into lots of little, easily solved ones.

A short while later, he followed the winding road to the house where Ms Hannah Hornby lived. After knocking on the door, he waited for several minutes before it opened to reveal a man with sunken eyes and large ears, and not much older than he. Unshaven and unsmiling, the man asked Felix's business.

"I'm here to speak to Ms Hornby."

The man stepped aside to let Felix in. Muffled footsteps issued from above and another man stood in the kitchen, staring at him. His eyebrows met in the middle and he concealed something behind his back. Felix hesitated before being shown into the little parlour with leaf-green walls and flaked gold accents, warmed by fat candles. Threadbare carpet underfoot did little to mask the thump of his boots. A book lay open on a sideboard.

"Ms Hornby," he said, "I don't know if you remember

me but—"

"I remember you perfectly well." Ms Hornby sat by the fireplace with a peeling knife grasped in her hand and a bowl of carrots by her feet. She wore a simple cornflower-blue gown with matching ribbons in her hair.

The scruffy man with sunken eyes who had let Felix into the house stood behind him, blocking the doorway.

"You're working with Vince. With the Watch," Ms Hornby said.

Felix's heart thumped and he began to feel dizzy. "No, no, I'm not with the Watch. Is that..." He pointed to her little knife. "Is that what this is about? I'm not here about Uncle Gregory or the Watch investigation."

Ms Hornby pointed the knife at him when she spoke. "Then what do you want?"

"We are. I mean to say, my cousin Dahlia and I are reopening the Star We Sail By for a show, and we were hoping you might return to tend bar."

Ms Hornby's eyes narrowed. Then she lowered the knife and laughed. "I thought you were here to drag me off into Vince's clutches."

Felix's shoulders sank, and he took a quick breath. "No, no, nothing of the sort." He put on a smile though he didn't really mean it.

She asked him to sit down before addressing the sunken-eyed man barring the door. "You can tell the others to relax."

He nodded and left the room, heading towards the kitchen. Felix felt glad not to have found out what the other man had hidden behind his back.

"Your husband was prepared for trouble?" Felix asked.

"Mr Sparrow is not my husband," Ms Hornby said. "He's just a lodger. They all are. And none of them have any great love for Vince or the Watch. I don't know what the council were thinking, putting him in charge. No one will cooperate with the Watch knowing he's involved."

"Does this mean you know something about Uncle Gregory's disappearance?"

She squinted at him again. "I thought you weren't here to talk about him. But no, I don't. I'm just saying if I did, I wouldn't have told him. For all I know, he did away with your uncle and is looking for someone to pin the blame on. He's the Watch Commander, who's going to stand up against him now? If he drags someone in front of the magistrates, they're not going to ask any questions. They all stick together, that lot. The magistrates, the council, the Watch, the greencoats..."

The same thought had occurred to Felix too. Vince's reputation meant he'd always be the first suspect in any crime he sought justice for. That couldn't be an easy position for him to be in. Felix didn't really believe Vince was involved in Uncle Gregory's disappearance. Did he? Did he honestly believe Vince was doing everything he could to find out what had happened? What if the culprit was a former associate of Vince's? A friend, even? Would Vince turn them in? Or would he bury the evidence? And if Ms Hornby was correct, and Vince couldn't rely on the help of the public, then Felix didn't know how Vince was ever going to find the truth.

He sank a little farther into his seat. "I'm...I'm sure Vince is doing everything in his power to find out what happened."

Ms Hornby set the peeling knife on the opening book. Spots of water dropped onto the page. "You have more faith in him than I do."

Felix gripped his cap more tightly in his hands. "What say you, then? Will you work at the Star once more?"

She tapped her fingers on her leg. "I suppose so. I

need the money."

FELIX RETURNED TO the Star to deliver the good news about Ms Hornby. He found Dick Tassiter behind the bar helping himself to some gin.

"I left money, Mr Diamond!" he said. "Honest!"

Felix was in a good mood so he left Mr Tassiter to it. He checked the lift. "No sign of Mr Huxham yet?"

Mr Tassiter swallowed some ale. "There's a card on the windowsill for you."

Felix lifted the little rectangle and read it to himself.

"Bad news?" Dahlia asked.

"It's from Iron. He said he's been unavoidably detained at his workshop and won't be able to come round today."

"Aww, do you think that's just a flimsy excuse, and he's changed his mind about you?"

Felix's legs twitched. "I didn't until you said it!"

Dahlia giggled.

"Wait," Felix said, pointing to the lift. "Has anyone

checked the shaft?"

"You mean for your uncle's...? You mean for your uncle?" Mr Tassiter turned white as a sheet.

"Calm down," Dahlia said. "I did. It's where I'd stash a body if I had to. There or the cellar."

Felix didn't know if he should be relieved or not. The thoughts of his uncle's body being stuffed into the lift shaft made him sick, but at least it would be an answer.

"I take it you've had no further word?" Mr Tassiter asked.

Felix hadn't seen Vince since kicking him out of the Star. Or at least, that was how he remembered it. He doubted if Vince would ever want to talk to him again.

Dahlia climbed onto the stage, pacing out a little dance routine. "I've spoken to some musicians I know, and they've agreed to play on the night."

"Some good news," Felix said. "I can cross that off my list."

"And they've agreed to be paid a week later."

"Even better news! We've got Ms Hornby back, as well."

Dahlia stopped in mid-step. "That still doesn't mean you get to hide away in the kitchens all night." Amongst other things Dahlia had discovered about herself while Felix had been away, she had apparently also found her second sight.

"Not all night, no." Part of his role as ship's cook had been figuring out ways to make a few measly scraps of meat last for weeks at a time. "But people will expect food. And it's an easy way to make some money. I can get some vegetables and cheap pork cuts, roast it all with some salt and nutmeg, and dish out a few dozen plates. We can charge whatever we want. I know how to feed a lot of people on very little money."

"I thought the C.T.C. were one of the biggest companies in the world," Dahlia said.

"They are, but it seems you don't get to be rich by spending a lot of coin on your workers."

"Speaking of which," Dahlia said, "where are you getting the money for all this?"

Before Felix could answer, the doors to the bar clattered open. "Well, well. Rumour has it the Star is back in business." Tenner, dressed in a charcoal frock coat emblazoned with an inferno of fine needlework flames and wearing bottle-green spectacles, sauntered in and grabbed a jar of gin from behind the bar.

Felix was over to him like a shot. "We're not." He grabbed the jar.

Tenner refused to let go. He smiled down his scabbed, snub nose at Felix, baring his teeth a little. "Looks to me like you are. And I hear you're preparing for a show." Though still bruised, his left eye had healed a little since yesterday. The marks on his unshaven throat had yet to clear up though.

Felix wrenched the jar from his grip and slammed it back on the shelf. "Who told you that?"

Tenner removed his spectacles and slipped them into his pocket. "Mr Marwood. He could hardly contain his excitement." He flared his coat wide and hopped over the bar. "Tell me this: if you're not open—" He pointed to Dick Tassiter. "—then what's he doing here?"

"He's part of the furniture," Felix said.

"This is where you've been hiding then," Tenner said to Dahlia. "We missed you at the last family gathering."

Dahlia rolled her eyes. "Getting drunk and picking fights with sailors at the Salt Pocket isn't a *gathering*."

"They love it," Tenner said. "Sailors can't resist a scrap. Isn't that right, Lucky?"

Felix clenched his fists. He hated fighting. The very

idea of it made his stomach lurch.

"When's the big show then?" Tenner asked.

"Wednesday," Dick Tassiter said.

Felix shot him a dirty look.

"Wednesday," Tenner said with a grin. "Well, I'll be sure to let the family know."

"There's no need," Felix said.

"Oh, now, what kind of family would we be if we didn't support one another? And you'll need some customers, won't you?"

"Not ones like you," Felix said.

Tenner leaned on the bar, his hands clasped, his knuckles red from fighting. One of his forearms bore evenly spaced welts. "You still don't understand how things work around here, do you? We're coming. All of us. Now, you can either accept that or get your friends in the Watch to come round and keep us away. And it won't just be us. You'll alienate all your customers at once. Because no one wants to drink with the Watch and *no one* wants to drink with Vince. Look at the Jack Thistle—the Watch has practically taken over the place and driven out all the regulars. You going to let them do the same to the Star, are you, Lucky? I'm looking forward to Wednesday." He sauntered over to the entrance. "I haven't had a proper night out in ages." He laughed and slammed the doors closed behind him.

CHAPTER FIFTEEN

THOUGH THEY HADN'T planned to, Sorcha and Vince patrolled the waterfront every afternoon. Vince liked to get out of the office and stretch his legs—and give Crabmeat a good, long walk—and Sorcha always insisted on accompanying him. He had complained a lot about it, at first, but he got used to having her around. Sorcha had only been working with Vince for a month, but she'd quickly discovered that if left to his own devices, Vince was prone to stewing on his own thoughts. This often led to his quick temper becoming quicker still. She didn't care so much about being on the receiving end of his ire as she knew how to diffuse it, but she could see the effect it had on the rest of the Watch.

The presence of patrolling Watch members helped to quell trouble. Something about the sight of approaching red and black uniforms had a calming effect on the populace of the town. Or, as Sorcha had often thought, the people were just waiting until the Watch had passed before committing whatever criminal act they were planning on. Fights were the main source of trouble on the waterfront. Be it over short supplies, shortchanging, or just short tempers there was usually a scrap waiting to happen.

Something had been troubling Vince all morning. Sorcha suspected it had something to do with the Star We Sail By. Ever since he'd left there yesterday afternoon, he'd been in a foul mood. So foul, he hadn't even been snapping at the Watch. He'd been very, very quiet. And that worried Sorcha more than anything.

"Here we go." Vince pointed to a pier.

Next to a docked sloop, two men squared up to one another. Sailors, Sorcha guessed from their clothing. The men were shouting, the people in the crowd around them were shouting, then Vince shouted and everyone fell quiet. He pushed his way through a mob made up mostly of other sailors. "Something wrong?"

The older of the two men wiped his nose on the back of his hand. "Nothing worth troubling the Knights over."

"It looks to me like you boys were about to knock seven bells out of each other," Sorcha said.

Crabmeat—wearing his black and red Watch collar—stood ready to snarl or drool at a moment's notice.

"Just some bad blood between us," the older man said. "You wouldn't understand. Lubbers never do."

"Well?" Vince pointed to the younger man. "Agree with him?"

The younger man cracked a knuckle. "Oh, I do indeed, sir. This has been brewing for a long time."

Vince addressed the onlookers in his loudest voice. "Stand back. Give them room."

The crowd were no fools and did as they were told, forming a ring around the men. Vince and Crabmeat walked away with Sorcha in tow.

"Are we not going to stop them?" she asked.

"Why? Not hurting anyone but themselves," Vince said without breaking his stride. "Both of them want to fight. Let them."

Sorcha dashed in front of him and stood staring up at

him with her hand out to his barrel chest. "Except one or both of them might just be trying to save face," she said. "They're not going to want to look weak in front of their crew, now are they?"

Vince looked down at her determined little face. "Hadn't thought of that."

He turned on his heels and hurried back along the pier. He broke the crowd up with a clap of his hands. "Move, move." He pointed at the men who had already landed a few punches. "With me. Now."

Sorcha followed them, puzzled. "Where are you bringing them?"

Vince led them to an empty boat shed, one whose wooden walls were coming apart at the seams. He shoved them both inside, then closed the door and bolted it. The men shouted for their freedom.

"Nobody around to see you now," Vince said through a gap in the walls. "Beat each other senseless if you want to. But you don't have to fight. Can just tell your crew you did. Talk to each other instead. Hash it out like men, not animals." He slammed his open palm against the door for emphasis and took a few paces back to give them some privacy. The crowd had remained on the pier, apparently fearful to approach. Which, Sorcha reasoned, was what Vince was counting on.

"On reflection, they did appear to be fairly passionate about beating lumps out of each other," she said. "You do know that when you open the door again one of those men could be dead?"

"Least we'll know who did it."

"Not like poor Gregory Diamond."

Vince huffed and crossed his arms. Not an easy thing for him to do, and it made them appear even thicker.

Sorcha fixed him with her steeliest stare. "You've not been right since yesterday, aul man."

Vince scowled and said nothing. He kept his gaze fixed on the ground.

"Somebody is after saying something to you. I can see it in your face. You get this little wrinkle between your eyebrows. Who was it?"

Vince snorted and said nothing.

Sorcha pushed her finger into his arm. "Come on," she said. "Who was mean to you? Who said mean things to you? Was it a bigger boy?" She stood with her hands on her hips and pouted, hoping to get a smile out of him.

"Are no bigger boys than me." His shoulders slumped

and his meat pie hands fell by his side.

"That's right," she said, poking his arm again. *Men are such fragile creatures. A little dent to the ego and their world falls apart.*

"Felix kicked me out of the Star," Vince said.

He tried to play it down, but he couldn't disguise the genuine hurt in his voice. Not much bothered Vince, but this had wounded him. "Why did he do that? Vince, what did you say to that nice boy to make him kick you out?"

Vince held his hands out and shrugged.

Sorcha raised her eyebrows and tilted her head.

"Might have suggested his cousin Dahila's opium debts provided good reason for her to kill their uncle."

Sorcha threw her head back. "What have I told you about tact?"

"Isn't always time to be tactful!"

"You have to *make* the time!" Sorcha said. "People already don't trust you, you don't have to make it worse by blurting out the first thought that comes plodding through your thick head."

Vince crossed his arms again. "Still think his family are involved."

"In fairness now, I wouldn't put it past Alma

Diamond," Sorcha said. "Getting Gregory out of the way leaves her as the head of the family. And you might have a point about Dahlia's debts. Money has a way of bringing out the worst in people."

Tired of standing around, Crabmeat slumped down on one of Vince's boots. A nearby gull pecked at a rotten cabbage. Crabmeat watched it intently, licking his wet lips.

"It might not be a bad idea to talk to the owner of the opium den," Sorcha said. "Lyton Marwood, isn't it?"

"Already did."

Sorcha threw her hands in the air. "And you didn't think to tell the rest of us? You're not working alone any longer, aul man. The Watch needs to be kept abreast of what you're up to. Well? What happened?"

Vince kicked at a shell, disturbing Crabmeat from his rest. "Marwood said he made an offer to buy the Star from Gregory. Then from Dahlia when he thought she was the new owner. Extended the same offer to Felix."

Sorcha's eyes narrowed. "He wants to buy the Star? Badly enough to do away with the owner?"

Vince looked out to sea. "Seems the type. But not this time. Didn't get the impression he was lying to me."

Sorcha was about to object, but if anyone could spot a

liar and a killer, she reckoned it would be Vince. "They're awfully quiet in there, aren't they? Go and check on them. Go on. Just in case." She gave his arm a little shove to encourage him to move, which was a little like saying she gave a tree a bit of a push to make it fall over.

As Crabmeat plodded over to sniff at the discarded cabbage, Vince scowled and marched up to the boat shed. Sorcha followed him in case he tried to use any more unsupervised tact. They both peered in through the gap in the wooden panels to find the two men locked in a passionate embrace. The younger man had his hands down the breeches of the older one. Sorcha turned away and covered her mouth to stop herself from giggling out of embarrassment. She had the distinct impression that had she not been there, Vince might have stayed and watched a little longer. Instead, he quietly undid the bolt and they both walked back in the direction of the Watch House with Crabmeat lazily trailing along behind them.

"That didn't go quite how I expected," Sorcha said.

"*Humph*, just some misplaced aggression," Vince said. "Might know a thing or two about it."

"Indeed," Sorcha said, kicking at the same shell Vince had booted. "Thankfully you don't have a problem with that any longer."

Vince shot her an icy look which only served to make her laugh.

CHAPTER SIXTEEN

SOME MORNINGS, THE town of Port Knot created its own mist as cold air blew in from the sea and dashed against the network of hot water pipes that crept across every building like copper vines. The mist would fade before long but for now it hid the harbour from Vince's view. His whole world consisted of Bibbler's Brook and the few roads around it. He'd had yet another sleepless night and wandered through town in a daze. A daze shattered when Felix charged around the corner and collided straight into Vince's belly.

Felix staggered back, the sack he held over his

shoulder slipping from his grasp and spilling its contents onto the wet cobbles. Withered carrots rolled and became wedged between stones. A few mushrooms tottered about while a small turnip made a break for it, rolling away down the road towards the harbour and, presumably, freedom. A passer-by, wrapped head to toe in fur to guard against the cold, curtailed its escape by stopping it with her foot. She handed it over to a grateful Felix before carrying on her way.

Vince stooped to help Felix retrieve more errant vegetables, but he didn't speak a word. Felix avoided looking at him, his cheeks reddening like a slapped arse. He swallowed hard, as though trying to work up the courage to speak. "I'm... I regret speaking to you so harshly when last we met."

It wasn't what Vince had expected him to say. He grunted a response, then straightened up and thrust his hands into the pockets of his claret-coloured Watch greatcoat. "In a hurry?"

Felix brushed a little spot of mud from some celery. "Dahlia and I have decided to open up the Star for a show," he said. "Tomorrow night, as it happens." He spoke with a little smile.

Vince frowned down at him. The creases in his fore-head tugged on the leather strap of his eyepatch. "That a good idea?" he asked. "Considering everything that's hap-pened?" His voice, usually harsh as falling rocks, had mel-lowed unexpectedly.

"I don't see why not." Happy to have cleaned the cel-ery as much as he could, Felix dropped it back inside the hessian sack.

"Might not be safe," Vince said. "Could be putting yourself at risk. Still don't know what happened to your uncle. Might be best you stay low until we do."

Felix shook his head and sucked in his lips. "I've been in Port Knot for a few days, if someone wanted to get me they've had ample opportunity. I need money. The Star needs money." He held his hands wide open. "This is the only way I can think of to get it."

"Still don't think it's worth it," Vince said.

"Well, Commander Knight, it really isn't up to you."

"Commander Knight now, is it? Fallen so far out of your favour already?"

"What makes you think you were ever in my favour?" Felix asked. "Come along and you can keep an eye on me yourself. Or don't," Felix said, walking away. "That, at least, *is* up to you." He stopped a few paces away. "I notice you didn't say anything about putting Dahlia at risk."

Vince stared at him without blinking. "Dahlia is not my main concern."

The mist swallowed everything of Felix's but the striking of his heels on the slick cobbles. Vince huffed and carried on his way but something made him stop. He pictured Felix in the Star, standing with trays of food and drink with no one to serve them to. He wondered what that would do to Felix, what it might drive him to. He ducked through an Entry and headed back up the hill towards Two Brothers Road.

He removed his tricorne and let himself into the offices of the Blackrabbit Courant. The reception of the newspaper building stood deserted. A counter stopped the public from wandering around but Vince flipped the hatch open and marched through. "Anyone home?"

The horological lift to his right clanked into life. "You're not supposed to be back here." Ms Emmeline Hawksmoor, in a pastel pink beaded gown, descended in the lift. When it reached the floor, she pulled the cage open and worked a lever on her clockwork wheelchair, thrusting her towards Vince.

"Thought you'd make an exception for me," Vince said.

"Presumptuous of you." She gestured towards a lime-green sofa. "What can I do for you?"

Vince sank heavily onto it. "Wondering if you might do me a favour."

Ms Hawksmoor crossed her bare arms. "The last favour I did for you left me with a head injury."

"Was hoping you wouldn't bring that up," Vince said, grimacing. "Not really a favour for me though. Know the Star We Sail By? Reopening tomorrow. Thought you might write about it in the paper. Give it a boost."

Ms Hawksmoor raised a black eyebrow. "Why was it closed? The Star?"

Vince fiddled with his cap. "Didn't you hear? Landlord went missing. Nephew has taken it over."

"And the Watch is investigating?"

Vince nodded. "Not here about that though. Felix Diamond is a good lad from a bad family. Deserves a chance at success. Thought you might be able to help."

Ms Hawksmoor lifted her chin. "What's in it for you?"

"Nothing. Honest."

She tilted her head.

Vince exhaled. "One Diamond gainfully employed is one less Diamond for me to worry about."

FELIX CARRIED ON to the Star, hoping the quivering in his stomach would settle down once he was inside. He couldn't believe he'd said it. About Vince Knight. To his face, no less! He had braced himself for a response and hoped he'd have a chance to duck or run away. But he hadn't needed to. Vince had just continued to frown at him. Felix thought back to what Tenner had said. What if Vince and the Watch did put people off from coming to the Star? Felix couldn't afford to lose custom. But then what was to stop the Diamond clan from taking over? The longer Uncle Gregory remained missing, the braver the Diamonds became. Only the threat of Uncle Gregory returning made them hesitate. Having Vince and the Watch in the Star would buy Felix more time but at what cost? Not for the first time in his life, he wondered what Uncle Gregory would do.

Dahlia was waiting for him. "What do you think?" She indicated to the tiara studded with emeralds on her head. "I was going to wear it tomorrow night. They're fake, of course. But enough to fool the uneducated, don't you think? Oh, before I forget, here." She presented him with a list of names. She had approached some of her more creative friends and offered them a spot on the stage.

"I don't know any of these people." He carefully set down the sack of vegetables, hoping to avoid another gaol-break.

"I didn't think you would," Dahlia said. "I'm just letting you know we've got some interest. Everyone on the list is going to bring someone with them."

"Hardly enough to fill the place."

Dahlia snatched the list from his hand. "It's a start, isn't it? And it's more than you've brought in."

"I was busy checking ale barrels for rats and lice all night," Felix said. "And lugging them up from the cellar. I haven't missed doing that, let me tell you. I don't remember the hatch being so tight."

Dahlia giggled and pressed his generous stomach, causing it to wobble. "You're bigger than you used to be, remember."

"Oi, enough of that, you," Felix said. "I'm a ship's cook and a good cook has to taste his food."

Dahlia hugged him tightly. "I'm just teasing, I love you like this, all cuddly and warm."

"Get off," Felix said, laughing. He opened the sack of vegetables at his feet. "I've got some provisions at the market."

Dahlia peered into the bag and pulled out a greying leek. "Nothing but the finest for the customers of the Star."

"This is all we can afford," Felix said. "And with the right amount of salt and pepper, no will notice. I've got some chicken bones to make a broth too. We need to make as much money as we can tomorrow night." He hadn't told her about borrowing money from Mr Marwood. He planned to pay him back from the opening night's takings. All being well, no one would ever know he'd borrowed it in the first place.

"What happens afterwards?"

Felix heaved the sack of vegetables over his shoulder once more. "We'll just have to wait and see how the show goes."

THE MOON HAD freshly risen when Vince spotted Tenner rifling through a coin purse and heading towards the Salt Pocket alehouse. Vince followed along, sticking to the shadows and doorways. Tenner's eyes were still puffy, his snub nose still marked with a red cut. He held his side as he walked, as though nursing a bruised rib or two. When he thought no one was watching, Tenner stopped and held out a hand to steady himself against a wall for a moment. Then he steeled his nerves and ducked into the Pocket. That was all Vince needed to be certain Alma Diamond was inside too. Tenner was the unofficial protector of the now-head of the Diamond clan. He was there to take the lumps and administer the beatings, a role Vince himself had played for someone else, once upon a time. He idly wondered if Tenner would ever be able to escape the role others had placed him in.

Sandwiched between two derelict houses on the west side of town, the Salt Pocket lived up to its name by being a tiny tavern popular with sailors. The Pocket was also a popular haunt of the Diamond family. Vince concealed himself in the shadows of a nearby Entry. He wondered if such a tactic would be possible in the glare of Sorcha and Iron Huxham's street lamps. He'd supported the idea but right then he could have been easily swayed against them. Darkness had its uses.

He didn't have to wait long before Alma Diamond appeared with Tenner in tow. She wore her usual fuchsia tones, with this particular garment decorated in a pattern of rose and black swordfish. She pulled on a pair of satin gloves and set off along the cramped road.

"Alma," Vince called out in his gruffest voice.

She stopped dead in her tracks and squinted in the wan moonlight.

Vince stepped forward, keeping his back to the moon. "Need a word."

"The widow Knight." She tried her best not to appear surprised. "Can this wait until morning? I have plans for the evening that don't include being harassed by a coarse-faced ox."

Tenner stiffened up behind her, lifting his chin and balling his fists.

"Private word," Vince said.

Alma cocked her head to one side. "Go on, Tenner. I'll catch up."

Tenner took a step closer to Vince. "But—"

"Go on," Alma repeated. "The widow Knight won't lay a finger on me. He wouldn't dare."

"Run along, boy," Vince said.

Tenner gritted his teeth and did as he was told.

When he was out of sight, Vince lowered his voice. "Need to ask about Gregory."

Alma stepped onto the path. "I rather thought you might."

"No secret his disappearance has been good for you. Put you up at the top of the family ladder."

"That wasn't a question," Alma said.

"Tell me what happened last time you saw him."

Alma snorted. "That wasn't a question either, you shambling oaf. The last time I saw Gregory was the day before he disappeared. We quarrelled over... Well, it's none of your business."

Vince set his balled fists on his hips and drew breath.

"Fine." Alma held up her gloved hands. "I asked Tenner to...monitor some competitors of mine. They were planning to hold a card game and, from what I'd been told, they weren't planning on inviting me. I happened to mention this in passing and Gregory took exception."

"Gregory didn't want Tenner to do it?"

"Oh no, Gregory wanted Tenner to beat them all black and blue. As a warning about what happens when one tries to muscle in on Diamond territory. Cards are our business. You know they say that's where we got our name from? Our great grandfather practically invented the art of card palming. Or so they say."

Vince couldn't care less. "Heated argument, was it?"

Alma laughed again. "Not so heated it came to blows, no. Or to murder. Arguments among family are hardly exceptional, now are they? Then again, maybe you don't know. It's not as if you have much family to speak of, is it?"

"Have some," Vince said. "Treat them better than you treat yours. Think Mariette Baxter would agree with me."

In a flash, all cordiality—insincere though it may have been—dropped from Alma's eyes. She all but snarled at him. "Mariette had it coming. She thought she could breeze in and use my family as her own personal guard. My stupid brother Billy had his head completely turned by her. Imagine—she really thought she could take on your gangs at the time!" Alma's teeth flashed and her fingers curled like claws. "I may not like you, but I'm no fool. I could see what she was doing. Mariette Baxter was ambitious to a fault, she wanted to oust your lot and take over your territory. The Diamonds survived as long as we have because we stayed out of your way. She would have ruined my family." She took a few steps along the path to gather herself, then turned back. "Does Felix know you personally ran his parents off the island?"

Vince dropped his fists.

The cold smile returned to Alma's rouged lips. "Did you tell him how I came to you that night? How I was the one who warned you what his parents were planning?"

"Felix won't hear it from me."

Alma's tongue poked into her cheek. "Well, well. So you've taken it upon yourself to protect him in more ways than one. Or so you'd have us believe." She took a step closer to him. "You might have pulled the wool over the council's eyes, but I've seen you, Invincible Knight. I've seen the real you. The one you're hiding beneath that uniform, that veneer of respectability."

"Knew me at my lowest point. Point where I gave in to my base urges. Not the same man any longer."

Alma licked her teeth. "I've seen you soaked in blood and knee-deep in the broken bodies of those who've crossed you. You haven't changed. You're not capable of it."

Vince lifted his chin. "Better hope I have. For your sake."

CHAPTER SEVENTEEN

THIS HAS TO go well, Felix told himself at sunset. He checked his reflection in one of the tilted looking glasses on the wall of the Star and smoothed out his tidy moustache. *This has to go well or I'll have no money, and no food, and no heat, and no lights. I'll be destitute and hungry and cold, and I won't be able to see the stairs properly, and I'll trip, and I'll fall, and I'll break my neck. So this has to go well.*

With a deep breath, he undid the bolts to the front doors. Dick Tassiter was first through, as expected, and took his favourite seat at the corner of the bar. People started coming in dribs and drabs and slowly the seats started to fill. A couple of sheepdogs wandered in and settled by the feet of their owners.

Felix welcomed as many people as he could in person, but he had to keep dashing downstairs to the kitchen to check on the food. He'd left three big pots bubbling with a stew of his own concoction. The less-than-fresh vegetables and a hessian bag of chicken bones had gone into the largest pot. He took some cheap cuts of fatty pork and rubbed them with pepper, salt, nutmeg, parsley, a little thyme, and some sweet marjoram. He tied the meat together and carefully dropped it into the boiling broth. His recipe had been for mutton, but the Star's budget wouldn't stretch that far.

The kitchen smelled the way Felix remembered it from his childhood, full of steam and fresh meat. Back then, the Star had a full-time cook called Mr Loxbeare—a surly chap who never let anyone into his kitchen without making them work. Sometimes it meant chopping a carrot, sometimes it meant mopping a floor. Felix often wondered if Mr Loxbeare was responsible for him wanting to be a cook himself. Certainly, Felix had never particularly liked him but he couldn't deny the impact he'd had.

When he returned upstairs, Felix found it a good deal busier than he'd left it. Ms Hornby had her hands full slinging ale and gin. "You should have hired more dashes!"

He grabbed as many empty glasses and tankards as he could from the tables. "I had no idea it would be so busy…"

"It's probably down to this." She pointed to a copy of the Blackrabbit Courant on the bar.

Felix unfolded the newspaper and spotted a mention of the Star. The story concerned the disappearance of Gregory Diamond and how in his absence, his nephew had taken over the reins of the "ailing alehouse".

"Playhouse," Felix muttered under his breath. He didn't know how to feel about his family business being splashed all over the newspaper for everyone to read. He certainly didn't like the insinuations made against the *notable Diamond clan*, though he couldn't in good conscience deny them.

He folded the paper and popped backstage to the dressing room—little more than a long chamber mostly used for storage these days. The performers Dahlia had acquired were in various stages of dress and undress. Some were slapping on thick make-up, others were struggling to fit into elaborate tunics, or searching desperately for a needle and thread to mend tears and missing buttons. One nude Chinese gentleman with a muscular rear end was having trouble fitting into a pair of hose the colour of holly.

Felix picked up the running order and ran his finger along it. "I thought Mr Zhang was going on first?"

"No, we moved him down a few spots," Dahlia said over her shoulder.

"I'm not going on before that mare!" Mr Zhang said, pointing to a skinny bald man at the far end of the chamber.

"You're only fit to follow where I lead, my darling!" the skinny bald man called back.

"But you now have two singers on in a row," Felix said.

"Yes, well, Ms Gastrel and Ms Hookway aren't here yet," Dahlia said.

"And then two jugglers? The crowd won't be happy. And why is Ms Gravillon's monologue on before the one-act tragedy? Couldn't you break those up? And shouldn't—"

Dahlia snatched the sheet from his grasp. "Felix. It's all in hand." She stared at him with one eye painted and the other still bare.

"Am I doing it again?"

"You are doing it again, yes," Dahlia said in a lighter

tone. "I thought you would have grown out of that by now."

"Yes. So did I." Felix left the performers to their preparations, making his way through the rabble of customers. He rubbed his palms on his thighs and told himself Dahlia knew what she was doing. *I don't need to worry. I don't need to worry. I do not need to worry.* Although, Felix thought she'd have an easier time herding cats. The ego and timekeeping of the average performer must have factored into his Uncle Gregory's decision to cut back on shows at the Star.

At the front of the bar, by one of the bay windows, Iron worked frantically to finish the repairs to the lift.

"I know I promised you it would be ready in time," he said, "but Mr Williams kept me working till all hours, and then I couldn't get this part cast in time and I—"

Felix reached out and touched his beefy arm. "Take a deep breath. All is well."

Iron's shoulders slumped. "It will be ready soon. Definitely, this time."

The front doors opened and Vince ducked inside. He removed his tricorne cap and looked around the room. The quality of the air itself noticeably shifted. The good-natured chattering crash of bonhomie from the crowd took on a sharper edge. Voices lowered and backs straightened. Vince's squat, drooling bulldog waddled in ahead of him and sniffed at one of the other dogs at the bar. A young Watchwoman—Sorcha, wasn't it?—pushed past Vince and found them a space to sit in a dark corner near the doors, whether to keep an eye on the whole place or so they could make a sharp exit, Felix didn't know. She seemed pleasant enough. Always smiling. Her big eyes watched everything though.

Another man entered with them. Older than Vince, with dark skin and some grey in his hair, he walked with a slight limp and wore a pattered brocade vest over a chartreuse shirt. He seemed jolly enough, and he laughed and joked with Sorcha. Vince sat on the bench against the wall so that there was no one behind him. He clicked his thick fingers, summoning his bulldog to his side; then he nodded to Felix.

Felix hurried over to take their order. He didn't want them moving about the Star too much. Already he'd seen one person leave after clocking them, and he could sense another two or three people getting ready to follow suit. At least they weren't in uniform. He hadn't seen Vince in his ordinary clothes before—a worn pair of coarse linen trousers and a navy blue woollen jumper with more than one hole in the chunky knit.

"Nice to see you again, Mr Diamond." Sorcha wore a simple gown, in shades of amber, tailored to fit her perfectly. "This is a fellow Watchman, Mr Clive Hext."

Felix shook Mr Hext's sinewy hand. This was how it would happen. This was how the Star We Sail By would be taken over by the Watch. Tenner had been right all along. Soon the Watch would be his only customers. He hoped they liked to drink. "I'll have some food ready in about an hour," he said. "Can I get you all something to drink?"

Sorcha insisted on following him to the counter to help carry the drinks back. She leaned on it patiently while Felix fetched a whiskey bottle from the shelf. He gave a moment's serious thought to poisoning Vince's drink, but immediately spotted two problems. Firstly, Sorcha was watching, and secondly, he didn't have any poison. "Can I ask you something? How can you work for him? Vince, I mean. He's a monster."

Sorcha drummed her fingers on the counter. "You are not the first person to ask me that. Listen, when I joined the Watch, my sister thought I was stone-hatchet mad altogether because I'd be putting myself up against Vince and his gangs. I spent years dealing with the aftermath of his crimes. His people controlled everything, *everything*. They took a percentage from businesses operating in his territory, they stole whatever wasn't nailed down, they smuggled, they blackmailed, they robbed. The Watch couldn't do anything about them. Nor could the greencoats. And it wasn't just the townsfolk who were frightened of him. He was a phantom, a scary tale criminals told one another. When he stepped down from that life, the gangs tore themselves apart trying to replace him. When the dust settled, they were even worse than before.

"Then the first week he took over the Watch, he put an end to the two most dangerous gangs this island has ever known and recruited the third—the Clockbreakers—into the ranks of the Watch itself. And they all follow his lead. He took a problem and made it a solution. He works longer and harder than any of us to make the town safer."

Felix leaned in to object but Sorcha cut him off.

"Yes, yes, I know," she said, waving her hand. "He organised the gangs of Blackrabbit in the first instance, he changed the way they operated forever, but he's cleaning up his own mess. I'm sure you've heard the stories about him and don't get me wrong, they're all true. But he's no longer the same person. He's trying to be better. Give him a chance and he'll prove it to you."

CHAPTER EIGHTEEN

FELIX RUMINATED ON Sorcha's words as Iron appeared from the lift, smiling and wiping his hands on a floral cloth. "All done! It should be—hullo, Ms Fontaine! Sorcha, I mean. I didn't know you'd be here." He stood beside her at the counter.

"I was just thinking the same. You've got the very best horologist in town working for you, Mr Diamond."

"Oh, stop," Iron said. "In a few minutes; there's no hurry."

Felix laughed as he poured the drinks. "I didn't know you two were friends."

Iron tucked the oily rag into his pocket. "Oh, we're... Are we...?"

Sorcha shrugged and took two glasses in her hands. "I like to think so. We worked together on the street lamps. Iron here designed them for me. And a wonderful job he did too."

"Well, thank you kindly," Iron said, taking a little bow.

"He's been fixing the Star's lift all week." Felix wiped up a spillage with a cloth. "I hope it hasn't kept him away from more important work?"

"Not at all," Iron said. "And besides, the repairs are complete. All that's left is to test it out."

"Oh, I know who should give it a lash," Sorcha said. "Clive. *Clive!* Get over here. I need you for a minute."

Mr Hext arrived and took his drink from the counter. "You could have carried this over yourself, you know."

"Not that," Sorcha said. "Come on, come here to me." She took him by the arm and led him into the lift.

Felix supposed his limp made him as good a candidate as anyone.

"It's because of this," Mr Hext said. He pulled down his stocking and pulled up the leg of his breeches to reveal a gleaming brass horological limb. Through gaps in the curling metalwork, cogs and springs sat tightly wound and ready to move.

Iron leaned down for a closer look. "May I?"

"Help yourself," Mr Hext said. "They assist the foot in moving up and down. They take the strain. Still, stairs can be a bit tricky."

"Wonderful work, just wonderful." Iron pulled across the gate and pointed to a lever inside the lift. "Just take it up to the first floor for now."

Mr Hext took a theatrically deep breath and pulled the lever. At first, nothing happened, but then the lift gave one sudden shudder and with a loud ticking, it slowly started to rise. To Felix's surprise, the crowd in the Star held their drinks up and gave a great cheer as Mr Hext and the lift disappeared from view. He supposed some feats transcended petty tribalism.

"Hope the Knight swine gets stuck in it!" someone shouted from across the room.

Felix slapped Iron on the shoulder. "Thank you," he said. "You've done wonders."

Iron slipped his arm around Felix's waist. "I'm happy to have helped." He held Felix's gaze for a moment.

"Mr Diamond," Ms Hornby said from behind the bar.

"You're needed." She pointed to Dahlia's head, which was poking out from the curtains on stage.

"I'd better go." Truthfully, all Felix wanted was to keep Iron's arm around him forever. Reluctantly, he plodded towards the stage. Another cheer went up when the lift reappeared and Mr Hext emerged, waving.

"Ah, I thought we got rid of him!" the man across the room shouted.

Felix climbed the three steps to the little stage where Dahlia hissed at him. "When do you want me?"

He threw his cloth over his shoulder. "I can have Ms Hornby announce you now, if you're ready?"

"You do it," she said.

Felix shook his head so rapidly he thought he'd break his neck.

"Go on," she said. "You're the new landlord, it'd be better coming from you."

"No, no, no," Felix said. "No chance."

He didn't think he'd ever get used to being called the landlord but he supposed it to be true. The Star was his now for good or ill. Its success or failure rested entirely on his shoulders.

Dahlia reached out and took his hand. "You can do

it. And remember—I'm on first."

Felix swallowed hard and puffed his cheeks out. Dahlia nodded enthusiastically and disappeared behind the curtain again.

"Um, everyone, if I...if I could please have your attention?" The bar had more than half filled and the mood had become rambunctious. "People of Port Knot? Please? Just a moment of your time. I'm delighted to see you all here tonight for the grand re-opening of the Star We Sail By, and I'd like to thank you for coming. My name is Felix Diamond and on behalf of myself and my cousin Dahlia, I'd like to—"

"Get on with it!" a man shouted from the back of the bar. He sounded liked the man who wished the lift would get stuck.

Some people laughed, others tutted.

"Um, yes, well," Felix said, "without further ado, let me introduce our first act, Miss Dahlia Diamond."

A smattering of applause welcomed Dahlia to the stage where, in thick white makeup, she performed a scene from one of Shakespeare's comedies. Felix had no idea if she did well or not but the crowed seemed to enjoy it. He kept busy behind the bar, helping Ms Hornby to serve drinks.

Dahlia's second performance turned out to be a good deal more engaging. With accompaniment from some musicians, she sang a song the whole room knew and chimed in with. Her voice was smokey and engaging, almost effortless in its melodiousness. When the rapturous applause for her had died down, she invited the next act on stage. The skinny bald man Felix had seen backstage put on a salacious skit about the council in which he played each part with the help of crude animal masks.

Next came Mr Zhang—the muscular gentleman in the tight hose—who performed an operatic aria, possibly of his own composing. After him, one young man played a fiddle while another sang a supposedly comical song; however their effort was somewhat off-key and came across as melancholic. Felix shot a look to Dahlia who whispered to one of the men. Their next song was a good deal cheerier and some in the crowd started swaying in their seats. The song after that was just about the filthiest thing Felix had ever heard on dry land, but it got everyone in the room laughing and singing along.

Felix had been dividing his time between serving behind the bar and checking on the food in the kitchen.

"Iron, are you...? Can you give me a hand? Please?"

Iron followed him downstairs, into the kitchen. He took all the bowls he could find from the cupboards and laid them out on the long table in the centre of the room. Each one had a chip out of the rim and no two were alike. While Felix dished out his stew and sliced up the fatty pork into pieces, Iron tore chunks from day-old loaves of bread.

Felix hurried along the line of bowls, dropping lumps of pork into each one. Broth splashed over the edges, and he cursed himself for his untidiness. He wiped the edges of them with a cloth, making sure they were perfect.

"I wouldn't worry so much," Iron said.

Felix didn't respond, he just carried on wiping edges. His hands had started to shake. He closed his eyes and tried to stop them, but that just made them shake more. The ladle fell from his grip, splashing his boots and trouser legs with broth. "Stupid," he said under his breath. He dropped to his knees to retrieve the ladle, then started wiping up the mess on the tiled floor. His ears had started to throb, his heart beat as though trying to escape his chest. "Stupid bleddy fool," he said again.

Iron knelt in front of him. "Leave it. It can wait until later."

"No, I have to do it now." Felix kept on wiping up the mess. He accidentally mashed a piece of potato into the cracks between the tiles and started trying to pick it out with his fingernail. "The crowd will be getting angry; they want food. Come on, come on." He picked and picked at the tiles.

"They've waited all night; they can wait another few minutes," Iron said. "Stop it; you'll injure yourself. Give me your hands. Come along. Don't be difficult. Now, take a deep breath."

Felix sat back on his heels, his face hot and turning redder by the second. "I can't."

"You can. It's easy." Iron held out his own hands, but still Felix refused.

"I can't. I haven't time. I need to get this food up there, and I need to help Ms Hornby behind the bar, and Dahlia must be having kittens by now, and I haven't even—"

"Felix, stop. Stop." Iron reached over and took Felix's hands firmly in his own. "Dahlia and Ms Hornby know what they're doing. Trust them."

Felix's eyes started to sting. "It's not easy for me. I just..."

"You think you have to be in control of everything?"

"It's not like that," Felix said. "If it all goes wrong and I didn't do *everything* I could, *when* I could, then I'll never forgive myself."

Iron smiled at him. "You mean you'll never stop blaming yourself."

"Something like that."

Iron squeezed his hands, gently. "Nothing is going to go wrong. The Star is almost full. The crowd are enjoying the show. The bar is taking in money. And, I don't know if this counts, but I'll be here all night. And if you need me for anything at all, you need only ask."

Felix's grip tightened. "It counts."

He carefully filled the rest of the bowls; then he and Iron took the first trays upstairs in the lift. The lift wobbled and jerked, but Iron managed to only spill a couple of drops which he promised to clean up before serving. They set the trays on the counter and shouted to the crowd to come and get it.

A rowdy line quickly formed and each person slapped their coins on the counter.

"Oi, landlord," one man shouted. "Haven't you forgotten something?"

Felix's brow immediately moistened.

"How are we supposed to eat this?" The man laughed and the line of people jeered. Iron gritted his teeth and fidgeted with his waistcoat pockets. Felix hurried down in the lift and raided the kitchen drawers for every spoon he could find.

"Stupid, stupid, stupid." His pits were damp, his legs were shaking. How could he have forgotten something so basic? He knew how, of course. He'd been distracted by Iron's beautiful brown eyes, by his warm grip, by the place where his shirt collar opened and revealed the top of his strong chest...

When he reappeared upstairs, the crowd were chanting, and they cheered when he splayed the spoons out for them to take. Iron handed out some to the people in the back of the queue.

After a few minutes, Dahlia appeared and nudged Felix in the ribs. "Look lively." She nodded to a wiry woman at the door. "Aunt Alma's here. And she's not alone."

CHAPTER NINETEEN

FELIX CLENCHED HIS fists as Aunt Alma marched to the front row of seats with a dozen of the Diamond cousins, including Tenner, Clarity, and Slate. They intimidated people out of their seats before dragging a handful of tables together and gathering around them, shouting their drink orders to Ms Hornby. All this, while a man on stage tried to ignore them and not lose his place in the somewhat rambling poem he'd been reciting before they arrived.

Vince stood and moved to interject, but Felix quickly shot him a look and shook his head. Vince huffed and dropped back onto his seat. The last thing Felix needed

202 - GLENN QUIGLEY

was for the Watch to weigh in.

He took a deep breath. "Aunt Alma," he said. "What are you doing here?"

She wore her hair in neat swirls and paired her high-necked fuchsia gown with a fuchsia jacket patterned with bold, white roses. Fuchsia satin gloves and brocaded fuchsia silk shoes completed her carefully cultivated appearance. "I thought we should come and support you, dearest nephew," she said. "It's so important to keep places like this alive. Why, aside from the theatre, there's hardly a decent playhouse left in Port Knot. Nowhere for the arts to thrive. You're doing a good thing, my boy. A good thing." She reached out and tapped his hand a couple of times. "Your uncle Gregory would be proud."

She pulled a deck of cards and dealt a hand for her and Clarity. Felix remembered well why those looking glasses on the back wall had been tilted. He was able to see her opponent's cards, and so could she. Tenner stifled a laugh and sloughed off his charcoal overcoat with the embroidered flames. He draped it over the back of a chair and something inside knocked loudly. The leather strap of a baton poked out from an inside pocket. From a heavy bag, Tenner handed out coin after coin to Clarity and the other cousins.

"There's no gambling in the Star," Felix said. "Where did you get all those coins?"

Tenner looked to Aunt Alma.

"Never you mind," she said.

Felix swiped one of the coins and examined it. "Are these counterfeit?" His face began to heat up and he stormed off a few paces, stopped, and turned on his heels. "No," he said.

Aunt Alma set down her cards. "I beg your pardon?"

"No," he said again. "I'm not having this. Uncle Gregory would never put up with your nonsense in his place, and I won't let you either."

Aunt Alma's eyes sharpened. "You won't *let* me? And just who are you to *let* me do anything? Listen here, you little bilge rat, this is my brother's tavern—"

"Playhouse," Felix said.

"My brother's tavern," Aunt Alma said, "and with him gone, I'm head of the family, so I decide who will and who will not be allowed to operate in this place. Count yourself fortunate I don't turf you out on your ear, boy. Gregory was always fond of you, and that's the only reason I'm letting you stay here."

Felix's face nearly caught fire. "You're letting me?" he said. " *You're* letting *me* stay here?" He spat the words out.

The man on stage had given up trying to recite his poem. A few people in the crowd drained their glasses and scurried out through the front doors.

Dahlia took his arm. "Come along, Felix. Leave them to it."

He broke free of her grip. "No, I won't leave them to it. You can see what she's doing, can't you?" He raised his voice so the whole room could hear. "She's marking her territory. She wants everyone to know this is a Diamond tavern. Well, it isn't. I won't have the likes of you running decent people off."

Aunt Alma's arrowhead eyebrows shot at the ceiling. "The likes of me? Gregory opened his doors to any Diamond in need. You of all people know that."

"Uncle Gregory knew you were poison; that's why he kept you—all of you—from doing business here. You're in need of nothing save for a good—"

"Dahlia, talk to him," Aunt Alma said. "Talk to him before he says something he'll regret."

"Come along, Felix," Dahlia said.

"Get out," Felix said.

Tenner braced himself and waited for word from Aunt Alma, who simply stared dead ahead, ignoring everyone.

"*Get out!*" Felix gripped one of the tables and turned it over. Tankards dropped, ale splashed, cards fluttered, and the cousins jumped to their feet, waiting for the word to strike. In a flash, Felix reached into Tenner's overcoat and drew the baton from it, holding it high overhead.

Aunt Alma calmly wiped some foam from her fuchsia gown and rose to her feet. She stood taller than Felix and looked down at him with her stone-grey eyes. "Felix, you need to remember how things work around here. This is a dangerous town. And you won't survive long without friends. Without family. We are all you have now. Gregory isn't coming back."

"What makes you so certain, I wonder?" He still held the baton, ready to strike.

Her eyes flashed and her voice dropped. "You have too much of your mother in you. Her temper got her in trouble too. I won't tolerate another outburst like this." In the complete silence of the bar, she walked to the front door with the cousins in tow.

Tenner knocked some drinks from people's hands as

he passed by, daring them to react.

Aunt Alma stopped and pointed to Vince, Sorcha, and Mr Hext. "I never thought I'd see the day when a Diamond wasn't welcome here but a bunch of Watchfolk were." She spat on the floor; then she and the cousins left without another word.

Felix finally lowered his arm and set the baton on the counter. His heart pounded as if fit to burst. He cursed himself for being so stupid, so reckless. Tenner could have attacked him, so too Alma, Clarity, and the rest of the cousins. They could have beaten him to a pulp. His set his hands flat on the counter to stop them from quivering. What if they came back when he was sleeping? He'd have to bolt every door and window. But then what if they set the Star ablaze? He'd have no way to escape.

His heartbeat gradually slowed, and though it had felt like many minutes to him, it had likely been only a few seconds since the Diamond clan departed. A young man with sunken eyes and protruding ears had stood aside to let them out before entering the bar himself. He looked around, puzzled. Sorcha waved him over to her table and he joined her company, shaking hands with Mr Hext. Felix was certain he'd seen the man somewhere but could not remember where until Ms Hornby spoke to him. The man with sunken eyes was Mr Sparrow, one of Ms Hornby's lodgers and the one who had opened the door to him at Ms Hornby's home.

He was also, Felix then realised, the town's lamplighter. He passed by the bay windows of the Star every morning and every evening with his lighting pole. He must work closely with both Sorcha and Iron. Speaking of, where was Iron? Felix spun around, hoping to catch sight of him. He hadn't gone to use the privy; he would have had to pass Felix to do so.

In the silence following the Diamond clan's departure, a clutch of other customers gathered their belongings and left. Felix's heart began to beat louder in his eardrums. Had he caused them to leave? He'd never flipped a table in his life before tonight. For all his talk, he'd done exactly what a Diamond would do. He'd been the one scaring away his customers, not Aunt Alma.

Vince marched to the bar and spoke loud enough for everyone to hear. "Think we can all agree that was unpleasant. No reason to let it ruin the night. Get the next act on, Felix. Everyone else, get a drink. On me."

The remaining people in the bar murmured and

mumbled amongst themselves. A couple more people left, but the rest took Vince up on his offer. A band started playing on stage and two portly men performed a very bawdy dance to much laughter, and within minutes one would swear nothing had happened at all.

"Where's Iron?"

Vince sucked in his gut, lifting himself up to great height. "Left after you flipped the table."

Felix's stomach plummeted to his feet. "What? Why?"

"Couldn't say. Seemed startled."

Felix pushed past Vince and bounded through the bar, out into the rain. He turned this way and that, but of Iron he found no sign. Resigned, he returned indoors.

CHAPTER TWENTY

A SHORT TIME later, at the front of the stage, Felix gathered some tankards from the floor as Vince righted the tables. "You don't have to," Felix said. "And you didn't need to buy a round for everyone either."

"Couldn't have your first night be a flop." Vince set some tankards on the bar and tried to hold back a yawn. Without his greatcoat and tricorne, he cut a less imperious though no less imposing figure and still stood a head taller than anyone else in the room. Felix noticed the holes in his knitted jumper were worse under his arms. Clearly, it hadn't been made to cover Vince's bulk. "None of you are in uniform," Felix said. "I take it you're not working to-night?"

"Thought you could use some support," Vince said. "Sorcha wanted to come too. Think she was secretly hoping to be asked on stage. Good singer, she is. Clive can't resist a night out either."

Sorcha sat with Mr Hext and Mr Sparrow, tapping her toes along to the music. She cheerily waved over when she realised she was being talked about.

"The Watch has changed while I was away," Felix said. "It used to be a bunch of bad-tempered old gits spoiling for a fight."

"Some of it still is," Vince said.

He might have been making a joke about himself, Felix couldn't tell, but he told himself to smile, regardless.

Vince dropped a rag onto a puddle of ale and mopped it with his boot. "Spoke to your aunt Alma about Gregory. Know they had a row before he disappeared?"

"I'm not surprised. They always fought like cats and dogs."

"Diamonds are no strangers to quarrels, it's true. Could have taken a nasty turn this time."

"I wouldn't put it past her." Felix dried a wet tankard

with a cloth. "You know I'm one of them? You never talk to me as if I am. Sometimes, if I didn't know better, I'd say you were trying to get a rise out of me."

"Doesn't sound like something I'd do." Vince wrinkled his nose. "Nothing like them, far as I can tell."

"Ah, but then you don't know me. Sometimes I think it'd be easier just to...I don't know, join in with them, I suppose. At least I'd have family around me instead of being alone."

He carried the empty tankards to the bar and gave them to Ms Hornby.

Vince leaned an elbow on the counter. "Thought you were a sailor? Crew is your family now, no?"

"Crews are family until they're not. Until you take a new commission and start over again. I started working in the galley to hide away from people. It's hard work but I'm not pestered from sunup to sundown."

"Not sure you're going to enjoy running an alehouse."

Felix moved to object, but Vince held up his hands. "Playhouse, playhouse," he said. "Lot of people here. Every night, if you're lucky. Which you are. According to Dahlia."

"I know. I know," Felix said with a laugh. "Maybe a

change would do me some good."

"Something else is worrying you."

Felix licked his own lips. "If Uncle Gregory is...gone, and if I stay here, it means being around the family and I just...I don't want to end up in the family business."

"Then don't."

"Come now, you know it's not so easy. It's insidious; it starts small. Turning a blind eye, holding onto some stolen trinket for a while. Before you know it, you're in it. I've seen it happen. I can't keep the family out of here forever, much as I want to. They don't respect me the way they respected Uncle Gregory."

"Not yet."

Felix cleared his throat. "I wish I had your optimism."

Vince grunted. "Not sure anyone's ever called me optimistic before. Got good instincts about people though."

"And what do they say about me, these instincts of yours?"

Vince shrugged his heavy shoulders. "Tell me you'll do the right thing."

"Really?"

"Really. Because you're smart enough to know that if you don't, you'll have to answer to me."

Felix clinked his glass against Vince's. The man had a point. "There's something I haven't told you. Something I haven't told anyone." He reached into his pocket and withdrew the little key marked with a star. "Uncle Gregory sent me this, along with the letter and the front door key. I didn't want Aunt Alma to know about it. If Uncle Gregory had wanted her to have it, he wouldn't have sent it to me."

Vince frowned. "Gregory must have a safe or vault?"

"I already thought of that," he said. "There is a safe but this key is too small for it. I just don't understand why Uncle Gregory didn't just tell me what it opened."

Vince reached over and took the key, weighing it in his palm. How small it looked in his meat-pie hand. "Gregory must have been worried about his letter being intercepted. Couldn't tell you what the key was for without alerting others, as well. Gregory was a Diamond. Must have had plenty of secrets. Plenty of enemies. Must have had a place to stash things away. Not a safe, then something else. Not the cellar?"

Felix shook his head. "I searched it thoroughly."

"Someplace else then. Know for a fact Gregory took in stolen goods from time to time. Didn't like his family working here but wasn't averse to doing some business on the side himself."

"Oh, I know," Felix said. "But you make a good point. I've checked his room and there's nothing up there. I've searched the Star, top to bottom. This key must open something special. Some hiding place of his."

"Might not be on the premises," Vince said.

"Hmm, no, I think it is," Felix said. "Uncle Gregory sent this to me and I no longer know Port Knot. It changes so quickly and I've been gone so long."

"Bits are funny." Vince touched the end of the key with his thick thumb. "Short. Odd shape. Might know someone who can help."

"A locksmith?" Felix asked.

"Something like that." Vince slipped the key into the pocket of his scruffy linen trousers. "Most of my new Watch were part of a gang of lockpickers and housebreakers."

Felix's eyebrows shot up. "I had heard some talk about it. The town's sentries are its former criminals. Well, what's the old saying? Set a thief to catch a thief. I don't think whoever came up with it meant it to be taken so literally, mind you."

Vince shrugged. "Working well so far."

THE MUSIC ON stage continued for a good hour or more, and the crowd happily sang and clapped along. A few people had cleared a space to dance a jig, slopping ale across the floor and laughing uproariously. A thick fog of tobacco smoke lingered, fed by the many clay pipes of the patrons. Vince added to it himself when he produced his pipe from his coat pocket and lit it at the bar.

Felix pushed his way through the crowd to clear tables. A few people stopped him to tell him how glad they were to see the Star open again and so full of life. He smiled at them and nodded sheepishly. Vince studied him carefully, noting the awkward way he moved around people. He kept his chin low, always looking at the ground, as though afraid to be noticed. There was a man comfortable in the background.

Sorcha took Felix by the arm and persuaded him to dance. Felix moved about, heavy-footed and cumbersome, until Sorcha took him by the hand and led him in an impromptu minuet. Felix laughed and tried to hide his face.

"I don't suppose I could entice you up for a dance?"

Vince turned his head to find the brawny Ms Briony Underhay standing on his blindside. "Not tonight, Ms Underhay. Surprised to see you here." He turned to rest both forearms on the bar.

Ms Underhay leaned out to get a better look at his rear end. She smiled. "I had to see what Gregory's nephew was up to. The whole docklands have been talking about it."

"Thought dockers preferred the Jack Thistle?"

Ms Underhay hopped onto a stool to avoid the now-drunk lamplighter, Mr Sparrow, who staggered into her on his way out to the privies in the backyard of the Star. "Nah, not since they brought in all those pub games. You can't have a drink in peace without hearing darts slamming into a board or the clattering of skittles. Mind you, this isn't much better." She nodded to Ms Gastrel and Ms Hookway, a double act who performed ventriloquism, with one acting as the doll spouting all manner of filth. "They're doing well but some of these other acts... If this is the quality of entertainment on offer, I'll take my chances at the Thistle." She took a drink and eyed up Vince's bum again. "Unless you're offering some entertainment, of course."

Vince looked at her and couldn't help but laugh. It had been a long time since a woman propositioned him so blatantly. "Not tonight, Ms Underhay," he said again.

She reached over and grabbed his bearded chin, giving it a squeeze. She squinted as she spoke, trying to focus. "Some other night, then, big man." She winked at him, finished her drink, and left.

"You've got an admirer there," Ms Hornby said. "But if I may offer a piece of advice? I'd steer well clear of that one."

Vince frowned at her.

"She was no good for Gregory. She only wanted free booze and a quick tumble."

"Don't we all?"

Ms Hornby laughed and returned to cleaning tankards.

The last act of the night cried off as he'd been left waiting so long he'd had far too much to drink. He staggered to the door in the arms of a woman who told him he'd regret overdoing it in the morning.

"I think we'll have to call it a night," Dahlia said from the stage. "Unless any of you lovely lot would like a go?"

"Sure I thought you'd never ask!" Sorcha pushed her

way to the stage and hurried up the little steps.

Dahlia bowed and left her to it.

Sorcha cleared her throat, started with a low hum to find the right key then launched into a haunting ballad, sung, Vince assumed, in her native Irish, for he didn't understand a word of it. Still, there was no denying the emotion in her voice. Once a fiddler joined in with the tune, he found himself swaying along, just a tad.

After a few minutes, she finished her song to heartfelt applause and joined Vince at the bar.

"Happy now?" he asked.

"Oh, yes," she said, positively beaming. "That's set me up for the week, that has."

"Should ask Felix for a regular spot." Vince turned his head to find Felix moping by the stairs. He felt a great swell of pity for the lad. His actions had frightened the object of his affections, Iron Huxham. Vince wondered if they were in the first throes of becoming suitors. Certainly to his eye, they had all the bungling vitality of young love.

Dick Tassiter was the last to leave and had to be gently encouraged out by Felix. Sorcha retrieved her coat and stood at the door, waiting for Vince. "Come on, aul man, I'll walk you home," she said. "I wouldn't want you walking these roads alone at this time of night. Sure anything could happen to you."

"Decent of you," Vince said. He turned to speak to Felix but stopped. He touched his pocket before thrusting his hand inside. He checked the next pocket and the next.

"What's the matter?" Sorcha asked.

"Key," Vince said. "Someone's taken it."

CHAPTER TWENTY-ONE

VINCE AND SORCHA scoured the floor of the bar, moving every table and chair while Felix checked the hallway and Dahlia searched backstage. Ms Hornby looked inside every tankard and glass in the place.

"Nothing," Dahlia said. "What key is it? Not the front door?"

"A second key," Felix said. "It came with the letter."

"Why didn't you tell me about it?"

"I thought it might be important and, well..."

Dahlia slumped onto the edge of the stage. "And you don't trust me."

Felix put his hands on the bar and lowered his head. "It doesn't matter now. It's gone. He lost it."

"Wouldn't say lost," Vince said. "Lot of people around us earlier. Ordering at the bar. Wouldn't have taken much to slip a hand in and pilfer the key."

"I saw you talking with Briony Underhay," said Ms Hornby.

"Can't have been her," Vince said. "Would have seen."

Felix pointed to Vince's eyepatch. "Would you, though?"

"Kept her off my blindside as best I could." He slammed his palm on the counter, rattling some bottles. "Can't believe I let this happen."

Nobody spoke for a moment until Dahlia cleared her throat. "I suppose it could just as easily have happened to Felix."

"Not the same," Vince said through gritted teeth. "Should know better. Old fool."

"But how would anyone have known you had the key?" Dahlia sat on the stage wearing a juniper banyan, her hair tied up and make-up scrubbed off.

Felix sighed heavily and clamped his eyes shut.

"Because I took the key out to show Vince, right here, in front of everyone."

"Wait though," Sorcha said. "Why would anyone think the key was important? I've got a key, most people here tonight had keys. How would anyone know that key was special?"

Vince withdrew his pipe from his coat pocket. "Because I took it," he said. "Because whoever stole it has been waiting for it to turn up. Think whoever took your uncle was here tonight. Think they'll be back too." He tipped tobacco into the bowl and lit it with a striker.

"What makes you say that?" Felix asked.

"Wager they've been waiting a while for the key to show up," Vince said, smoke billowing from his nostrils. "Suspect they took Gregory to make him give up the key. Think me and Crabmeat should stay here tonight."

"I can stay too," Sorcha said.

"Need you back at the Watch House in the morning," Vince said. "Go home. Get some rest. Might need it."

She left with Ms Hornby and once they'd gone, Vince helped lock up, checking every door and window was properly barred and fortified.

"Presumably, whoever took the key knows what it's

for," Felix said. "So either they've got whatever it opens—"

"Or they'll be back here," Dahlia said.

"Fantastic," Felix said. "We've got—at best—a kidnap-per and—at worst—a murderer coming here at some point. And it's all your bleddy fault." He pointed to Vince.

"Don't wallow," Vince said, frowning.

"Shouldn't you get more Watchfolk here?" Dahlia asked. "To protect us, or catch the thief in the act?"

Vince shook his head. "Don't want to scare them off. Might work to our advantage, this. Force their hand. Get them to reveal themselves sooner rather than later. Safe enough with me here. Can promise you that."

VINCE TOOK A low, empty crate from backstage, stuffed it with rags, and put it at the top of the stairs then clicked his fingers twice. "Crabmeat. Bed."

Crabmeat waddled over to the crate, sniffed it a few times, and looked up at Vince with wet, sad eyes.

"Don't start," Vince said. "Need you to keep an eye out for burglars." He bent down and scratched Crabmeat behind the ears. "Bark if you hear anything."

Crabmeat climbed into the crate and turned around three times, then a fourth, before collapsing into a sleeping position.

"Good boy," Vince said.

Dahlia appeared at the top of the stairs in a long, jade velvet overcoat. Candlelight from the nearby sconce glittered in her perfect raindrop earrings. "Don't wait up, boys."

Vince put his hand on the far wall, blocking the stairs and stopping her from passing by. "Don't think it's a good idea."

Dahlia stood with her arms crossed. "May I ask why?"

"Thief is probably watching. Might get you like they got Gregory."

"I have been out quite often since Gregory vanished," she said. "They haven't abducted me yet." She tried to push past him, but he didn't budge an inch.

"Different now they've got the key," Vince said. "Going to use it."

"As far as I can see, the only one holding me against my will is you, you great lout." She hit his arm, half-heartedly.

He leaned down and whispered to her. "For all I know, you took the key. Going out to pass it off to an accomplice."

She pulled her coat tightly around her throat. "And why would I do that?"

Vince glanced upstairs to make sure Felix wasn't listening. "Still a Diamond, aren't you? Maybe Alma took advantage of your history with Felix. Got you to worm your way in here, into his good books."

"You think very little of me."

"Think very little of your whole family," Vince said. "Maybe you're thinking of selling it. Need money, don't you?"

Dahlia stood back and held her overcoat open. "Go on, then. If you think I have it, search me. I won't stop you."

Vince's hand remained firmly planted against the wall. Dahlia closed her coat and tied it with a belt. She tried to duck under his arm but he lowered it, quickly.

"Still not letting you go out." He kept his voice low. "Can manage one night without opium, can't you?"

She glared at him before stomping back upstairs and slamming the door to her bedroom.

With the Star We Sail By locked up tight and Dahlia retired to her bed, Vince and Felix sat in the tiny parlour on the top floor. Nestled at the back of the building, through a large, half-moon window it offered a view of the cemetery and the moonlight falling on the gravestone globes within. A bucket had been left in the middle of the room to catch drips coming from the ceiling. In one corner, a patch of black mould grew with gay abandon.

Felix set a bottle of cheap whiskey on the table between them. "I thought we should have a drink, settle our nerves. Or my nerves, at least." He poured two glasses and pushed one over to Vince.

Vince shifted about on the worn tawny settee. "Wanted to..." The words caught in his throat. "To say...sorry about what happened with the key." He took a swig of whiskey from his glass.

"I have to say, I'm surprised it happened at all." Felix leaned back in the ratty brown armchair, arms splayed outwards, glass held between two fingertips and his thumb. "I would have thought you'd be a bit too long in the tooth to fall victim to a pickpocket." He never once took his eyes from Vince.

Vince's left hand reflexively touched his eyepatch. "Must have come up on my blindside." His ears reddened and burned, just a touch. He wasn't used to being the victim of crime.

"You're going soft," Felix said. "I heard the stories about you, growing up. There was a time when no one would dare steal from you."

"Times change."

"So I keep hearing."

There was something in Felix's voice, a sharpness that wasn't present when he spoke to anyone else. Vince could hardly blame him. Felix was a Diamond and the Diamonds had plenty of stories about Vince, he was certain.

"Big lad, you are," Vince said. "Probably do a lot of fighting at sea? Heard there's always a scrap to be had on a long voyage. All those people, locked up together for weeks and months. Plenty of bad blood to be stirred."

Felix sucked in his own bottom lip. "There is but I try my best to avoid it." He paused there and Vince knew he was struggling with how much to say. Felix seemed to Vince to be the guarded type. He knew it well, the need to protect oneself, the urge to push away people and not reveal too much. The more people knew, the easier it became for them to hurt you.

"Already a boxer by the time I was your age," Vince said. "Worked as an enforcer too. Bigger you are, more fights other people find for you."

Felix sighed. "I feel the same. I could see how Uncle Gregory was feeding me up. A Diamond who can fight it worth a dozen who can't."

"Didn't want that life?" Vince asked.

Felix shook his head and refilled their glasses.

"Probably shouldn't take too much more," Vince said. "Need our wits about us in case the thief comes back."

"You have the bearing of a coach horse," Felix said. "Surely it takes more than a few glasses of bad whiskey to get you drunk?" He squinted, trying to focus on something in the far corner of the room. "What is that? Is that a panel? I've never seen it before."

Vince slid from the settee and crept over to the dark corner. "Fetch a lantern." He clicked his fingers. "Might just have found what we've been looking for."

Felix stood up from the shabby armchair and grabbed the baton he'd taken from Tenner. He heaved it and with every ounce of strength in his body, he swung it at Vince's head. The baton cracked. Or Vince's skull did. Vince slumped to the floor, fingers twitching. He rolled, turned, and tried to get up, his boots slipping from under him. Felix struck him again. Vince's lone eye wandered, unfocused. Lights popped and sparked in front of him. Another whack to the head sent him reeling.

CHAPTER TWENTY-TWO

HIS MIND A fog, Felix closed and locked the parlour door to prevent Vince from summoning Crabmeat, then he took some rope from a drawer. He tried to wrestle Vince's hands behind his back but gave up and settled for tying them together in his lap. He paced the floor while he waited for Vince to regain his senses, unable to stop his legs from shaking. Vince stirred and muttered something foul under his breath. Felix grabbed the baton again. He had checked it for blood and been relieved to find none. Vince blinked a few times, shook his head, winced, and spit. He tried moving his hands apart, pulling on the rope.

"I wouldn't bother," Felix said. "I'm a sailor, I know how to tie a good knot."

"Know you're angry about me losing the key," Vince said. "Still a bit extreme."

Felix paced and paced, his insides in turmoil, his forehead damp with sweat. "Do you know how I came to live with Uncle Gregory?"

Vince lifted his head to talk. "Diamonds always dumped their children off with him. Only responsible one of you."

"Uncle Gregory had space for us and work for us," Felix said. "He taught us skills, skills to help us survive."

"Didn't stop you running away."

"I wasn't a child by then."

"Barely fourteen, I hear," Vince said.

"Old enough to make my way," Felix said. "You knew my parents, didn't you?"

Vince twisted his wrists again. "Aware of them. Billy and Mariette."

Felix pointed the baton at Vince. "You were more than just aware of them. I know what you did. I know you're the reason my parents left Blackrabbit."

Vince remained as impassioned as the masthead of

the Star's balcony.

"My mother gathered a bunch of the family together," Felix said. "She was planning to ambush one of your gangs, to get rid of them. You found out. I don't know how, but you did."

Vince's lips parted, just a touch, then snapped shut. He lifted his chin and frowned. "Knew everything that happened in this town back then."

"You were hardly ever seen in public at the time. You preferred to do everything through your intermediaries. You made an exception for my parents. Why?"

"Diamonds rarely joined my gangs," Vince said. "Preferred to keep to themselves. Let them work in Port Knot because they were useful to me. Mariette was brighter than most Diamonds. More cunning. More charismatic. Already turned a couple of my people to her way of thinking. Thought she had a chance of success. Couldn't allow it. Rot has to be excised. Quickly. Before it spreads. Best way to send a message to everyone else was to do it myself."

"But they escaped your clutches."

"Message was sent though. No one else dared to defy me. Not for a long time."

Felix started pacing again. He swung the baton by its

leather strap handle. "I remember the day I came here to the Star. I remember my parents talking to Uncle Gregory. I remember him lifting me out of bed early the next morning and running to the harbour with me in his arms. We watched a ship sail away, and he looked at me with such pity in his eyes. I don't think he knew my parents were planning to leave without me. You were coming after them. They left me with Uncle Gregory because they knew I'd be safe with him. Then they went on the run. They left Blackrabbit, the only home they'd ever known, and they never came back."

Vince shook his head and instantly regretted it. He winced at the pain in his skull. "Felix, those parents of yours were bad people. Highwaymen. Used to rob coaches at gunpoint."

"And that makes it acceptable to run them off the island, does it?"

"Trying to say violent lives often end in violent deaths. Parents could have had it much worse."

"What would you have done if you'd caught them? Would I still have grown up without my parents, even if they'd stayed?"

Vince sighed, his brow dropping. "Perhaps."

Felix tightened his grip on the baton. "This is why you've been so nice to me. You feel guilty."

"Course I do. Have to be a monster not to. Caused you a lifetime of suffering. Least I can do is try to help you now." Vince studied his every move. "Didn't realise you knew I was responsible for what happened to your parents."

Felix stopped pacing. "I didn't until a couple of years ago. Uncle Gregory would never talk about why they left. Would you have told me yourself?"

Vince exhaled, loudly. "Like to think I would have. Suppose we'll never know."

"Not long after my parents fled, they wrote me a letter. The only letter they would ever write to me. They told me they'd reached America and started trading furs. They were making a good living for themselves. I remember my hands trembling when I read it, waiting to hear when they going to bring me out there to live with them, or when they were coming home. But they didn't do either. They told me Uncle Gregory would look after me." Felix's eyes welled up, and he sniffed away some tears. "When I went to sea, I always had a plan—to get to America. It took a few years to get the right ship, but I made it to Grand Portage.

I found where my parents lived. I knocked on their door and, ah, they were not happy to see me." He sniffed again, holding his wrist under his nose. "They told me what happened, why they had to leave. They told me they feared what would happen should you get your hands on them.

"They had this gold bracelet, a wedding gift from my father to my mother. My mother blamed all their rotten luck on it. She said everything started to fall apart as soon as she slipped it onto her wrist. Firstly, the plan to attack your gang fell apart. Then you, personally, came after them. They had to sell the bracelet to a ship's captain to pay for their travel to America."

Felix grabbed the baton in both hands and twisted it, squeezed it as though trying to rinse it of his anger. "The journey was rough, they said. Fraught with danger. When they arrived in the Americas, the ship they were on came under fire from Spanish raiders. My parents barely escaped with their lives. They saw one of the raiders take the bracelet from the dead hands of the captain. They'd planned to steal it back themselves, of course. Planned to sell it again to make some money so they could have a fresh start. But my mother said the bracelet was bad luck. Cursed. She was glad to be rid of it." Felix's stomach turned to lead, his blood ran ice cold. "They'd built a new life for themselves, and they didn't want any reminders of their old one. They even had more children. They thought the letter made their position clear; they saw it as a way of severing ties with Blackrabbit, with the Diamonds, with...with me. So I left them to it."

"Blame me for it," Vince said.

Felix's reddening eyes turned hard again. "You're damn right I do." He shook the baton when he spoke. "If they hadn't left, if they hadn't been afraid of you, afraid of what you'd do, maybe...maybe..."

"Maybe you'd be knee-deep in the Diamond family business instead of a career seaman."

"What, am I supposed to thank you for saving me from a life of crime?"

"Course not," Vince said. "Sorry won't ever be enough but I am sorry, Felix. Truly."

Felix was silent for a few moments. He weighed the club in one hand and then the other. "When I was young, I used to imagine killing you," he said. "I imagined shooting you, or stabbing you, or pushing you off the end of a pier and watching you drown. In my imagination, you were this great, big, wild animal with fangs and blood-stained claws. Barely human at all. Over time, I stopped thinking about you quite so much. Other things in my life took priority. But then I came home to Blackrabbit. And I went looking for help. And I found you. The monster from my fantasies, wearing a uniform, and on the right side of the law. I didn't know whether to laugh or cry. It sounded so...absurd. The very last person who should be in charge of the Watch—the person with least moral authority imaginable—was telling the rest of us to obey the law."

"Not wrong," Vince said. "Don't have a leg to stand on. Done worse things than even you know. Why I'm best suited to warn you all to stay away from that life. Why I'm best suited to rounding up those who still live it. Know it inside out. Know the harm it causes. Know the toll it takes. Regret it ever happened though. To them. To you. Were only a boy back then. Four? Five years old? Parents just leaving you? Horrible. Unthinkable. Not shirking the blame. No one's fault but mine. Can't change what happened. Why I'm with the Watch now. Trying to make amends. Trying to help as best I can."

His damned strained manner of speech, his skipped words, his burring, rumbling, voice, it all grated on Felix's ears. "Lucky you, you got a second chance."

"Yes," Vince said. "Lucky me."

Felix started pacing again, swinging the baton almost absentmindedly. He'd gone too far, and he knew it. Vince knew it. What was he going to do now? How had it come to this? He'd been so angry at Vince for losing the key but more than that—he'd been angry at Vince for most of his life. After resisting his temptation to shove Vince off the cliff above Chancewater, he thought he'd buried his anger, thought himself incapable of such callous violence, but the baton in his hand suggested otherwise. "You're the reason my life turned out the way it did. You shaped my whole future. How is that fair? Why should you have so much power over me yet I have none over you?"

"Not fair. Not right."

Felix whacked the baton against a wall, taking out a chunk of plaster. It crumbled to the slatternly carpet. "Stop being so bleddy reasonable!"

"Listen, Felix. Not the first person who's said something like this to me. Have had an impact on the people of this town. This island. Very little of it good. Why I joined the Watch. To make up for it the only way I know how." Vince looked to the baton. "Now what? Going to use that again? Bash my brains out? Leave me for dead?"

Felix let the baton hang by his side. He'd lost his way; he knew that. He knew it even as he'd lifted the baton the first time. This was not the waves breaking over him; this was the waves overpowering him, drowning him, dragging him under. The baton slipped from his hand and clattered to the floor. "Sorcha told me you weren't the man I thought you were. She told me you'd changed. I didn't believe her."

Vince nodded. He flexed his massive arms. The rope twisted, turned, frayed, and snapped. He stood and brushed the dust from his loose, linen trousers.

Felix didn't move. "You could have freed yourself at any point?"

Vince nodded again. "Knots are only as strong as the rope they're made from."

"You weren't actually unconscious either, were you?"

"Could see there was something you needed to get off your chest, so I let you. Feels better, doesn't it?"

Felix took a deep breath, trying to keep his composure. Before he could speak, Crabmeat began barking wildly.

CHAPTER TWENTY-THREE

VINCE BURST OUT of the parlour door and took the stairs three steps at a time. He passed the empty crate and discovered Crabmeat at the glass-panelled doors to the sail-boat balcony, barking as loudly as he could, gobs of hot saliva flying from his mouth. Vince went to throw open the balcony doors but found them locked. As he rattled the handles, Felix arrived and took the ring of keys from his pocket. He unlocked the doors and Crabmeat pelted through, scrambling to climb the concave walls of the sail-boat. Vince leaned over the side, scanning the road below but even in the light of the street lamps, he could find no trace of an intruder.

He held the back of his own head, checking for blood. He winced when he touched the bruise left by Felix's clubbing. Crabmeat plodded about, sniffing at the cold night air, before lying down in the middle of the balcony.

Dahlia arrived, holding a heavy candlestick. "They came in through here?"

"The doors were still locked," Felix said. "Crabmeat probably scared them away before they could get in."

"Must have climbed up the outside of the building," Vince said. "Not so unusual. Known people to climb up to get at the bedworkers stationed here."

"Stationed," Dahlia said. "You make it sound so formal. As if they were soldiers manning the battlements."

Vince's boot accidentally kicked something across the floor. Dahlia bent down to pick it up. She held up to the light. "It's the key," she said. "Well, it's most of the key." She held in her hand the bow and stem of the little key stolen from Vince's pocket.

"Burglar must have dropped it," Vince said.

"Didn't you see it when you—" Dahlia's voice trailed off when she looked at Vince's eyepatch. "Can't your dog follow the scent? He could lead us right to the burglar."

"Not a bloodhound," Vince said.

Crabmeat's nose leaked as they talked about him and he licked at it, happily.

Vince took a striker-lantern from one of the private booths, lit it, and crouched down, checking every inch of the sailboat balcony.

"What are you looking for?" Felix asked.

"Burglar came up here with the key." Vince rubbed his hand across the wooden walls of the balcony, with its globs of decades-old thick brown paint frozen in mid-drip, like wax down a candle. "Broke it when Crabmeat scared them off. Must mean..." The sharp, pointy end of a broken key stem stung his hand.

"They were using it in the keyhole." Felix took the lantern from Vince and held it so they could all get a close look. Wedged in where the floorboards met the concave walls of the sailboat balcony, he found a piece of panelling the size of a matchbox. He held it up to the lock and found the wood covered it perfectly. So perfectly, in fact, if one had not already known of its existence, it would have been virtually undetectable. "So the burglar already knew the lock was here."

"I assume you believe me now?" Dahlia asked.

Felix stood up quickly. "Believe you about what?"

Vince continued poking at the lock. "Not important."

"Mr Knight here thought I might have stolen the key," Dahlia said.

Felix thought about it for a moment. "Seems fair enough to me."

Dahlia stood open-mouthed. "What?"

"Well, you are a Diamond," Felix said.

Dahlia tutted and sighed. She pointed to the lock. "What does it open?"

Vince searched the floor of the balcony, knocking on the level wooden boards with his fist.

Felix held out his hand. "Stop. Did you hear that?"

"Something under here," Vince said. "Metal."

"It's just the support beams, I imagine," Dahlia said. "They'd have to hold the weight of the sailboat. And all the people."

Vince searched for some crack to work his stubby fingernails into, some seam to burst open. "Sealed tight."

"Now what do we do?" Dahlia asked.

Vince stood and huffed. "Know someone who's good with locks. Will get him in the morning."

Felix covered the lock once more. "I doubt the

burglar will return tonight."

"In which case," Dahlia said, "there's no reason I can't go out. Is there, Mr Knight?"

Vince grumbled and clicked his fingers for Crabmeat to follow him inside. "Burglar will be angry. Frustrated. Might be looking for someone to take it out on."

"I'll take my chances." She dashed upstairs to change and within minutes she was out the back door and on her way.

Vince touched his head again and winced.

"It's probably better if you stay here tonight." Felix turned the key in the back door. "Just in case anything happens with your injury. I assume you don't have anyone at home waiting for you? No one to keep an eye on you."

Vince grunted and followed him upstairs.

Felix led him into Uncle Gregory's bedroom. "There are nightshirts in the drawer over there, but they'll hardly fit you."

While Felix went to fill a jug with fresh water, Vince pulled off his navy blue jumper, slipped the braces off his shoulders, and stripped out of his linen topshirt, revealing his tattooed torso. With one hand holding up his linen trousers, he sat on the narrow bed, testing it could hold his bulk. He wrestled with his scuffed black boots and pulled them off, letting them thump to the floor. Crabmeat settled on a tatty rug at the end of the bed.

Felix returned and set the jug next to a white bowl on the dressing table. "I think I should apologise. For attacking you."

Vince snorted. "Pass my pipe."

Felix rummaged in Vince's coat and found the pipe, packet of tobacco, and a silver striker.

"Young men act rashly." Vince took the pipe. "Not as if you planned it. Would have done the same thing in your shoes. No real harm done. Won't hold it against you."

Felix sat on the end of the bed. It sank under his weight. "That's very... I don't know if I would be so magnanimous."

Vince clicked open the clockwork striker, making it spit sparks. "Wait till you get to my age, then see." He puffed on his pipe. "Wasn't just me you were angry with."

Felix's gaze dropped to the floor. "If I hadn't let the key out of my sight, this wouldn't have happened."

"Don't know that," Vince said. "Can't know that. Not worth dwelling on."

"Hah, if only it were so easy."

"Thoughts can be tamed. Takes time. Takes patience."

"You're not the first person to tell me something like that," Felix said. "And I try, I really do. A captain I served under once taught me a technique to calm myself down. I needed to use it a lot when I was around him."

Vince studied Felix's handsome face. He kept his cards close to his chest, but every now and then, his expression flickered, revealing a glimpse behind the curtain. "Wasn't just any old captain, was he?"

Felix licked his own lips. "Oh, no, he definitely wasn't. I was in love with him. Head over heels, butterflies in the stomach... I couldn't think straight when he was around. I was tongue-tied whenever I had to talk to him. And I might have gotten over him if we hadn't had our romp in the captain's quarters."

Vince leaned forward a little. "Romp?"

"He shouldn't have done it, professional ethics and all, but he wanted to, and I wanted to, and so we did." Felix clasped his hands between his own thighs and shrugged. "It didn't mean anything to him though. But it meant the world to me. Stupid, I know."

"Not stupid." Vince puffed on his pipe. "Young hearts

burn brighter. Nothing to be ashamed of. James should have known better."

Felix shot him a look, his mouth open. "How did you know who I was talking about?"

"Had an inkling. Way you flinched when you saw his portrait in my office. Meant you either loved him or hated him."

"I've felt both ways about him."

"Captain Godgrave has that effect on people."

Felix's shoulders relaxed and his attention wandered over the tattoos on Vince's bare chest and arms. "How do you know Jim?"

Vince blurted out a short, harsh laugh. "Never heard anyone call him Jim before. Can't imagine calling him Jim. Met him a couple of months back. Here, in Port Knot. Got himself appointed by the greencoat admirals to create his own version of the Watch. Gave him a new headquarters in the harbour. Same time as I took over the real Watch. Blew up in his face though. James left the island soon after."

"Were you and he...close?"

"Close?"

"You know what I mean. Were you lovers?"

Vince nodded and scratched his own chest. "Can't say if there was any love involved, mind you. On either side."

Felix toyed with a fold in the blanket. "And are you two still...close?"

"Written me a couple of letters. Haven't replied."

"Why not?"

"Been busy," Vince said. "Thought you were in the merchant arm of the C.T.C.? James is military. Greencoat."

"The captain of the C.T.C. vessel I served on was arrested for murder, and Jim took over his duties for a time so he could investigate the murder himself. He turned over every square inch of the ship, gave us all a right bollocking."

Vince snorted a laugh, sending smoke shooting from his nostrils. "Sounds like James."

"But while we served together, I fell in love with him." Felix's eyes glazed over a little, and he smiled in a way Vince hadn't seen him do before. "He's so big, and strong, and handsome. And confident too. There's something very appealing about a confident man. He has such a commanding presence. Everyone listens to him. He's..."

"Annoying. Overbearing. Bullish."

Felix laughed. "All those and more. The man's an absolute nightmare. Still. There's something about him."

Vince nodded. "Certainly is."

"When he left I gave serious thought to signing up as a greencoat so I could serve under him again. So to speak. But I'm no fighter."

"Could have fooled me." Vince touched his bruised head. He finished his pipe and set it on the bedside table. He swung his legs past Felix and stretched out on the bed. "Ask me, you're better off without him. James is a liar and an amoral opportunist."

Felix stood and nodded. "He looks good in a uniform though."

"Certainly does." Vince settled himself lower on the bed. "Looks even better out of it, mind you."

Felix laughed and held the door handle. "Sleep well. And if you think you might die from your head wound, do call for help, won't you?"

"Be the first to hear about it," Vince said. "Promise."

CHAPTER TWENTY-FOUR

VINCE LEFT THE Star We Sail By at dawn, just as a flock of gulls squawked overhead and as Dahlia was teetering up Bibbler's Brook. He held the door open for her. "Made it back in one piece then."

She smiled at him, her eyes unfocused.

"Come in and I'll make you breakfast." Felix took her by the hand. "Are you certain you won't stay and eat with us, Vince?"

Vince shook his head. "Keep the place locked up. Crabmeat, stay and look after them." He bent down to pet Crabmeat's head. "Don't feed him any cheese. Doesn't agree with him. Will be back soon."

Nearby, the lamplighter, Mr Sparrow, extended his long, knobbly lighting pole and pushed the tip into a slot in a lamp head. Inside the lamp, a snuffer lowered and smothered the candle flame. With a twist, the lighting pole retracted to half its length and Mr Sparrow used it as one might a walking stick. He nodded to Vince and Felix as he passed by. "I wish I'd called it a night sooner." He winced and rubbed his temple. "Tell Sorcha I might be late for our meeting today, Commander Knight."

A mizzling rain cooled Vince's skin on his walk back to the Watch House. Dazzling white and with a glass turret overlooking the water, it sat nestled at the edge of the harbour like an albatross waiting to take flight.

He sat in his cramped office and closed his eyes for half an hour. He never needed much sleep but had started awake multiple times at the Star. Partially from worry about the burglar returning and partially from worry that Felix's attack had done more damage than Vince had realised. He grumbled when Sorcha burst in and woke him to find out what had happened at the Star after she'd left.

He told her about the burglary and finding the hidden lock, and he told her about Felix and James.

"He knows Captain Godgrave?" She sat on the corner of his desk.

"Intimately."

"My, my. It's a small world, isn't it?"

Vince shrugged. "Both work for the C.T.C. Both good-looking. Both like men. Suppose it's not so strange."

Sorcha screwed up her eyes and pursed her lips. "And how are we feeling about this, hmm? Not...I don't know...jealous, at all?"

Vince adjusted his eyepatch. "Nothing to be jealous about."

"Of course not." Sorcha rose to her feet. "After all, it's not as if you and Captain Godgrave were ever suitors."

"Right."

"You and he were simply ships passing in the night. A mere bed-game."

"Correct."

She ran her finger along the framed charcoal portrait of Captain James Godgrave which Vince had drawn during their brief time together. "Nothing but the briefest of dalliances."

Vince set his palms on his desk. "Wouldn't be jealous even if I did have feelings for James. Not that sort of person."

Sorcha held onto the doorknob and smiled at him. "How fortunate."

Vince wrinkled his moustache at her. "Any Clockbreakers on duty?"

"Don't call them that," Sorcha said. "You know they don't like it. There are no longer any Clockbreakers; they're just Watchfolk."

Vince held up his hands. He never called them Clockbreakers to their faces; he just enjoyed getting Sorcha's hackles up.

"Celeste was here but I think she's out on patrol with Clive," she said. "Flowers is downstairs though."

"Send him up in an hour or so," Vince said. "Got a little job for him."

VINCE SHOWED FLOWERS to the hidden lock on the sailboat balcony of the Star We Sail By. Flowers, named for the horticultural tattoos adorning his body, set down his bag of tools and cracked his knuckles. He ran a hand across the crown of daisies inked onto his bald head.

Vince opened the bag. "Thought you'd gotten rid of all this?"

Flowers slapped his hand away. "I knew it would come in handy someday," he said. "Besides, shouldn't we know about all the tools the criminals are using these days?"

He lifted out a Ticking Ginny, a horological device used for cracking window locks, as well as half a dozen other elaborate implements Vince couldn't name—all the tools of the trade formerly used by the Clockbreakers gang.

Vince left him to work and plodded downstairs to the bar.

Felix eyed him and frowned.

"Whiskey." Vince settled himself onto a stool. "Bottle. Two glasses." He slapped some coins on the counter.

"Bit early, isn't it?" Felix said but brought him his order, regardless.

Vince poured some whiskey into each glass and pushed one towards Felix. "Watered-down rubbish, this. Barely fit for a baby."

Felix didn't respond, he just leaned on the bar and stared off into space.

"Dahlia upstairs?"

"She's trying to teach Crabmeat how to follow a scent," Felix said.

"Best of luck to her." Vince drained his glass. "Something on your mind?"

Felix inhaled deeply. "I find myself unable to move away from the thought of how useless I've been. Uncle Gregory asked me to come home. I don't know why, but I doubt he wanted me to just stand around getting drunk."

"Doing the best you can under the circumstances," Vince said.

"I should be out there searching for him." Felix stood up straight, possibly for the first time since Vince had known him. In the gloomy light of the shuttered bar, he cut quite a dashing figure.

"Safer here," Vince said.

"I don't need to be safe," Felix said, "I need to be... I don't know, useful. Active."

"Might get your wish sooner than you think."

Felix looked to him with narrowed eyes. "What makes you say that?"

Vince cleared his throat. "Been thinking about the burglar. Way I see it is this: Gregory gets kidnapped. Kidnapper wants something from him. Suppose whatever it is, it's hidden behind the lock on the balcony. Gregory confesses he sent the key to you. Kidnapper can't dig into the balcony without being noticed, so decides to wait for you and the key to show up. Reads in the newspaper about you putting on a show at the Star and thinks it's a good opportunity to find the key. Kidnapper sees me taking the key from you. Steals it from me. Breaks back in again last night. Gets disturbed by Crabmeat before they could open the lock. Breaks the key in the shock of a slobbering bulldog trying to get at them."

Felix nodded along, frowning the whole time, his heavy brow covering his nut-brown eyes.

Vince tried to think of a nice way to say his next piece but failed. "Means the kidnapper will be desperate. Desperate and dangerous."

Felix walked around to the front of the bar and paced about before sitting on a stool next to Vince. "But what could Uncle Gregory have hidden that would be worth all this?"

"Suppose we'll find out once Flowers has worked his magic," Vince said. "Been a rough couple of days. Can see you're still beating yourself up. Need someone to talk to, go visit your friend, Mr Huxham. Or talk to me if you're really desperate."

Felix looked at him. "Why are you being nice to me? I clubbed you over the head last night. You should lock me up."

Vince touched the bruise under his short, snowy white hair. His shoulders slumped and he cupped his glass in both hands. "Was right, what you said last night in the parlour. Feel guilty for what I did to you." He looked over Felix, from head to toe. "Could tell something was wrong with you. Weren't acting like yourself. Were colder. More distant—in your eyes."

"It was as though someone else had taken over my body. I was sitting at the back of my own mind, watching it all unfold."

"Maybe it was the Diamond in you finally coming out."

"I certainly hope not." Felix rubbed his own forearm. "I don't ever want to feel that way again. I'm sorry I struck you. That's not who I am, I swear. I could have killed you."

Vince couldn't help but snort a short laugh. "Hate to break it to you, but I've been hit a lot harder in my time," he said. "Wanted to kill me, would have kept hitting me with your baton. Tied me up instead. Waited. Wanted to talk. Knew you had a good reason. Glad you let it out. Doesn't do any good to keep feelings bottled up. Poisons you. Poisons your life." He rubbed the back of his own head again. "Still stings, mind."

Felix looked to see if he could find the mark he'd made. "I didn't even break the skin."

"Tough as old boots, me," Vince said. "Know you said you didn't want to get stuck in your family life, but anything in particular make you leave and go to sea?"

Felix sighed. "It sounds silly now, but there was this one day, nothing special about it, nothing unusual, just this one day where suddenly I saw my whole life unfold in front of me. I saw my mornings cleaning the bar. I saw my afternoons restocking the ale barrels. I saw my evenings dealing with drunks and fights. I saw the thieving, and the gambling, and the fencing, and the beatings. The constant looking over my shoulder and never being able to truly relax, never being able to truly escape the life of a Blackrabbit Diamond. Not if I stayed. Uncle Gregory is the best of us—which isn't saying much, admittedly—but even he has his dark side. He didn't want me to go. He tried to talk me out of it. Then he tried to frighten me out of it. I wanted something better for myself. And he didn't. I wish there had been another way to handle things, but I couldn't see one at the time."

"Life is seldom so neat. Just have to play the hand we're dealt."

Felix breathed out, his eyes damp.

Vince frowned. "Probably could have been more tactful. Never been my forte."

Felix laughed and sniffed away a tear. "I cannot get used to this. To you. Talking to you like...like you're a normal person."

Vince straightened up.

"I didn't mean it that way," Felix said. "You're so different from the man I thought you were. The man I was told about."

"Used to be that man. Spent too long being him. Even old dogs can learn new tricks. Sometimes."

Felix shrugged then as if the business with his uncle was all ancient history and powerless to touch him, but Vince could see the pain behind Felix's eyes. It had become clear to him Felix didn't tell his story often and it hurt to drag the words up from the little dark box in his heart. Vince's instinct was to hug him, to tell him he'd done the right thing. Vince knew the Diamond family, and Felix was dead right—he would have ended up in that life. No matter how high he climbed, his family would have dragged him back down into the gutter. But Vince didn't hug him. Of course he didn't. He hadn't known Felix very long, and it wasn't his place. Instead, he laid a hand on Felix's shoulder and squeezed ever so gently. "Only get one life to live," he said. "Don't regret trying to make yours better."

"If you're done drinking and sharing," Flowers said from the hallway. "I've opened your lock."

CHAPTER TWENTY-FIVE

FELIX TOOK A moment to compose himself. He stoppered the bottle of whiskey, then followed Vince upstairs to the sailboat balcony. The mizzling rain had eased and left the wooden floor slick.

"What did it open?" Felix asked.

Flowers—a lithe young man of Indian heritage, Felix guessed—knelt and found a crack in the floor. "It popped when I opened the lock." He worked his fingertips in and tugged open a hatch about the size of the one leading to the cellar. Flowers banged his fist on the metal lining of the hatch.

"No wonder Vince couldn't break it," Felix said.

"Would have worn it down eventually," Vince said.

"It wasn't an ordinary lock." Flowers ran his hands along the edge of the hatch. "If I hadn't been able to get the broken bit of the key from the lock and use it, I might not have been able to pick it. It was designed to break if tampered with."

Behind the hatch, Felix peered into a large cavity carved into the masthead itself.

"It's not simply lined with metal." Felix ran his hand along the inside. "It's an iron chest inside Atlas." He reached in and withdrew a wooden box intricately carved with dozens of blossoms and curling leaves. He knelt on the balcony floor and set the little box in front of him. Whatever this was, it held the reason he'd come back to the island, the reason his uncle had sent for him. He opened the lid.

"Well?" Flowers asked.

"It's a bracelet," Felix said. "A cuff bracelet." He held it up to the light. Wide and gold, patterned with frolicking rabbits and copses. Embedded with pearls, too, in places, and sapphires. "There must be something more." Felix frowned and turned the box, again and again, the lid clattered on its hinges. He scrambled to the cavity in the prow and thrust his hand inside, searching for something else, anything else. "There has to be! Why would Uncle Gregory send me the key just for this?" His breathing had become heavier.

Vince set a hand on Felix's shoulder. "Breathe," he said. "Take a moment. Breathe. Gregory must have had a good reason for hiding this. Probably worth money."

"Enough to kill for?" Flowers asked.

Vince turned the heavy bracelet for a better look at the inside. "Something engraved," he said, squinting. "*To Mariette. I will give you the world. Your Billy.*"

Felix's face dropped.

Flowers clicked his tongue. "Well? Who are Mariette and Billy?"

"My parents." Felix took back the bracelet. "How can this be here? Vince? I don't understand... How can this be here? This was taken by Spanish raiders years ago, how could it possibly be *here?*"

"Kidnapper knew about it," Vince said. "Bracelet is what they've been looking for. Why they took your uncle. So he could tell them where to find it."

Felix stood wide-eyed, his heart thumping at a rate of knots. "But how did they know about it? How... Wait.

Wait. The day I arrived, Tenner searched my bags while I was talking to Aunt Alma. He was looking for something."

Vince's brow furrowed. "For the second key?"

"No," Felix said, "if Tenner knew about the key, he would have searched my pockets." He held up the bracelet. "I think he was looking for this. And there's something else—his injuries were fresh."

Flowers started packing up his tools. "If I had to guess, I'd say Tenner stole it from someone, and they put up a fight."

Vince rubbed his chin. "Or whoever he stole it from found out about it. Attacked him, trying to get it back?"

"I suppose he could have already given the bracelet to Uncle Gregory by that point," Felix said.

"Sold it to him, most likely," Vince said.

Felix stood and rested his arms on the gunwale of the sailboat balcony. "It's worth a fortune. Uncle Gregory wouldn't have paid him very much for it. Maybe he took it with an eye to selling it on? Does this mean Tenner is the burglar? And the kidnapper?"

"WHERE ARE WE going?" Felix hurried to keep up with Vince who was marching through the narrow, winding streets of Port Knot at full speed.

"Don't need to come with me." Vince dashed down a set of stone steps jutting out from a bridge carved with clam shells. "Safer to stay at the Star."

"I'm tired of sitting around and doing nothing," Felix said, side-stepping a large pile of horse dung. "I don't understand how my father was able to afford the bracelet in the first place."

Vince cleared his throat. "Felix, think about it, lad. Mariette and Billy were highwaymen."

"Oh." Felix came to a halt next to a mangy cat. "Oh, of course. They stole it. Or Dad did. He stole it, had it engraved, and gave it to my mother as a gift. Then they sold it to a ship's captain and Spanish raiders stole it from him off the coast of the Americas. But how did it end up back here?"

"Hopefully we'll find out." Vince led them around a

corner and down a puddle-strewn alleyway at the side of a bakery and silently indicated to Felix to slow his pace. Vince pulled up the collar on his own claret overcoat, puffed out his chest, and hollered at the top of his lungs. "*Tenner!*"

A quaking Tenner spun on his heels and held out his spade like a sword. He swung it from side to side. "Get away! I didn't do anything! I wasn't doing anything!"

Ash powdered his clothes like the first snowfall of winter, and he wore a piece of cloth across his nose and mouth. He clawed at his dusty goggles, trying to clear the lenses but settled for pulling them off entirely. They left behind a cloud of dust in the air about his head. "Vince? What are you shouting at me for? I nearly had an accident! Felix, why are you lurking about?"

"Could ask you the same thing." Vince launched himself at Tenner and grabbed his collar. With his other hand, Vince easily wrenched the spade from Tenner's grip and threw it across the yard.

"I'm not lurking," Tenner said. "I'm working! Oh, that rhymes, that does."

"Likely story," Vince said.

Close by, a donkey stood unfazed by all the noise and harnessed to a cart half-filled with ash.

Felix pointed to it. "I think he might be telling the truth."

Vince looked back and forth but refused to let go of Tenner.

"Come out," Vince said over his shoulder.

From behind the cart, Clarity and Slate slowly appeared. They, too, were coated head to toe with ash, though they lacked any goggles.

"Hullo, Felix," Clarity said. "We weren't doing anything. Honest."

"We've been clearing away ash from the bakery ovens," Tenner said. "Has to be done, doesn't it?"

Vince leaned in closer. Tenner tried to put on a brave face, but the closer Vince got the less convincing it became.

Vince pulled a handkerchief from his pocket and rubbed Tenner's face with it, cleaning away the dust and ash.

Tenner spluttered and tried to pull away. "Ah, stop, what are you... Stop!"

Vince stuffed the handkerchief back in his pocket and tapped a red mark on Tenner's forehead. "Been in a fight?"

"Ow! You know us Diamonds, Vince. We can't resist

a scrap."

Vince poked him in the ribs, and once on the thigh. Tenner winced each time.

"Someone got you good." Vince pulled up the sleeve of Tenner's striped shirt to reveal several evenly spaced welts on his bare forearm. "Not a scrap, someone gave you a right beating. Saw you limping last night, at the Star. Saw your cuts and bruises."

Tenner tried to tear himself away again. "Let me go, and I'll tell you."

"Let you go *when* you tell me," Vince said.

Tenner huffed but realised he wasn't in any position to barter. "Someone attacked me with a metal bar."

"Why?" Vince asked.

"Who knows? There are a lot of angry, violent people in this town."

"Including me," Vince said, rolling his voice even lower so it almost turned to a growl.

Tenner blanched, his beady eyes widening. "I came into possession of something last week. Something I couldn't sell without people asking questions, so I took it to the Star. Gregory gave me a good price for it."

"The bracelet?" Felix asked.

Vince shot him a look that turned his belly to ice.

"How did you know about it?" Tenner asked. "Gregory didn't send it to you, did he? Wait, have you found it?"

"Never mind," Vince said. "Someone came looking for the bracelet? Owner, perhaps?"

"I don't know who he was," Tenner said. "I never saw his face."

"Where did you find the bracelet?" Felix asked.

"Found? Stole, more like," Vince said.

Tenner tried again to pull himself free from Vince's grip. His shirt popped a few stitches. Vince's grip didn't loosen. "Come on, be reasonable. You can't expect me to admit that in front of the Watch!"

Vince grunted and let him go. He took a step back into a pile of ash. If he wanted to run, he'd have to get past the cart, Felix, and most of all Vince.

"Listen," Vince said. "Bracelet was stolen long before you got your hands on it. Don't care about thieves stealing from one another. Just need to know where you got it."

Tenner eyed Vince up, trying to decide if he could trust him or not. "We were working at the back of the sailors' shelter, down at the waterfront. Clearing away some rubble from a shed they'd knocked down. I took a break and sat by the back wall of the first cottage."

"It's true," Clarity said. "He takes a lot of breaks, does Tenner."

Tenner stared at her before continuing. "I had a quick look in the window and saw something glinting in a bag under one of the beds. There was no one around so I helped myself."

"No better than a magpie," Felix said. "This was last week? When?"

"Tuesday, I think," Tenner said. "No, Monday. It was Monday."

"And you went straight to Uncle Gregory?"

Tenner nodded. "While Clarity and Slate took the cart back home, I took the bracelet round to the Star. Ever since the Watch put paid to the Pennymen gang, there's been a dearth of reliable fences in this town. I knew Gregory would be able to shift the bracelet, so I let him take it. He told me he'd get a pretty penny for it and split the profits."

"And you believed him?" Felix said.

Tenner just sneered at him. "That night somebody attacked me from behind, wanting to know what I did with the bracelet."

"What did you tell them?" Felix asked.

"I told him I gave it to Gregory, of course," Tenner said.

Felix threw his hands up in the air. "Oh, you halfwit. You sent some maniac after Uncle Gregory!"

Tenner played with the rip in his shirt and stuck his bottom lip out. "Better him than me."

"What is all this shouting about?" A woman appeared at the back door of the bakery. She wore a lace cap over her black hair and an apron. She clapped her hands lightly, knocking free a cloud of flour.

Vince's whole demeanour changed, his shoulders dropped, and his grimace vanished. He nodded to her. "Hester," he said. "Sorry for the ruckus. Needed a chat with Tenner."

"Be quick, Vince," Hester said. "I need this ash cleared away right now. I can't have it piling up."

"Couldn't find anyone more suitable?" Vince asked, pointing to Tenner. "Hard work and low money. Probably just doing it to get a look around. Come back later, steal anything not bolted down."

Clarity and Slate exchanged a glance.

"Charming," Tenner said. "A man tries to earn an

honest day's pay and this is the thanks he gets."

"Wouldn't be surprised to hear someone is missing a donkey and cart," Vince said.

Slate held up a finger. "Actually, he won those fair and square in a card game. Well, mostly fair. He only cheated once."

"Let him get back to work," Hester said. "Tenner, I want this lot cleared in the next hour or you'll not see a shilling." She walked with Vince and Felix along the covered alleyway to the road. "Is he up to no good?"

Vince scowled a little. "Usually. But nothing too serious this time."

"I haven't seen you about in a while," Hester said. "And who is this?"

"Felix Diamond," Vince said, "meet Hester Farriner. Felix here is a sailor."

"Another Diamond," Hester said, shaking his hand warmly. "I hope you won't give Vince too much trouble."

"I wouldn't dare," Felix said. "How do you two know each other?"

"We're family," Hester said. "In a manner of speaking. My late husband's brother is married to Vince's half-brother. So we're...whatever that makes us."

"Confusing," Felix said, with a polite laugh. "Do they live on Blackrabbit as well?"

"Merryapple," Vince said.

Felix had never been to Merryapple, the second largest of the Pell Isles, though he'd passed its lighthouse more than once.

"Keep an eye on Tenner," Vince said to Hester. "Don't trust him for a second."

"The boy is trying to earn an honest living," Hester said. "I would have thought you of all people would understand." She touched him lightly on the arm and smiled. "Good day, Commander. Felix." She returned to her bakery, leaving Vince and Felix in the street.

"How did you know where to find Tenner?" Felix asked.

Vince hooked his thumbs into his braces. "Helps to know where all the troublemakers are."

"I suppose," Felix said. "Now what do we do?"

Vince shuffled off down the road. "Owner of the bracelet came back to the shelter, found his bracelet missing. Assumed—correctly—Tenner had stolen it. Went looking for Tenner. Think it's time we went looking for the owner."

CHAPTER TWENTY-SIX

FELIX FOLLOWED VINCE to the waterfront, aware of the stares from the townsfolk they passed by. One usually had to brush past the people of Port Knot, but every one of them stood back to make space for Vince. Not simply due to the size of the man—tall as a shire horse and thick as an oak tree—but because his reputation preceded him like the prow of a ship, parting the sea of people. Felix was aware, too, that by being seen in Vince's company so often, he was garnering a reputation of his own. Whether for good or ill remained to be seen.

The Chase Trading Company headquarters consisted

of a large compound on the waterfront with their offices, warehouses, dry docks, and draughting office. On the far side of it lay a row of small cottages.

"The C.T.C. shelter for sailors," Felix said. "I was offered a place in one when I told my captain I was leaving."

"Didn't know you'd left them entirely," Vince said. "Assumed you were going back."

Felix thrust his hands into his coat pockets to warm them up. "My captain said she'd stop at Port Knot on her return to Falmouth. She said if I'd changed my mind, I'd be welcome back on board."

"Given it any thought?"

"I haven't really had a chance," Felix said. "She only wants me for my food anyway. There's no better cook than I in the whole fleet."

"Going to stay and run the Star with Dahlia?" Vince asked.

"I haven't decided yet." And he hadn't. Since he'd arrived in Port Knot, he'd bounced from one moment to the next, always at someone else's whim. If not Aunt Alma's, then Dahlia's, or Vince's, or the Star's. He was used to taking orders but the niggling thought at the back of his head—the thought that someday he was going to have to take control of his own life—wouldn't leave him alone.

And then there was Iron. In the quiet moments before falling asleep, Felix had let himself imagine what his life might be like with Iron by his side. How happy they could be together, even in Port Knot. He had complicated Felix's decision about whether or not to return to sea. Though after Iron's reaction to the altercation in the Star last night, that particular complication had apparently been resolved.

The sailor's shelter sat neat as ninepence in a line facing the sea. Thatched and whitewashed, their upkeep was a condition of occupation.

"Which one did Tenner say he found the bracelet in?"

"Found?" Vince removed his tricorne cap and banged on the door of the nearest cottage.

A sandy-haired woman with a ruddy, weather-beaten face opened it.

"Need to look around." Before the woman could speak, Vince had ducked his head and barged in.

Felix sheepishly followed him. "Don't worry, he's the Watch Commander."

"I know who 'e is." The woman held her hand at her throat. "Everyone knows who 'e is. You're not wearing a

Knight uniform though."

"Ah, no, I'm not with them. I mean to say, I am with them today but I don't..." He held out his hand. "Felix Diamond. I run the Star We Sail By playhouse."

"Ms Clover Stock," she said, shaking his hand. Her grip was firm, her skin rough. "I thought the Star was a tavern?"

"Wouldn't call it that," Vince said, his voice still rumbling. "Felix doesn't like it being called that."

The cottage had a small kitchen and two rooms, each with a handful of beds. Vince stood stooped the whole time to keep from banging his head on the low ceiling. "Other residents?"

Ms Stock thought about it for a heartbeat. "Just me, at the moment. The last occupant moved out yesterday."

"Moved to where?"

"I couldn't say. She didn't tell me. I've been 'ere for a month. I've seen six, maybe seven people come and go." She sat on a chair by the crackling hearth and stirred the pungent contents of a blackened pot hanging over the flames.

"Seen any of them with a fancy gold bracelet?" Vince asked.

"No, nothing like of the kind," she said, shaking her head. "Most of us come 'ome with just the clothes on our backs. If we 'ad any fancy jewellery, we'd sell it, most likely."

Vince nodded to her and left. Felix thanked her for her time. He wondered if the reason Sorcha followed Vince so closely was so she could apologise to everyone he encountered for his brusque behaviour.

Vince crossed the compound and bundled into the nearest office where he barked at a quivering little man behind a desk dressed in the emerald and white uniform of the C.T.C. "Register of shelter occupants," Vince said, slamming his open palm on the table. "Last month. Make it two."

The little man sat wide-eyed. "I, um, Commander Knight, isn't it? I would, um. I would need to get approval for—"

Vince barked at him. "Head of the Watch! All the approval you need!"

Felix had started to wonder if the unusual way in which Vince spoke was entirely involuntary or if he played it up sometimes. Certainly, it had a perplexing way of disarming a person, especially when roared at high volume and accompanied by Vince's menacing scowl. The little man scurried off to fetch the list, almost tripping over his own feet.

Vince turned away and winked at Felix. At least Felix assumed he was winking. With Vince's eyepatch, he found it difficult to tell.

"Good to keep the greencoats on their toes," Vince said quietly.

Felix smirked back at him. Aside from Captain James Godgrave, Felix had no particular love for the greencoats either.

The little man returned some minutes later with a sheet of paper and a woman in the much more elaborate uniform of an admiral. On her belt hung a musket and a sheathed officer's sword with a fish-scale grip. Felix's back stiffened—a reflex from serving on C.T.C. ships for so many years. She cut a matronly figure, stern-faced and dimple-chinned. Had she not been an admiral, she would have undoubtedly been a judge, or perhaps a schoolmistress. Hers was not the face of one destined for subservience.

"Ah, Commander Knight, is it? Admiral Valentine Boon." She nodded curtly to him and fixed him with a scowl. "I wonder if you might be so good as to tell me why you require this information?"

Vince didn't appear fazed by the admiral's presence and lazily turned to look her in the eye. "Looking into a disappearance," he said. "Might be tied to a robbery from one of your sailors."

"Which one?" Admiral Boon asked.

"Trying to find out." Vince snatched the list from the little man's hands.

"If someone has stolen from one of my sailors then my soldiers will look into it."

Vince didn't bother to look up from his reading. "Don't need help," he said. "Soldiers aren't much use without their weapons. Haven't forgotten that you can't take them into town, have you?"

Admiral Boon's frown deepened. "No, I certainly have not forgotten, Commander Knight."

Vince marched out of the office. Felix considered apologising for Vince's curtness but thought better of it.

"Greencoats haven't forgiven me for banning firearms from the island," Vince said.

"Wasn't Admiral Boon wearing one on her hip?"

"Greencoats think their compound is exempt. Happy to let them believe it for now." He read the list as he marched along the harbour towards the Watch House. "Will get some Watchfolk to check these names. Might take a while." He stopped at the doors.

"Those cottages are for sailors who've just come back from being at sea," Felix said. "For people with no accommodation. A place where they can take some time to get back on their feet. How did a sailor, freshly arrived on the island, get his hands on the bracelet?"

"Could have stolen it," Vince said. "Probably planned to sell it. Buy a house."

"Is it really worth that much?"

"Must be," Vince said. "Worth enough to pay for the passage of two people to America. Worth enough to abduct your uncle for."

"A sailor at sea, dreaming of a nice house in the town, has his only means of paying for it stolen out from under his bed. It's enough to make anyone angry," Felix said.

"Angry and dangerous," Vince said. "Make sure the bracelet is well hidden. Will let you know when I hear anything. Get some rest. Better still, go see your friend. Huxham."

Felix's ears warmed up. "I doubt he'll want to see me again. And who knows, maybe I'm better off. If he runs when things get loud, he won't last long around me. Not with my family."

Vince rubbed his own chin and gazed out to the harbour. "Don't judge people by how they react when frightened. Isn't fair. Fond of him, aren't you?"

Felix shrugged and kept his hands in his pockets.

"Worth giving him the benefit of the doubt, then." Vince straightened up. "Will say this though: fewer people who know about the bracelet, the better."

"I trust Iron. Or I did, at any rate."

Vince looked him up and down. "Enough to bet your life?"

As he walked back towards Bibbler's Brook, Felix started to wonder.

CHAPTER TWENTY-SEVEN

FELIX AMBLED ALONG Bibbler's Brook, lost in thought. He stood outside the Star, looking up at Atlas, the masthead of the sailboat balcony. He imagined his Uncle Gregory in a panic, hiding the bracelet in the concealed metal chest. It must have happened after closing time, as the balcony was always frequented by bedworkers plying for trade. There was a thought. What had happened to the bedworkers who used the balcony? Had the Watch spoken to any?

"Penny for them?"

Felix hadn't noticed Iron approaching from behind.

"You came back. When you ran out last night, I didn't think... Vince told me my actions alarmed you. The table...the shouting..."

Iron stood with his hands behind his back, his chin raised. "Over our dinner, I told you I couldn't risk garnering a reputation, a mark against my name through our association."

"You did." Felix splayed his hand on his own chest. "And it was never my intention to sully you with my actions. I have never turned over a table before in my life. I am not prone to outbursts of that nature."

Iron lowered his head and turned, just a fraction. "It frightened me, Felix. You frightened me."

Felix took a step back. "I never... I didn't..." He rubbed his hands over his face. "I am so sorry, Iron. I just... I just kept picturing Uncle Gregory returning and seeing Aunt Alma in the Star and being so angry, so disappointed that I let her in, and I cannot... I cannot... I don't know where he is, and I..." He covered his eyes to shield his tears. "I shouldn't have done it. I shouldn't have given in to that part of myself." He took hold of the front door handle.

"Wait," Iron said. "Don't leave. Not yet." He

swallowed hard and cleared his throat, his eyes dampening. "I, uh, I shouldn't have left so abruptly last night. I should have been, well, a better friend, I suppose. I could see you were upset, and instead of helping, I ran."

Felix wiped his own eyes with the indigo handkerchief about his neck. "No one could blame you for protecting yourself. You don't know me very well."

"That's true." Iron's hands dropped by his sides. "But I would like to." As the rain began to pour, he stepped forward, gently took Felix's hand in his own, and sheltered by the dripping sailboat balcony above their heads, they kissed. A brief kiss, one of reassurance more than passion.

Still, it made Felix's heart leap. "I feel like I should thank you. Is that strange?" He chuckled a little and sniffed away the last of his tears.

Iron squeezed him tighter. "What would you like to do now?"

"This may seem like an odd question, but I don't suppose you know where the bedworkers from the balcony might have gone?"

Iron let go of Felix's hand. "Ah, no, no, I don't. How would I...oh. Actually, I assume they went to the cherry house."

"Which one?"

"There is only one nowadays. Over in the Tangles. If they're anywhere, they'll be there. Why do you ask?"

Felix scrunched up his face. "I'd like a chat with them. One of them may know something about what happened to Uncle Gregory." He started off through one of the Entries, heading south and deeper into town.

Iron hurried after him. "Is it safe? If they're involved, they might be dangerous. Shouldn't you alert the Watch?"

"There's nothing to alert them to...yet." Felix ducked under some sheets drying on a line.

The cherry house, squat and wide, stood sandwiched between other, taller buildings in the Tangles. Constructed of the same honey-coloured stone of the rest of the town, with white-painted window frames, only the wrought iron fence which fronted it marked it as anything out of the ordinary. Felix knocked on the blood-red door and a woman with painted hands opened it.

She welcomed him inside. "And will your handsome friend be joining you?"

Iron hesitated on the road outside before stepping in. He hung his coat beside Felix's on the rack in the deep-red hallway. The cherry house was a private establishment

where consenting adults could meet, and while bedworkers often plied their wares there, the cherry house was not
a brothel. Crystal sconces and gilt looking glasses lined the
walls, scattering the flickering candlelight across the black
floor and gold ceiling. In a lavish reception room, a small,
naked band of elderly, overweight musicians played bowed
instruments.

Before Felix and Iron, three rooms waited. One
marked with a cockerel, one a hen, and one with both. Felix hesitated for a moment before approaching the cockerel door.

"We should try the mixed room," Iron said. "No
sense in limiting our options."

Felix followed him through the last door on the right
and found himself standing in an indoor pleasure garden.
A vast space, open to the upper floor, with curving balco-
nies of white and gold. High walls painted with trees in full
bloom, augmented with living branches that, thanks to a
clever use of hidden clockworks, hung overhead and made
one believe they swayed in an unfelt breeze.

People flocked about in various stages of undress.
Long couches held entwined couples who groped and
kissed each other. Pillories without locks held all-too-

willing captives, whipped across their bare buttocks by gleeful patrons. Playful men pushed swings holding nude, giggling women, maidens in diaphanous gowns danced with crowns of vivid green holly about their heads, a couple rutted like animals against a water fountain whilst others watched and stoked their own fires. At one end of the room sat a table laden with fruit and bread. Full grapes and warm crust to fill the sails once more.

And in the centre of the cavernous space, a tall pole, thick as the trunk of a sweet chestnut tree. Long, robust chains hung from the top of the pole, attached to wooden horses at the base, and painted in flamboyant colours.

Felix pointed to it. "What is it?"

Iron took his hand. "Wait and see."

Riders—women, men, and those who claimed allegiance to neither—climbed onto the horses. In a moment, the pole started to turn, moving ever more quickly, clicking and ticking as it went. Looking glasses on the pole caught the candlelight, dazzling Felix as the pole turned. Slowly, the wooden horses and their bare riders lifted from the ground, flying through the air. The riders giggled and hollered with delight.

Felix's heart thumped. He'd never been in a cherry

house before, though when he and Tenner were young they tried to peep in the windows of one until an irate cherrykeeper had chased them off. He kept his voice to a whisper. "How am I supposed to find anyone in here?"

"The bedworkers usually keep to the private booths at the back," Iron said. While Felix had been surveying the room, Iron had stripped and was placing his clothes inside one of the empty baskets which lined the muraled wall.

"What are you...?" Felix's gaze wandered over Iron's beefy frame, taking in every curve and dip, every perfect inch of him.

"It's bad etiquette to remain clothed," Iron said, his hands hanging loose by his side. "I thought you knew that? Come along, no need to be shy."

Felix first removed the handkerchief from around his neck. Next came his boots, jumper, trousers, and finally his drawers. He covered his privates with one hand and blushed so bright he thought himself a lighthouse in the dark.

Iron took Felix's free hand once again and led him through the crowd, up a set of winding stairs, and into a domed, looking glass-lined hallway peppered with doors. Nude people walked up and down the corridor, smiling and stroking their own chests and faces.

Felix hadn't expected the cherry house to be quite so overwhelming. He'd pictured a single dark room with perhaps a handful of folk waiting in a corner for someone to make a pass at them. This was something else entirely, more akin to a society party.

Some of the bedworkers wore expensive masks, others jewellery or fine silks. Most had oiled bodies, glistening in the candlelight and scented with sandalwood or other spices. And then there was Iron. He tried not to look and tried not to let his excitement show. Iron had no such compunctions and left his body free to do what it may. His member, no longer than Felix's own, though more bulbous at the end, bobbed about with impunity.

"Hullo, boys." An athletic young man stood with an arm up, like a cat stretching. He had oiled his rich, tan skin to show off every muscle, every curve. Shiny black curls fell past his jawline, and he wore only a gossamer-thin piece of blue fabric around his waist which hid nothing and accentuated everything.

Iron waved at the man while pursing his own lips and trying not to look down. "My friend, Felix, here would like to ask you something."

The athletic man put his hands on his own hips. "A comely chap like him can ask me anything he likes."

Felix's mouth turned dry. "Have you...? I mean to say, do you usually work the sailboat balcony at the Star We Sail By?"

The young man's smile faltered for a heartbeat. "I have been known to, yes."

"I was wondering," Felix said, "if you might know anything about what happened to the landlord? Gregory Diamond?"

The man's smile faded entirely. He pushed open the door behind him and beckoned Felix and Iron to follow inside. The little private room, painted to resemble the inside of a huge birdcage hanging in an opulent garden, held a wide bed, big enough for three or four. "Shut the door. Why are you asking me about Gregory?"

Felix started to wish he had gone to the Watch first but then he pictured standing here with a nude Vince and found little comfort in the idea. "He's my uncle. And he's missing." In the confines of the room, Felix's exhilaration faded, and he allowed his hand to resign from its duty.

The young man's gaze snapped straight to Iron.

"It's true," Iron said.

Felix couldn't understand why Iron's word held more water than his own. "Is there anything you can tell us? Anything unusual about the days before he disappeared?"

"Nothing whatsoever," the young man said, crossing his arms.

Iron sighed and leaned forward. "Please, Rudyard. This is important. Was he still taking the Diamond Cut?"

Felix set aside his confusion for the moment. "What's the Diamond Cut?"

The young man, Rudyard, threw his hands in the air and sat on the edge of the plush bed. "It's what we called the extra percentage your uncle swiped in exchange for letting us work at the Star. We all rented a spot on the balcony at an agreed price but every week there was something extra he said we needed to pay for. Spilt drinks, or tarnished woodwork, or stubborn stains. Some excuse to trim some money off the top. He'd always done it and, well, we got sick of it. All of us. We started talking and wondered if there was anything to be done."

"Such as?" Felix asked.

"We talked to Gregory, but he didn't take it well, and so he stopped bothering with the excuses at all. He just demanded more money from each of us or else we'd lose our position on the balcony. And believe me, there are plenty of other bedworkers waiting to take our place."

"I'm sure that was well-received," Felix said. "What were you going to do about it?"

Rudyard's eyes sharpened. "You cannot tell anyone I told you this. If she finds out, my life won't be worth living."

"If who finds out?" Felix asked.

"Gregory's sister, Alma, approached us. She suggested that if she were in charge of the Star things might improve for all of us."

Felix clenched his fists. "What did you do?"

Rudyard held his hands up. "Nothing. Nothing, I swear. We were all talk. Your uncle can be quite intimidating when he wants to be. None of us wanted to rile him up. It never went any further than idle talk and dreams of ousting him. But how could we? The Star belongs to him."

"No longer the case," Iron said.

Rudyard adjusted the ribbon around his waist. He pointed to Felix. "You mean you...? Well, some good news at last. Have you started renting the balcony yet? Because I—"

Felix shook his head. "I haven't decided what I'm

doing."

Rudyard stood and prowled over to Felix, running a finger over his soft, hairy belly and up to his chest. "Do say you'll keep me in mind, won't you? Now, if there's nothing else, I have money to earn." He winked and left the private room, leaving Felix and Iron alone.

Felix sat on the bed. "You know him? Rudyard?"

Iron leaned his shoulders against the papered wall. "I know him."

"Because you're...not a friend of his. So, a customer, then?"

"I'm not a customer, no. I'm sure you've already guessed." Iron's head hung low, his gaze on the floor. "I worked the sailboat balcony for a few months. I needed money to become a horological apprentice. That was the fastest way to get it. Are you upset?"

Felix shrugged. "Of course not. Work is work. I do wonder why you didn't tell me you knew Uncle Gregory?"

Iron put his hands on his bare thighs, where his pockets would be. "I have no great love for your uncle. I felt it uncouth to speak ill of him, and since I could not speak of him in any other way, the safest action was not to mention him at all."

"What did he do to you?"

"Nothing he didn't also do to every other bedworker on the balcony. I confronted him once about the Diamond Cut and he turned quite nasty. He never struck me, but he didn't have to."

"Uncle Gregory has a temper. It's a Diamond trait."

"So I've come to appreciate."

Felix sucked in his lips and thought of the bruise on Vince's skull, of the table lying on the floor of the Star. "I like to think I have it under control."

Iron cleared his throat. "There is something else. He heard I liked to tinker with clockworks, and he ordered me to build something for him. A waterproof tank for holding his 'fleeting plunder', as he put it. When I told him I wasn't about to help him in his smuggling endeavours, he made it quite clear that he wasn't asking. But he also paid me for it. Fairly, more or less. Which meant I didn't have to work the balcony for as long as I'd expected to."

Felix wasn't sure how to respond. "What was it like? Being a bedworker?"

"I was never very good at it," Iron said. "When one looks the way I do, customers expect a certain...persona. Most bedworkers are slight and toned, and the ones who look like me tend to be dominating. Domineering. And that just isn't me. So I always felt like I was a tad disappointing to them."

"I'm sure no one left your company disappointed," Felix said. "I know I never have."

For the first time since entering the room, Iron looked at him. Felix sat up straighter, his excitement rising once again. Iron put his hand on the side of Felix's face and leaned down. Their lips met lightly, tenderly. Iron sat beside Felix, his arm around Felix's shoulder. With his free hand he stroked Felix's hairy chest, moving lower, over his belly, grasping his stiff member. Felix gasped as Iron deftly worked at his manhood. They kissed again, more forcefully than before, and lay back on the welcoming bed.

CHAPTER TWENTY-EIGHT

THE MANY-PANELLED glass turret of the Watch house bulged from the sheer, jagged rocks of the harbour, like a varicose vein. The whitewashed walls of the Watch house proper hugged the turret, as though to keep it from toppling into the crashing waves below.

Vince rapped the curved glass with his knuckles and wondered how long it would be before the sea finally claimed the turret. Whoever had built it had given no thought to its upkeep. How was anyone supposed to clean the glass without hanging above a dangerous drop into the sea? How were the glass panes, small and dense though they were, meant to withstand the force of a storm?

He'd had no say over the Watch house's construction. It had been a vanity project by the C.T.C. A shiny modern eyesore built just where the harbour began to rise steeply to become the famous white cliffs of the eastern coast. He found it hard to argue with the view, mind you. The sea, pitted with ships, stretched out before him: To his left, the expanse of docklands swept around like a crescent moon. To his right, the little rocky outcrop home of the gaolhouse and lighthouse.

Crabmeat plodded beside him and slumped over his boots. Vince leaned down and rubbed his ear. "Thought I left you at the Star?"

"He wandered in the front door about an hour ago," Sorcha said. "He misses you. You've been leaving him in your office too often."

Sorcha had spread out roll after roll of lamp plans on her desk in the Pit—the area of the Watch House seeded with chairs and tables where the rank and file worked.

"Won't get out of his bed half the time. Lazy sod." He jabbed his finger at a drawing of an ornate five-sided lamp head. "Been meaning to ask you. Lamplighter you hired. Jason Sparrow. Best man for the job, was he?"

Sorcha scratched the back of her head. "More or less. He was no worse than any of the other candidates. But I wasn't the one to make the decision in the end. One of the C.T.C. admirals paid us a visit. I think you were out dealing with a bar fight at the Lion Lies Waiting. The admiral wanted to check on our spending, since the greencoats were footing the bill, but she made it very clear she wanted Mr Sparrow to get the role. He's a former greencoat himself, a navy man. He'd been retired due to an injury and was seeking gainful employment on land."

Vince straightened up. "Admiral who?"

"Boon," Sorcha said. "Hefty woman, round face. All bosom and bluster, you know the type."

"Met her recently."

Flowers leaned over her shoulder and picked up a sheet of schematics. "I still think a double head would be better."

She grabbed it from his tattooed hand. "Yes, I know you do, you've said as much every other day for weeks."

Flowers was a tinkerer, an amateur horologist. When he'd been part of the Clockbreakers gang, he'd trained them in the use of clockwork housebreaking devices, among other things. He had wanted to work on the designs for the lamps and had his nose put out of joint when he'd been told the council wanted to use a professional. "A double head would give more light."

"And cost twice as much. Do you want to go to the greencoats and tell them?"

Flowers shrugged. "Fine. It wouldn't bother me. What are you looking so worried about?"

"Every day there's someone complaining about how the light is keeping them awake at night, how the noise of the lamps being installed is disturbing them, how they're being blinded by the glare from them. The glare! I ask you!"

Flowers laughed. "People love to complain about anything new. Look how many articles there have been in the Blackrabbit Courant complaining about the Watch running during the day. As if we're going around peering into people's windows to make sure they behave. Don't let them get to you. For one thing, these lamps will cut down on housebreaking. Trust me on that. Oh, Vince, I nearly forgot. Clive Hext tracked down the packet ship that carried Gregory Diamond's letter. They run day and night. It took him a while, but he spoke to the woman who took the letter from Gregory. She said he looked skittish, nervous.

He hurried away as soon as he could. And we spoke to almost everyone on the list the C.T.C. gave us. Two old men, who should have retired a long time ago, and four women. The men had family who said they were with them at the time Tenner was beaten. The women all had people who vouched for them, as well. One of them was in the C.T.C. offices when it happened. None of them knew anything about a bracelet."

"Said you spoke to almost everyone?"

Sorcha pulled the list from her pocket. "There's one we still haven't found. A man named Rob Evans."

"I've got a feeling I know who he is," Flowers said. "I knew a Rob Evans from back before I joined the Clockbreakers. He never stayed on the island for too long, but if he's in town now, I bet I know where he'll be."

"Coming with you," Vince said to Flowers. "Both of us." He clicked his fingers and Crabmeat lumbered after them.

VINCE FOLLOWED FLOWERS to the Tangles, and into *Helen's Salve.* Once again, Vince ignored the greeter at the door and plodded along the lush, red carpet. Ahead of him, the giant copper squid, its lantern eyes blazing, rattled as it pumped smoke through its long, outstretched, segmented tentacles and into the den's many stalls.

Vince and Flowers climbed one of the black spiral staircases to the first mezzanine. There, Vince removed his tricorne as they searched each stall, many of which were occupied by vacant-eyed men and women lost in a haze of smoke. More than once, Vince had to pull Crabmeat away from lapping at some suspicious-looking puddle on the floor. "Confident he'll be here, are you?" Vince asked.

Flowers peered through the fog. "I worked with his sister once or twice," he said. "She introduced me to him, and he introduced me to the delights of opium."

He walked backward as he spoke, batting away billowing silk garlands and peering through plumes of sweet, floral smoke.

"Didn't know you were a hazeman."

"I'm not, these days. But there was a time when you couldn't drag me out of this place."

Of all the former Clockbreaker gang members who

Vince had recruited into the Watch, he found Flowers the most difficult to understand. Everyone else treated Vince with a mixture of fear and reverence, but Flowers? Well, Flowers seemed to find Vince vaguely amusing. He talked to Vince as though he were in on the joke, though Vince had no idea what the joke might actually be.

The stalls, not unlike those as might be found in a stable, were made of polished maple wood topped with curving stained glass depictions of the den's squid, or scenes from Greek mythology.

Flowers poked his head into one of them. "Aha!" He stopped by a tattered duck-egg blue divan and kicked the foot of the man lying upon it.

He stirred, opening his baggy eyes and running a hand over his high forehead. "Flowers? Ha! Ha! I've not seen you for many a day! Come, sit." A copper tentacle ran along the wall above the man's head, and from it descended a delicate pipe which the man held to his mouth. He gathered his legs beneath himself to make room. Flowers flared out his red and black Watch greatcoat and duly sat next to him.

"You've added some more ink since last we spoke," Mr Evans said, examining the blossoms on the back of

Flowers's hands and the crown of daisies around his head.

"We all have our vices, Mr Evans."

Mr Evans laughed. "So we do. So we do." He took another drag of his pipe.

Vince just grunted.

"You were staying at the sailor's shelter," Flowers said. "At the harbour? You didn't happen to have anything stolen while you were there?"

Vince studied Mr Evans's reaction. In his current state, it would have been virtually impossible for him to hide anything from them.

"Not a thing," Mr Evans said. "Except perhaps my heart."

"Oh, what's this?" Flowers asked. "Has some pretty bird finally caught your eye?"

"Less a bird and more a stallion," Mr Evans said. "A beautiful stallion with the softest skin and the sweetest kisses." He closed his eyes and swayed, lost in the memory. "We spent the most wonderful afternoon together. But alas, t'was naught but the most fleeting of dalliances. We pass through one another's lives like...like...fish through a net, do we not?"

"Nets catch fish." Vince balled his hands on his hips.

"Whole point of them."

"You've been living somewhere else?" Flowers asked.

"With my dear, dear sister," he said. "She says I'm no burden at all since I'm hardly ever home."

"Sounds about right," Vince said under his breath.

"Do you remember where you were on the twenty-seventh?" Flowers asked, swaying slightly to match the movement of the man.

"The twenty-seventh? Why, it was the blissful day I spent in the arms of my beloved stallion! We spent all morning and afternoon in bed, making all manner of shapes with our limbs and our members."

"Yes, fine," Flowers said. "I understand. Where was this?"

"At the sailor shelter," Mr Evans said. "I had to share my room there, of course, but my bunkmate, Mr Roskilly, had thankfully departed before sunrise."

"How fortunate," Flowers said. "And can you per-chance tell us the name of your stallion?"

"Of course!" Mr Evans said. "His name is Iron Hux-ham. Port Knot's very finest horologist."

CHAPTER TWENTY-NINE

WITHIN THE PAINTED birdcage of the private cherry house booth, Felix and Iron lay naked, their limbs entwined.

"We shouldn't really be here, should we?" Felix frowned as he spoke. "Shouldn't we be in the cockerel room?"

Iron lightly kissed his arm. "You have quite the most hirsute back I've ever seen. And chest, for that matter." He ran his hand through Felix's chest hair, catching tufts of it between his long fingers.

Felix's face must have betrayed how he was feeling

because Iron pulled him closer and smiled. "I don't mean it in a bad way. I like it. It's cosy and warm." He ran his hands along Felix's downy arm.

Felix stroked Iron's muscular leg, squeezing lightly every now and then, admiring its tautness. Iron lifted his leg slightly, allowing Felix to run his hand to the inner thigh and farther still, until he grasped the concealed rigidity. "I see now why you're named Iron." Felix firmly stroked the poker in his hand, making Iron groan. "You've not softened one crumb."

Iron laughed a little. "If you hadn't received your uncle's letter, what would you be doing now?"

"I was in Falmouth when it arrived, on the Cornish coast," Felix said. "It's only a few hours sailing away. I was preparing for a voyage to India with the rest of the crew."

"And then? Did you want to be a sailor forever?"

"I don't know. I hadn't given it much thought." Felix shifted, putting his arm behind his head. "What's that look for?"

"You don't strike me as the type to blunder through life. I imagine you are the sort who makes lists. Plans. You never once daydreamed about what you'd do when you're old? Where you would live? What's the most beautiful place you've seen on your travels?"

"I would have to say...the Greek islands. Undoubtedly. Perfect white beaches, crystal clear water, beautiful food, beautiful weather, beautiful men." He laughed a little then. "Their houses are blinding white on the hilltops, with roofs a shade of blue I've never seen anywhere else."

"I would love to see them for myself someday. I'd love to see anywhere, in fact. I've never left Blackrabbit. I don't suppose I ever shall."

"What about you?" Felix asked. "What do you want to do when you're old?"

"I want to finish my apprenticeship. Become a journeyman. Take over the cogsmithing business. I want a nice house in Gravel Hill with a garden like this one." He gestured to the mural on the walls around them. Rolling green lawns, perfectly kept, and surrounded by tidy, clipped trees. "I want to travel. I want to never worry about how I'm going to keep a roof over my head, or where my next meal is coming from. I want shoes on my feet and clothes on my back. I want to be safe, I suppose. Properly, completely safe. But then doesn't everyone?"

"Some people like a touch of danger. My cousins seem to."

"They're fools," Iron said, stroking Felix's chest. "Life is short enough and difficult enough without seeking danger. It finds us all, eventually. They should try being more patient."

Faint strains of music from the nude band in the cherry house's entrance wafted through the room. Felix didn't recognise the tune. "What made you change your mind about repairing the lift?"

"I told you."

"Yes, you did. And I'm asking you what really happened." His hand glided over Iron's smooth body, over his long, hefty limbs, onto the finest pair of thighs Felix had ever laid eyes—or lips—on. Iron wore a single, simple gold hoop through one ear and it caught the candlelight just so. If Felix could have spent all his days kissing Iron, he would gladly have done so.

Iron looked at him with a sappy grin. "Promise me you won't take offence?"

Felix leaned back. "I promise nothing of the kind."

Iron chuckled a little. "Well, to be completely truthful, once you'd left I found I...um...well, I found I couldn't stop thinking about the little gap between your front teeth."

"That's all it took?" Felix said, laughing. He whistled

through it and laughed again.

"Well, the gap and your eyes," Iron said. "They're so kind. So gentle. You have such a youthful face. Innocent, almost. It seems unthinkable you should possess a fiery temper. Or have known any suffering."

"I've been luckier than some in that regard. Luckier than most, maybe."

"Have you ever had your heart broken?" Iron asked.

"Not by a lover. By unrequited love, perhaps."

"By life, then?"

Felix chewed his own bottom lip. "By life, as you say. I learned early on not to rely on anyone but myself."

"As did I," Iron said. "But sometimes it can be...overwhelming." He paused then, considering his next question carefully. "How do you stop it all from becoming...intolerable?"

"You'll think it foolish, but I have this refrain," Felix said. "This maxim. *It is the waves which break—not I.* A burly and well-travelled captain I served under once taught me the technique."

"Might this be the unrequited love?"

"However did you guess?"

Iron chuckled a little. "I'm familiar with the signs. My

first bout of lovesickness came courtesy of the coal man at the orphanage. He'd come every few days with a heavy sack over his shoulder. And one in his breeches, from what I could tell. He had silver in his hair, and he was big, and he was bearded, and he didn't talk, and I was hopelessly in love with him, of course."

"Did you ever speak with him?"

"Not even once," Iron said, shaking his head. "I was never brave enough. And I was a child, I didn't even know what I was feeling, exactly. I just knew it felt powerful. Even after I left the orphanage, I'd go back when I knew he'd be there, just to catch a glimpse of him. Of his chest hair billowing up from his collar, of his big, hairy forearms dusted with coal. I'd just stand and watch him from a street corner. But then one day he didn't show up for his delivery. Someone else did, someone I did not like at all. And he never came back. I never did find out what happened to him. Ever since then, I've found myself unable to resist the charms of a thick-wristed patriarch. Take Commander Knight, for example. I've never been so attracted to someone I was so terrified of."

Felix's eyes popped wide. "Really? Vince?"

"Oh yes," Iron said. "He's so..."

"Scruffy? Lumbering? Impertinent?"

"Carnal," Iron said with a wiggle of his shoulders. "Don't you think so?"

"While I have nothing against men who've had their noses broken a half dozen times or could easily wrestle lascivious bulls, I find Vince a touch too...tarnished. Morally speaking."

"A fair point," Iron said. "I doubt he'll ever escape the consequences of his past, no matter how hard he tries."

"I wanted to hate him," Felix said. "A little part of me still wants to hate him. However, I find I'm unable to. I attacked him, you know. Just last night. I clobbered him over the head, and I tied him up, or so I thought. It transpires that he could have burst free of his bonds at any moment—burst free and beaten me to a pulp. Had he chosen to. But he didn't lay a finger on me. He just let me talk."

Iron struggled to find words. "You attacked him?"

"I'm not in habit of doing so. Please don't be alarmed. A lifetime of anger forged an arrow I aimed squarely at him. It's spent now."

"For what it's worth," Iron said, "I think he's serious about turning over a new leaf. These past couple of months, since he took over the Watch, he's worked night and day to clean up the town. The newspaper often details his exploits and a good many townsfolk would still gladly see the back of him. He's turned in people he used to work side by side with. He's burned every bridge with the criminal underbelly. There's no going back for him, I would say." Iron sat up. "You assured me the incident with the table was also outside the boundaries of your usual habits."

Felix rubbed a hand across his own mouth. "It was. I can see how it must appear to you. I think this town might be bringing out the worst in me. Just as I feared it would."

Iron turned to look directly at him. "I imagine it's the weight of your history with the people who live here. Your anger with Vince, with your aunt. The disappointment you feel your uncle will express in your actions. Perhaps your refrain isn't quite up to the task. It seems to me as though you are breaking along with the waves. How is it supposed to work?"

"The captain who taught it to me, Jim Godgrave, learned the skill in India, or thereabouts," Felix said. "He told me in times of great stress to picture myself as the strongest thing I could imagine, the strongest thing I'd ever known. I told him about how when I used to live at the Star, I could see Blackrabbit Lighthouse from my bedroom window. I used to watch it at night, watch the light sweeping out across the waves. I thought of the storms it must have seen and survived. Jim Godgrave told me to see the world—my problems, my trials—as the violent sea, as waves breaking on the solid and immovable lighthouse. When I feel under pressure I repeat the refrain to myself, over and over again. It's a way of shutting the world out and holding my mind and heart together."

"And you find that effective?" Iron asked.

"Perhaps I should be using it more often."

Iron lay by Felix's side once more, facing the ceiling where the gold trompe l'oeil bars of the birdcage met beneath a cloudy blue sky.

"What do you do when the world gets too loud?" Felix asked.

"I hide in a book. Or between someone's thighs. Whichever is closest to hand. Mostly books, these days. When I was younger I had no problem talking to people, I could talk to anyone about anything. Now, though... I don't know, maybe I've worked alone too long and fallen out of practice."

Felix turned and lay with his head on Iron's chest. "I thought you worked under a Master cogsmith?" He draped his arm across Iron's belly, feeling it rise and fall as Iron spoke.

"I do, but he isn't much of a conversationalist. And he leaves me to my own devices for much of the time."

"Do you ever think about taking on an apprentice of your own one day?"

"Me? No. Well, I hadn't really considered it." His brow furrowed. "I suppose I should, one day. It's expected that we pass on these skills to the next generation."

"Just like Uncle Gregory did with me. I don't think playhouses have apprentices, though."

"I can't imagine those skills were of much use at sea," Iron said.

Felix rubbed his own eyes, his chest tightening. "There were times, plenty of times, when I thought I shouldn't have left. I made the decision in the heat of the moment. And now I'm back, I just... I don't know how to feel. It's a huge responsibility, owning the Star."

Iron stroked Felix's arm again. "You don't have to keep it, you know. You can give the Star to someone else in the family."

"Dahlia will sell it. Aunt Alma will turn it into a squalid gin house for thieves and reprobates. Uncle Gregory didn't want either to happen. He said it all the time—he wanted the Star to stay in the family forever. Generations of Diamond landlords. I think he wanted to create an institution. My family has never stayed in one place for too long, one house, I mean. We're forever getting evicted for one reason or another. Uncle Gregory wanted the Star to be a constant in our lives."

"Hence the name, I suppose," Iron said. "Didn't he have any children of his own?"

Felix shook his head. "I think he really wanted to be a father but it never happened for him. His wife died in childbirth, he was never the same afterwards. Who could be? I felt sorry for him but he hated that. He didn't want anyone's pity."

"You're talking about him as if he's gone," Iron said.

"Am I? I hadn't realised."

Iron kissed the top of Felix's head as Felix closed his eyes and buried his face in the warm skin of Iron's chest.

CHAPTER THIRTY

TIRED BUT GIDDY and filled with a glow deep down inside, Felix sauntered back to the Star. Dick Tassiter was in his usual seat, being served by Ms Hornby.

"It's good to be back working," she said. "The lodgers barely pay enough to cover the rent."

"You need to find yourself a good husband," Dick Tasstier said. "Someone reliable who can take care of you."

"I've never met a reliable man in my life."

"You've met me," Mr Tassiter said, beaming.

"And you can be relied upon for one thing and one

thing only." Ms Hornby slung a cloth over her shoulder. "Drink your gin, Mr Tassiter."

A handful of patrons filled out the bar, some of whom Felix recognised from attending last night's show. He nodded politely to them, then walked to the rear of the bar and upstairs. Dahlia lounged in one of the private booths, turning the gold cuff bracelet round and round on the table in front of her.

Felix slid into the booth, on the opposite side of the table. "Vince thinks we should keep the bracelet hidden," he said, checking around for prying eyes. This part of the Star had yet to be officially reopened and so they were alone. But better safe than sorry. "It's caused enough trouble already. If word were to get out we had it, we might be in danger. We might already be. My mother thought it cursed."

"Maybe she's right."

"You've been taking too much opium," Felix said. "It's muddled your brains."

Dahlia sat up straight. "No, think about it. Whoever owned this bracelet originally had it stolen by your parents, probably at musketpoint. Your parents were then chased off the island and had to sell it to save their lives. Tenner had it for less than a day and got himself beaten black and blue because of it. Gregory had it and now he's...missing." She slipped the heavy bracelet onto her thin arm and held it up to the light. The golden curves grew warmer and glinted in the late afternoon sun. "That sounds cursed to me. What a life this thing has had. I wonder how many hands it's passed through?"

Felix drummed his fingertips on the table. Someone had long ago carved their initials into it. "Do you think Uncle Gregory is still alive? Because Vince doesn't."

Dahlia kept her gaze on the bracelet. The low sunlight caught behind her garnet earrings, making them glow as lanterns do on rainy afternoons. "I hope he is," she said. "But I don't know. I thought if anything ever happened to him I would feel it, you know? Inside." She tapped her chest as she spoke. "I lived here for a long time. Longer than anyone else, except for Gregory. And still, when it came time to hand the Star over to someone new, Gregory chose you." Her eyes turned hard as glass, her lips pressed shut.

Felix refused to look away. "Can you really blame him?" He reached over and quickly slid the bracelet from her arm. "I'm going to put this somewhere safe."

"Don't you trust me with it?" She gave him a look he found hard to name.

All he could think of was what Vince had told him about Dahlia's debts. "Like I said, it isn't safe." He had no idea where to hide it, but he thought it best if Dahlia was kept in the dark.

He walked up to the top floor of the Star and into his room. He closed the door and sat on the edge of his bed, staring at the bracelet in his hands. How heavy, how golden, how beautiful. He thought about his parents stealing it from the arm of some wealthy person in their carriage. He thought of the screams, the shouts. He wondered if they'd fired a musket. If anyone had died to protect this trinket now in his hands. But then someone had died for it, on the vessel which had carried his parents to the new world.

Perhaps Dahlia was correct. Perhaps the bracelet was simply cursed. There were tales of that, weren't there? Of gold cursed by piskies or bucca, jealous of its beauty or angry at its theft from the ground, from the world below? Where could he hide it now? Where would it be safe from the ruffian who was willing to beat, kidnap, and perhaps even kill to secure its return? His head grew lighter, the room began to lurch, and he held his breath. He held in his hands a target.

All of a sudden, the events of the past few days began to press upon his chest—they filled his ears, his nostrils, and forced themselves into his every pore, threatening to drown him. His eyesight wavered, his legs buckled, and his breathing became hurried and forced. He scrambled to the window and flung up the sash. The choir of town life flooded in and washed over him. In his hand, he clutched the bracelet and held it, ready to fling it out, to fling away this cursed, wretched thing.

He imagined himself a lighthouse in a storm, with the waves of misfortune and chaos crashing about him. He did not throw the bracelet but instead let it drop by his feet. It thumped onto the dusty old floorboards. He gripped the window sill with both hands and squared his shoulders. "*It is the waves which break—not I.*"

He repeated the line over and over until the chaos retreated. He breathed deeply of the fresh air, tinged with brine though it was.

Under his bed lay the box carved with blossoms which his Uncle Gregory had kept the bracelet in. Felix threw the lid open and shoved the bracelet inside, then he hid the box under a loose floorboard. It had been the place where he had hidden his money as a boy. Perhaps Dahlia knew of it; perhaps she didn't. But he could think of no safer place, and for the time being, it would have to suffice.

FELIX HURRIEDLY STUFFED some of the previous night's takings into a bag and tucked it inside his coat. He dashed along Bibbler's Brook and through to the Tangles. He found *Helen's Salve* tucked neatly between two houses, the door closed but unlocked, and so he let himself in. He passed between mauve curtains lined with tassels where a woman with wrinkled jowls and small, angular ears greeted him, wearing a sparkling turquoise gown with peacock-feathered shoulders. It took Felix a moment to gather his thoughts. "I...um...I would like to speak with Mr Marwood." She looked ready for a night at the opera, not an afternoon working the door at an opium den.

She smiled and beckoned him to follow her along a red carpet so plush his boots sank. Ahead of them, a great copper squid rattled and bellowed as its attendants fed opium and coal to keep it burning. Something in the squid popped, and he near jumped out of his skin. The attendants—almost wholly naked—paid no mind to either him or the cacophony from the giant squid. He wondered if their time spent in the haze of second-hand opium had dulled their senses entirely. Already he started to sway where he walked, his head starting to list like a ship tossed at sea.

The woman in the sparkling gown led him to an ordinary office door, made obscene by its extravagant surroundings, and knocked three times. She turned the handle and ushered him inside.

Mr Marwood sat at his desk, writing in a ledger. "Ah, young Mr Diamond! Come, sit, sit."

Felix thought the walls of the poorly lit and tawdry maple-wood office would close in around him. He fidgeted in his chair. "I-I've brought you your money." He set the bag on Mr Marwood's desk.

Mr Marwood scoffed and poked about inside the bag. "Well, blow me. You actually did!"

"Despite your attempts to derail the Star's opening night, it was a success."

Mr Marwood laughed. "Your family would have found out about your event sooner or later." His mouth smiled but his eyes did not. "A Diamond who pays his debts is rarer than hen's teeth." He sat back with one hand on his armrest and the other flat on the desk. "Your cousin should take a leaf from your book."

Felix squeezed his eyes shut, trying to clear the haze from them. "Dahlia will pay you back as soon as she is able. I'm certain of it."

"Mmm, well, as much as I would like to take your word for it, I need something a little more substantial." Mr Marwood's smile widened, showing more and more teeth. "You tell her from me she has forty-eight hours to pay back what she owes me. And if she doesn't— Listen, boy. Look in my eyes. If she doesn't pay, I will come down on her like a hurricane and she may not live to regret it."

CHAPTER THIRTY-ONE

SEVERAL CLOCKS TICKED in unison as Iron brushed aside some tools and set out a blue-and-white porcelain teapot with three cups. "I didn't have time to properly tidy up."

Sorcha moved some boxes of cogwheels. "Now, don't be worrying about that," she said. "This is your workshop, not a tearoom."

Someone knocked on the door to his quarters and Iron shouted for them to let themselves in.

"Apologies for my lateness," Jason Sparrow said. "The line for hot water grows ever longer in my lodgings."

He leaned his lighting pole against the wall. He was a small-mouthed, willowy man of twenty-five, with large ears and sharp cheekbones. He kept his hair slicked back and his expression serious. He wore his white lamplighter great-coat, its embroidered seafoam-green oak leaves still vibrant in the winter light.

"We were just discussing the next iteration of the lamps," Sorcha said. "The automatic lighting and extinguishing of the candles. Iron has created some exquisite mechanisms."

Mr Sparrow sat down and flicked through the pages on the table. His shoulders slumped and he exhaled. "I just wonder if perhaps we are making more work for ourselves than is strictly necessary. The current system is working, is it not? And would it not provide more employment if we were to avoid automating the process too much?"

Iron poured some tea into each of the cups. "If you are concerned about being put out of work, let me assure you that as the town's first lamplighter you will always have a place in this endeavour." He popped into the little kitchen and returned with a milk jug.

"I am grateful to hear it," Mr Sparrow said. "What I

meant, though, was when this scheme is extended throughout the town—as it surely will be—there will be a need for more lamplighters like myself. More people who would be grateful for the opportunity to work."

"I hadn't thought of it like that." Sorcha drowned her tea with milk.

"But surely a cheaper and more reliable system would be preferable, in the long term?" Iron asked.

"I hadn't realised I was an expensive liability," Mr Sparrow said.

Iron's tongue grew two sizes larger. "No, um, no, I didn't... I..."

"I'm sure Iron didn't mean it in a disparaging way. But a mechanism cannot become ill, for example," Sorcha said.

"But it can break," Mr Sparrow said. "And if only you or another skilled horological specialist can repair it, then that will take time. And what if something happens to you? Another lamplighter can take over from me at a moment's notice. How long would it take to replace you, Mr Huxham?"

Iron moved to speak but found he had nothing to say. Mr Sparrow made a good point.

"Perhaps it would be best to shelve these plans for the time being," Sorcha said. "We have enough on our plates with the current scheme."

"I think you're right," Mr Sparrow said. He leaned forward with his hands clasped. "Please don't feel put out, Mr Huxham. I am not attacking you or your ideas. Ms Fontaine is correct—these designs are wonderful, and I have no doubt they would work. But it can be easy to over-look the human element in these endeavours. People need to work. I was raised in privilege and never thought I would need an occupation, but here I sit, a victim to the whims of fate and grateful for the opportunities your lamps pro-vided. I am certain there are many others who would feel the same, many others would be ever thankful for gainful employment. Just because a machine can perform a task does not mean that it should."

Only the striking of the hour broke the silence which followed.

"Now, I am sorry to dash off, but I must, or I shall be late for my rounds."

Iron pursed his lips and nodded as Mr Sparrow re-trieved his lighting pole and took his leave. Iron closed the door and hesitated, his hand on the frame.

"Don't be too disheartened," Sorcha said. "All this means is you're a little too good at your labours."

Iron held up his hands in mocking celebration, eliciting a short laugh from Sorcha.

"I can see why Admiral Boon pushed so hard for him to get the role as lamplighter," she said. "He's certainly passionate about the position." She rolled up the plans on the table and tucked them under her arm.

Iron lifted his teacup. "Who did you want for the role?"

"Me? Oh, I assumed someone from the Watch was the obvious choice, though no one relished the idea. The council suggested someone outside the organisation ought to fill the position. I thought Vince would object, but he doesn't want the Watch to become so entrenched in the townsfolk's everyday lives." She puffed out her chest and her cheeks, and lowered her voice as far as it would go. "'Not their nannies', he said to me. 'Not here to hold their hand.'" She held her arms out to simulate Vince's gait.

Iron laughed and clapped. "Uncanny. You sound just like him. I, uh, I don't suppose you'd like to join me for dinner this evening? At the Jack Thistle?"

"Oh, I would but I can't," Sorcha said. "My sister is having some people from the C.T.C. round to her house, and she made me promise I'd come for moral support. They want to change the oak leaf design of the lamplighter coat to something more in keeping with the trade. She made Mr Sparrow's coat, did I tell you that? She makes the Watch uniforms too."

Iron forced a smile and saw her to the door. "And a fine job she has done with it. Well, good day."

When he was alone, he slumped into his chair. His ears burned, and his whole face tingled. He kept rolling up his sleeves and lowering them again, over and over. He considered visiting Felix but knew he would be busy at the Star and he didn't want to be a burden. They had spent a wonderful couple of hours together in the cherry house yesterday, and Iron didn't want to spoil the memory by annoying Felix with his sudden, unannounced presence.

And then there was the doubt. The niggling doubt in the back of his mind. He couldn't get the image of Felix's face as he turned over that table out of his mind. The anger in it, the fire as he shouted at his aunt. Iron couldn't help but imagine being on the receiving end of it, and it made him shudder. Then to discover Felix had attacked Vince?

Felix was either especially brave or especially foolish to have done so.

Iron shook his head. He wasn't being fair. Felix must not have been in his right mind at the time. With everything that had happened to him over the past few days, who could blame him? Iron could not honestly say he would have fared any better in Felix's shoes. He rubbed his eyes and wished he hadn't gotten out of bed that morning.

A heavy thump on the door roused him from his wallowing. "Did you forget something?" He opened the door to find Vince Knight towering over him.

"Thought I was someone else?" Commander Knight asked as he entered, wholly uninvited.

A smaller man followed him, someone Iron's age with a band of daises tattooed around his bald head. Both of them wore the claret-and-black uniforms of the Watch.

"Your companion, Sorcha Fontaine was here a few minutes ago," Iron said. "I thought perhaps she had left something behind."

Commander Knight immediately begun rifling through Iron's belongings. The papers stacked neatly on his desk, the little boxes of cogs and wheels, the tins of oil and grease. He lifted a lighting pole about as long as a man's arm. The pole was covered with apple-sized knurls—swollen lumps cast into the body of the rod itself—each set less than a hand span apart from the next. The knurls marked segments of the pole where it could be taken apart and held clockwork mechanisms necessary for its operation. Vince twisted a grip near the end. A thinner, threaded pole automatically screwed itself out from the top, ticking loudly as it went. When it had finished, the pole had doubled in length, and the tip ended in a triple-edged key, the standard for most horological devices. Each time Mr Knight turned the pole in his hands, no matter how gently, something inside rattled loudly. He held it close to his single, icy blue eye and turned it over and over again. He shook the pole and from within came a rattle and ticking so loud it vibrated through the entire rod.

"It's the first version of the lighting pole I made," Iron said. "It's a lot noisier than the one I made for Mr Sparrow. Why, um, why are you here?"

"We were wondering if you knew a man named Evans?" the tattooed man asked. "Rob Evans."

Commander Knight turned the grip on the pole, and the threaded end ticked, clicked, and rattled its way back inside its sheath once more.

"And you are?" Iron asked.

He held out his hands. Tattoos of rhododendrons adorned the backs of them. "Call me Flowers."

"However did you come by such a name?" Iron asked with a little laugh. It wasn't reciprocated. "Ah, no, I'm afraid I don't know who you're talking about."

With his back to them, Commander Knight suddenly slammed the pole down onto the workbench, causing Iron to jump.

"He seems to know you," Flowers said. "In fact, he knows you very well. Do you, by any chance, remember where you were on the afternoon of Monday the twenty-seventh?"

"I expect I was here," Iron said. "I'm always here. Well, downstairs, I mean. In the workshop. I'm usually always there. Am I making sense? Can someone usually always be somewhere?"

Commander Knight's head disappeared from sight as he leaned on the workbench, heaved his shoulders, and began breathing more heavily. Iron's palms turned clammy, and his throat ran dry.

"Mr Evans claims to have been with you," Flowers said.

"Does he? How strange. I'm certain I would have re-membered if he had."

Commander Knight flung a box of gears at a wall. It clattered to the floor, scattering pieces all around. Iron al-most jumped out of his skin. Before he had time to speak, Commander Knight was in front of him, towering over him, his hot breath on Iron's face.

He grabbed Iron's lapel and held it fast. "Don't appre-ciate having my time wasted. Don't appreciate being lied to."

Iron gibbered and shook. This huge bearded man with a leather eyepatch and gritted teeth filled his view. "I don't know who he is!"

"*Don't*," Commander Knight said, hurling globs of hot saliva into Iron's face.

Iron's nerve cracked. "Fine. Yes, I know him!"

"Well? *Well?*"

Iron's whole body quivered, and he blinked rapidly. "We shook the sheets in his room at the sailor shelter," he said. "Most of the morning and afternoon. I left before sunset."

Commander Knight stared at him. He finally let go of Iron's lapel and took a step back. His whole demeanour changed. He hadn't really been angry at all, Iron suddenly realised. It had been an act. How horrific to be able to turn into *that* so easily.

"Lied to us," Commander Knight said.

"It's not... It isn't lying," Iron said. "It's respecting someone else's privacy." He put his hand on the wall to regain some composure. "I didn't know how much he had told you. I don't know his personal circumstances, and I didn't want to land him in hot water."

"Considerate," Commander Knight said.

"How well do you know him?" Flowers asked.

"Not very well at all," Iron said. "We met on the street, at the market. We exchanged glances, a few words, and then we...took it from there. You know how it is."

Commander Knight grunted and nodded a little.

"We had our fun together and went our separate ways," Iron said.

Commander Knight hadn't taken his eye off of Iron. "Know a man named Gregory Diamond?"

Iron's eye twitched. He rolled up his shirt sleeve. "I know of him. Felix's uncle. Have you found him yet?"

Commander Knight's shoulders dropped a little. "Apologies for the mess," he said, pointing to the gears on the floor.

"Think nothing of it," Iron said. He saw them both to the door and bolted it once they'd left.

CHAPTER THIRTY-TWO

HOPING TO KEEP the momentum going and capitalise on the success of two nights ago, Felix threw open the doors to the Star. He had booked a number of performers to appear on stage, and the show began with a red-haired woman playing a crowdy-crawn drum and singing about the sinking of a pirate ship off the coast of Blackrabbit. She had initially refused Felix's offer to perform in Wednesday's show, but having heard about its success, she leapt at the chance to perform tonight. The rest of the playbill consisted mostly of acts who had performed earlier in the week. Felix hoped the customers wouldn't mind.

He found Vince in a dark corner of the playhouse, drinking alone. "You look miserable. Moreso than usual, I mean." His attempt to wrangle a smile out of Vince failed utterly.

"Hit a wall."

"I sincerely hope you're speaking metaphorically." Felix said. "Although with you, I wouldn't be surprised."

"Not used to looking so hard to find criminals. Used to be I knew everything that happened in this town. Not so much as a pocket got picked without my say-so."

The front door opened, and Iron poked his head in to scan the room before entering. He looked about and waved to Felix before taking a seat at the bar.

"Made up your differences then?" Vince asked.

"We've gotten to know one another a little better. He's a nice fellow. Interesting."

Vince took a drink of ale. "Checked up on everyone who was at the sailor refuge when the bracelet was pilfered. None of them knew about it."

"They could be lying?"

Vince shook his head. "Don't think so. All of them had explanations for where they were when Tenner was attacked. Had people to vouch for them. Including your horologist friend."

"Who, Iron? Wait, have you spoken to him? You don't seriously think he's involved in all of this, do you?"

Vince fixed him with a glare. "Iron flinched when I mentioned Gregory."

"Hah! That's it? That's all you have to hang this fanciful notion on?"

Vince's shoulders rolled. "Listen. Iron was at the sailor shelter with a man just before the bracelet was stolen. Could have seen it when he was there. Maybe he planned to steal it himself. Maybe Tenner beat him to it. Maybe Iron beat Tenner."

Felix shook his head. He didn't believe a word of it. "All you have are a pile of maybes."

"Help me narrow them down. Talk to him."

"Of course I'm going to talk to him but not because you told me to. Is there anything else you think I should know?"

"Iron lied at first," Vince said. "Claimed not to know the man I was asking about."

Felix's spine straightened. "Why would he lie?"

"Told me he did it to protect the man's privacy."

"That's not so strange, is it?"

With the back of his hand, Vince wiped some ale from his moustache. "Wouldn't be if you hadn't flinched when I said it. Lied to you as well, I take it?"

Felix said nothing for a moment and considered not saying anything at all. "He told me he'd never been here before, to the Star, but he has. He knew Uncle Gregory. Not very well, but still."

"Take it he wasn't fond of your uncle?"

Felix took a deep breath through his nostrils. "He was not."

Vince squinted at him. "Tell me everything."

Felix drummed his fingertips. The red-haired performer shifted her singing to something more crowd pleasing. Several women in the crowd joined in.

Vince sat up and lowered his voice. "Understand there's something blossoming between you two. Clear as day. Don't want to scupper your chances with him. But need to know everything. Might help me find your uncle." His voice had softened in a way Felix hadn't heard before, becoming warmer, richer.

He looked about to make sure they wouldn't be overheard. "Iron used to be a bedworker. He worked the balcony."

"Fell prey to the Diamond Cut?"

Felix shivered and his ears tingled. "You know about it?"

"Common knowledge in my circles."

"The bedworkers had enough of it. They spoke to Uncle Gregory, but he wouldn't relent. And then...well, then Aunt Alma got involved."

Vince's snowy white eyebrows jumped up.

"Don't get excited, nothing came of it. But it seems she approached the bedworkers and suggested if she were to take over the Star..."

"Diamond Cut would be no more."

"Precisely."

Vince clamped his brawny hand on Felix's arm, his voice turning to silk. "Take some advice from an old man—believe for one second you're getting dragged into something...nefarious? Run the other way. Fast as you can."

Felix didn't know what to say. He gently excised himself from Vince's grasp. Vince swirled the ale in his tankard before swallowing the last of it. With that, he lifted his tricorne cap and left.

The woman with the drum finished her piece and yielded the stage to a trio of actors performing a scene from a play Felix didn't recognise. Apparently, it necessitated two of the actors being shirtless and one being trouserless. The bare-chested men chased the other around the stage with a couple of parsnips. The crowd approved of their bawdy shenanigans and vociferously expressed as much. The town's lamplighter led the cheers, seconded by an uncharacteristically animated Dick Tassiter. Evidently, this sort of act was just Dick's taste.

Felix stood behind the bar and served one waiting customer. To his surprise, most of the attention in the room was on the acts, and had been all night. The chairs, usually gathered around tables, mostly pointed toward the stage at the back of the room.

Iron hadn't really looked up from his glass of gin. He cupped it between his hands as though it was warming him against a cold night.

Felix leaned on the bar. "Are you unwell?"

Iron stirred as if woken from a deep dream. "Oh, ah, no, no. Good evening, Felix. No, I was simply...reminiscing. Against my better judgement."

"Ah," Felix said, "one of *those* nights."

"Of all *those* nights, this is the most *those* it's possible to be."

Felix frowned, then laughed a little. "How much have you had to drink?"

Iron smiled. "Not enough, I can assure you."

Felix left Ms Hornby to attend to the customers and sat next to Iron. "And just what is so special about tonight?"

Iron licked his own lips and returned to staring at his drink.

"It's fine," Felix said. "You don't have to tell me. I shouldn't have asked, really. We don't know each another very well. I hear you had a visitor today."

"Ah, yes, I saw you speaking with Commander Knight," Iron said. "I don't mind telling you he scared me witless. I almost wet myself."

"Yes, I can imagine," Felix said. "Do you still find him attractive?" He chuckled a little then and wrought the tiniest smile from Iron.

"Must I answer the question?"

"Not right away," Felix said. "He was annoyed about you lying to him."

Iron cocked his head and fixed him with a curious gaze. "I imagine he expected you to be more discreet about what he told you."

Felix waved his hand. "I don't work for him. And I

see no reason to be coy around you."

"I've seen you being coy." Iron covered his own crotch with his hand in an echo of Felix's behaviour in the cherry house. "I found it charming."

The act on stage had become boisterous, with the trouserless man still being chased by the two shirtless ones, one of whom now held a wet rag at the end of a stick, for some reason which escaped Felix.

"I lied to protect someone else, not myself," Iron said.

"The same reason you lied to me about knowing my uncle."

Iron nodded before sipping his gin. "It's, ah, it's the anniversary of the day the orphanage kicked me out onto the streets," he said. "I believe it also to be the day of my birth. The orphanage only held children until the day they turned thirteen, so it makes sense."

"No wonder this is a difficult time for you," Felix said. "You had no family to take care of you?"

"None whatsoever," Iron said. "Today has a tendency to drive home just how...alone I am."

Felix quickly tapped his fingers on the counter. "Well, you can be surrounded by family and still feel alone. You truly have no inkling as to where you came from?"

Iron leaned his chin on his hand. "I used to dream I was actually the lost son of some baroness or lord, ferreted away in the night by a jealous butler and they would come and sweep me off the streets and into some grand palace full of food and warm clothing. I fancied I would have, not just a family, but a noble family, a great heritage stretching back centuries. Something to be proud of. Instead of just being...me."

"You started with nothing, and you're a skilled horologist. I'd say you have plenty to be proud of."

Iron smiled at him then. "That's kind of you to say. This has always been a...difficult day for me. I had asked Sorcha if she was available this evening but she had other plans."

"Why didn't you ask me?"

Iron cupped his glass again. "I knew you'd be busy. And it's fine, truly. I-I usually spend it alone. I'm used to it."

Felix reached over for a bottle and refilled Iron's glass. "Have you considered getting blind drunk with me instead?"

"You just want me to fill your coffers."

"Amongst other things." Felix raised his eyebrow and

smirked.

Iron almost choked on his gin. "Mr Diamond, your sailor's candour is a sight to behold."

"Amongst other things," Felix said again.

Iron laughed and wiped the gin from his own shirt.

As the night wore on, Felix found his attention being drawn to various jobs that needed doing. Spilled ale needed to be mopped up, a rowdy patron needed to be forcibly ejected, a performer refused to go on stage until the lighting had been set just so. All the while, his gaze kept drifting back to the striking Iron, perched on a stool at the end of the bar.

By the end of the night, the acts had finished, and the customers had started to wander outside. Felix and Iron stood by the bottom of the stairwell.

"Thank you." Iron wasn't drunk at all. Despite Felix's encouragement, he'd taken very little gin. "This is often a difficult time for me. Your company has made it much less so."

A customer staggered downstairs and pushed past them. Iron stood close to Felix, so close their boots touched. He leaned down and kissed Felix on the lips. Gently, at first. Felix grabbed his collar and pulled him in closer. They leaned back against the peeling, dark green paper of the wall, lips locked and hands exploring. Felix started to moan when Iron kissed his neck.

"I feel as though I have hardly spent any time with you this evening," Felix said.

Iron set his hand on Felix's cheek and looked him in the eye. "I knew you wanted to, though," Iron said. "And that's what counts."

CHAPTER THIRTY-THREE

FELIX STOOD WITH one hand on the door of Dahlia's bedroom as she folded her clothes and dropped them into a tattered trunk. As a gravestone concerns a person but contains nothing of them, so Dahlia's room stood unique to her yet absent of her touch. Bare walls and floors, plain bedclothes and curtains, not one trace of her could be found. Whether she'd always lived this way or Uncle Gregory had scrubbed every morsel of her from the room, Felix couldn't say. On the wall hung the black military jacket she'd been wearing when Felix had first returned to the Star. He took it from its peg and held it open. "Wherever did you come by a C.T.C. jacket?"

Dahlia huffed and flicked a strand of blonde hair from her eye. "A lover gave it to me. He was a greencoat officer. I thought we had a future, but it transpired he was already handfasted to another."

Felix held one of the brass buttons stamped with the letter "C" intertwined with a ship's wheel—the mark of the Chase Trading Company. "I would have thought you'd want to get rid of it."

"After I gave him a piece of my mind, I dyed it black. There was no sense in letting a fine garment go to waste. Give it here." She held out her hand, intending to pack the jacket away.

Felix hung it back on the peg. "You've been here almost a week, and there's been no major catastrophe of your making."

Dahlia performed a little curtsy. "Thank you, m'lord, I've been on my best behaviour; so I have, m'lord."

Felix didn't rise to the bait. "I think you should stay. Permanently."

Dahlia hesitated before squinting at him. "Why are you being nice to me?"

Felix rubbed his hand over his nut-brown beard.

"Dahlia, Mr Marwood wants his money."

Dahlia shrugged. "I expect he does. I'd like it too." She proceeded to remove clothes from her trunk and laid them in a drawer by the window.

"I can talk to Vince," Felix said.

"And tell him what? I do owe Marwood money. If anything, the Watch will lock me up."

"You're being very nonchalant about this."

With her hand, Dahlia tried to smooth out the wrinkles from a jade-coloured robe a la Francaise. "You think Alma will let Marwood touch me?

"Does she know about your debts?"

"Not as such, but..."

Felix held his hands open. "But what? You think she'll protect you? You think the family will protect you?"

Dahlia put a hand on her hip. "Are you saying you will?"

"I... If I can, I..." He took a step backwards.

"Listen, Lucky, this isn't the first time I've racked up a little debt, and it always sorts itself out one way or the other. Maybe Marwood will go out of business, or maybe whoever took Gregory will take him too. I don't know." She set down her dress and took his face in her hands.

"But you don't need to worry so much. I don't want you losing sleep over this. Not everything is your problem."

AFTER SPENDING MOST of the night sitting on the floor by his fireplace with a bottle of whiskey in one hand and Crabmeat snoring on his leg, Vince had climbed into bed but gotten very little sleep. Something in the back of his head kept niggling at him. Part of it was pride. He knew that much. He'd always been at the heart of activity in the town and found it difficult to accept he'd been sidelined so completely.

He still found his thoughts snagged on the night the key had been stolen from his pocket. There was another kick to his pride. That he'd fallen so far from people's estimations that anyone would *dare* steal from him. And what was worse, he still had no idea who'd done it. There had been a lot of customers in the Star at the time, too many to interrogate after the fact. And then there had been the ones who hadn't stayed for more than one drink. And the ones who had just popped their heads in to see what was happening. And the ones who had left as soon as Vince and the Watch arrived. Who's to say one of them didn't slip back in later?

He threw off his bedclothes. He always slept naked and without getting dressed, he stomped to his little kitchen. He took four eggs and cracked them into a blackened pan with a knob of butter. The stove heated slowly. He waited by his window. In the distance, the street lamps glowed, little beacons against the dark. By the time his eggs started to fry, pink fingers crept over the horizon, bringing with them a new day. He slid his eggs onto a chipped plate and dug out a fork from a drawer. In the distance, one of the street lamps dimmed until it disappeared entirely. Vince sat at his narrow table and after the first mouthful, he realised what had been niggling at him all night. He scoffed the rest of his breakfast, splashed some water on his face, dressed in his Watch uniform, and hurried outside.

FELIX MOPPED THE stage of the grime from the night before. How performers managed to get it into such a state, he'd never understood. As much as he'd like to have kept the doors to the Star locked until the evening, or even until the next performance on Sunday night, he needed the money and so had opened before dawn. Ms Hornby wouldn't be in until the evening but he didn't mind. He expected he would be able to cope without her. He hoped to catch some freshly docked sailors who weren't able to get into the Jack Thistle, but so far his only customer had been Dick Tassiter.

Mr Tassiter had taken his usual seat at the corner of the bar, delighted at the early opening. "I think this is a fine idea, lad! There's many a sailor would be glad of an early house!"

Iron hadn't stayed the night, much as Felix had wanted him to. Felix had kept him in bed for as long as he could, but Iron said he needed an early start as he couldn't face the questioning from Mr Williams should he be even one minute late.

Dahlia had been out all night at, Felix assumed, the opium den, and had arrived back in the early hours of the morning. She crawled into her bed with strict instructions not to wake her until the sun was beginning to set. "I know all I want to know of sunshine," she said. "Wake me when dusk arrives."

A woman with a weather-beaten face shuffled through the doors and took a seat on the bench against the wall.

"Good morning, Ms Stock," Felix called over to her. "I don't think I've ever seen you in here before."

"I've been 'earing a lot about this place for the past few days," she said. "A glass of blue ruin, please, when you get a minute." Her voice was raspy, cut to pieces, no doubt, by the roaring ocean wind. When Felix brought her gin to her, she bade him sit awhile. "Apparently you put on quite a show the other night."

This remained the one aspect of life in the Star We Sail By which he had never warmed to. He was not, by nature, a conversationalist, and though he recognised the need for it in this business, he felt himself ill-suited to the role. Nonetheless, he sat facing her.

"'Ow did you get on with finding the owner of the bracelet?" she asked.

Felix sighed. "The greencoats gave the Watch a list. A bunch of old men and women who should have retired years ago. The Watch spoke to every one of them, but no one knew anything about it."

"What about the young man?" Ms Stock asked.

Felix thought for a moment. "What young man?"

VINCE MADE A beeline for the C.T.C. office where he loomed over the little man at his desk. "Want to speak to Admiral Boon."

The little man tried not to look up at him and, instead, rifled through some papers. "I'm sure we can help you there, Commander Knight. The admiral has an opening on Thursday afternoon, and I believe— Wait, Commander Knight, wait. Where are you—? You can't just—"

Vince had stormed past the little man's desk and through a heavy set of doors into a honey-marbled corridor. He opened every door until he found Admiral Boon sitting behind her desk, reading a book.

"Mr Knight," she said, slamming it shut. "How dare you barge in here?"

"Commander Knight, as it happens," Vince said. "Here on official Watch business."

The little man scurried in behind him, apologising profusely for allowing Vince to get past.

"Well, let's be honest," Admiral Boon said, "it's not as if you could have stopped him."

Admiral Boon wore the traditional emerald-green-and-white uniform of the Chase Trading Company. She cut a matronly figure, with a dimpled chin and brown hair. "Now you're here, I suppose you might as well stay. Sit, won't you? Anton, please fetch us some tea."

The little man hurried away, closing the door behind him. It swooshed shut with all the heft of a tomb being sealed. The walls of the admiral's office held many framed maps, nautical charts, and paintings of important-looking military types with stiff upper lips, hard eyes, and extravagant uniforms.

"Wanted to ask you about the lamplighter," Vince said. "Sparrow."

"Jason Sparrow, yes, a good man. What about him?"

"Something's been bothering me. Only just realised what. Hear you were very insistent on him getting the job. Want to know why."

Admiral Boon's brow fluttered as she tried to follow

his meaning. As, no doubt, she tried to uncover some hidden agenda to his question. She looked at him as a cat would a lame dormouse. "Mr Sparrow is a C.T.C. man. A navy man. He was injured recently while serving his company and his country. As he can no longer sail, I thought it the least I could do to ensure he was gainfully employed on land. The C.T.C. is paying for the street lamps, so I feel we've rightly earned some say in how they're run, don't you?"

Vince didn't move a muscle. He gave nothing away, but he could tell she was hiding something. His instinct was to grab an object from her desk and throw it against the wall, but firstly, he suspected the admiral wouldn't fall for such cheap theatrics, and secondly, he wasn't sure how far his authority would stretch. The C.T.C. had challenged his law banning the use of firearms on the island by claiming their headquarters constituted something not unlike an embassy. That within its grounds, the C.T.C. could make its own laws. The council were still trying to disprove this notion, something which was likely to take years, and until they did, Vince needed to do something he was wildly uncomfortable with—he needed to tread carefully. "Sparrow ever live at the sailor's shelter?"

The corner of Admiral Boon's mouth twitched, just a touch. "He may have done."

Vince remained still as stone, not taking his eye from her for an instant.

She leaned back in her leather chair. "Yes, yes, I believe he did. For a short spell. Until he took up his role as our first lamplighter."

"Would have been at the shelter recently, then," Vince said. "Strange how his name was absent from the list you gave me."

Anton, the little man from the front desk, arrived with a silver tray laden with a teapot and two bone china cups. He set it on the desk between them. He lifted the pot and poured. The light from the window behind Admiral Boon caught the tea and the steam curling from it.

Admiral Boon smiled wholly without warmth. "You must understand, Commander Knight, the C.T.C. is a large organisation. A very, very large organisation. Sometimes, things become misplaced, names slip through the cracks, oversights are made, entirely without malice or intent." She lifted her cup and sipped, noiselessly.

She was definitely lying to him. Right to his face. He clamped his jaw tighter. He thought of Mr Sparrow touring through the town with his lighting pole, the one Iron Hux-ham had made for him. Vince thought about what he could do with something like that, the heads he could crack, the legs he could break. He wondered if Mr Spar-row ever had cause to use the pole in defence of his per-son. After all, he walked the streets of Port Knot at night, rarely a safe prospect for anyone. Especially in Pudding Quarter, with all those Diamonds about. In a flash, he gripped the armrests and flung himself to his feet. At the door, he paused when she called to him.

"Commander Knight. Won't you be staying to have your tea?"

He didn't look back, just marched through the honey-marbled hallway and out into the docklands. He had a name and at last he knew what he needed to do.

CHAPTER THIRTY-FOUR

"CAN'T YOU TELL me his name?" Felix asked.

Ms Stock clamped her eyes shut as tightly as she could. "It'll come to me; bear with me now; it'll come to me. It was a bird, I'm sure of it. Starling, his name was. Or Swift? Could it have been Sparrow? Sparrow sounds right."

"I don't remember any of those names from the list the C.T.C. gave us." Felix racked his brains trying to think if he'd heard them before.

"Pah, the greencoats can't be trusted with that sort of thing." Ms Stock's voice had risen an octave. "They lie all the time. They told me if I worked 'ard on their ships, I'd see the world. Well you don't see much when you spend your days scrubbing decks and fetching gunpowder, I can tell you. Now, Mr Sparrow, 'e was a greencoat, for a little while. Until 'e got shot in the belly. 'E told me all about 'ow 'e'd been forced to retire. 'E was only in the shelter for about a week, if even. The greencoats probably didn't want to mention 'im because it looks bad for them, you see? If they provide a shelter that's not safe?"

"Why isn't it safe?" Felix asked.

"Mr Sparrow, well, 'e 'ad a blazing row with Boon, one of them greencoat admirals you see swanning about the harbour. All medals and shoulders but never done an 'ard day's work in 'er life. And it doesn't look good for them, does it? Their admiral 'aving a row with a sailor, threatening all sorts?"

Felix leaned in. "I'm sorry, you're saying Admiral Boon threatened this Mr Sparrow?"

"Oh yes," Ms Stock said, waving her drink around. A drop slipped out and ran down her cracked fingers. "Well, I think so. She was very red-faced, I can tell you. I couldn't 'ear too well. They were all muffled because I was outside at the time—watching but not watching—you know 'ow it is.

And my ears aren't what they used to be. I got too close to too many cannons. They ring all the time now, from day to bleddy night, I can 'ardly get a wink of sleep. But they nearly came to blows, Boon and Mr Sparrow. I'm sure of it."

The sun had risen and Felix turned off a striker-lantern on a nearby table and the one on the wall above Ms Stock's head. As he went to turn off the one in the nearest bay window, he spotted the lamplighter in his white greatcoat at the bend in the road.

The lamplighter extended his nobbled lighting pole and inserted it into the lamp head. The candle within flickered then faded to nothing. The lamplighter caught Felix's eye as he twisted the end of the pole. The top half screwed itself down into its sheath until the whole pole was no more than the length of a scabbard. A scabbard with ridged, apple-sized lumps running the whole length of it. Each one set barely a few inches apart. Just like the marks on Tenner's arm.

Felix's face dropped. He suddenly remembered where he'd heard the name Sparrow before. In a flash, the lamplighter was at the Star's window. Felix staggered back.

The door opened and the lamplighter, Mr Sparrow,

stepped inside and removed his cap. He smiled at Felix, a cold smile, all artifice. "Mr Diamond," he said. "Might I have a quiet word?"

He waited for Felix to walk to the bar before moving away from the door.

Ms Stock waved to the lamplighter. "Oh, there 'e is! It's so funny I was just talking about you!"

"Were you, indeed? How strange. Are you still at the shelter?"

"Oh yes, no luck in convincing my ingrate nieces and nephews to let me stay with them." She took a drink of her gin. "I don't know what's become of the youth of today."

Mr Sparrow nodded politely and joined Felix at the far end of the bar, away from Mr Tassiter, with their backs turned and voices kept low.

"What's this about?" Felix asked.

"I can see in your face you know who I am," Mr Sparrow said. "So let's not pretend. You have the bracelet. I would like it returned to me."

"It isn't yours," Felix said. "It belonged to my parents."

Mr Sparrow's mouth opened, just a touch. He smiled again but more genuinely this time. "Is that so? They are the ones who stole it? Who had their names engraved upon it? Hah. What a small world we live in. Just think of it, Mr Diamond, all those years ago your parents put us both on a course that led us here, today, to this place. We were destined to meet. Hah. Nevertheless, I would like it back."

"Where is Uncle Gregory?" Felix asked. "You did something to him, didn't you?"

Mr Sparrow said nothing for a moment. "You can have him back," he said. "When you give me my bracelet."

"He's still alive?" Felix's heart thumped faster and faster.

"Of course," Mr Sparrow said. "I'm not a monster. Bring the bracelet to Chancewater. Let's say in one hour? Time enough for me to finish my rounds." He laughed then, his eyes wide, and white teeth bared. His thin eyebrows never lifted, not even once. "You give me the bracelet, and I give you your uncle. And let's leave your friends in the Watch out of this, yes? And your family, while we're at it. At present, your uncle is restrained and hidden. If I think the Watch is coming, he will remain that way until he starves. I'll see you soon, Mr Diamond." He took his cap, nodded to Ms Stock, and left the Star.

Felix's heart didn't stop pounding. He wanted to tell Iron, tell Vince, tell anyone. He gave a moment's thought to telling Aunt Alma. She'd know what to do, but would she help? Or would she just make things worse? He ran upstairs to wake Dahlia.

Bleary-eyed, she wrapped a banyan around herself and followed him out of the room. "You're not actually going to meet him?"

Felix knelt on the floor of his own bedroom and prised the loose floorboard up with his fingertips. "I don't have any choice. This is our only chance to get Uncle Gregory back." He pulled out the little wooden box carved with flowers.

Dahlia tugged it from his grip. "Wait, *wait.*" She held it out of his grasping reach. "Stop and think for a moment. You said yourself that Vince doesn't believe Gregory is still alive and he'd know—he's probably kidnapped more people than either of us has ever met. This is just a way to get the bracelet and probably kill you too."

"He doesn't have any reason to want me dead." Felix tried to grab the box, but Dahlia deftly kept it just out of reach, just as she used to do with his shoe when they were children.

"He doesn't need a reason," she said. "And, listen, this will sound cruel, but isn't the bracelet worth more than Gregory?"

Felix stopped trying to retrieve the box. He felt as though he'd been slapped in the face. "What an awful thing to say."

"Do you think Gregory would hesitate to sell you in the same manner?"

He finally succeeded in grabbing the box from her hands. He took his overcoat and cap and hurried to the stairs.

"You've been away too long!" Dahlia called after him. "It's made you soft!"

VINCE'S HEART THUMPED as he sped along the Entry towards Ms Hornby's house. He all but battered the front door down until she opened it.

"Did you forget your—? Oh, it's you."

"Sparrow about?"

"Mr Sparrow? No," Ms Hornby said. "He was here,

but he left. Where are you going? Commander? Commander!"

Vince pushed his way inside, frantically darting around the kitchen and parlour. "Sparrow's bedroom?"

Ms Hornby pointed upstairs, and Vince took the steps three at a time. Mr Sparrow's room was a tawdry yellow in colour. His single bed was unmade. The floor tidy. A wardrobe door hung open. Vince peered inside then slammed it shut. He pulled open every drawer in the chest by the window. "Empty," he said. "Sparrow goes about nude, does he?"

"Oh, how odd," Ms Hornby said. "He didn't have much with him when he moved in, but he must have packed everything up. Come to think of it, I did see him with his kit bag."

"When?"

"Just a few minutes ago," Ms Hornby said. "You only just missed him."

Vince's belly filled with ice. "Felix," he said.

CHAPTER THIRTY-FIVE

FELIX TOOK A moment to compose himself before returning to the bar. He didn't want to tip off Mr Tassiter or Ms Stock that anything was wrong. "I need to get another whiskey barrel," he said. "It's cold down there." He opened the hatch behind the bar and climbed down the stone steps into the damp cellar. He pulled on the dented cannonball, swinging open the hidden door to the smuggler's tunnels. He wished he had a musket but there were none in the Star, and thanks to Vince's new law, they were almost impossible to acquire on Blackrabbit these days. He hid the baton he'd taken from Tenner in the inside pocket of his long, corduroy overcoat. With a solitary striker-lantern to guide his way, he set off into the bitter, dark tunnels.

The coldness of the air caught his breath. The walls of the narrow tunnel were damp and a sickly, pale green in colour. He had room to stand straight, but just barely. His footsteps echoed along ahead of him. He wondered if the tunnels had been specially cut to stop Vince Knight from passing through them, but realised they likely were far older than him. The tunnels weaved and undulated, and Felix wondered at what point he'd passed under the cemetery. The thought of countless bodies lying still and sightless above his head made him shudder. The light from the lantern caught on stumps and protuberances, casting shadowy faces here and there. He tried not to look at them.

At last, he came to the end, to little Chancewater Cove. And there waiting for him in a sailboat was Mr Sparrow. Felix's hand touched the baton, just to reassure himself that he hadn't dropped it in the caves.

"Did you bring it?" Mr Sparrow asked.

Waves crashed, ringing though the cove.

Felix held up the box. "Where is Uncle Gregory?"

Mr Sparrow took his lighting pole and twisted the

handle. The top half screwed out automatically, clicking all the while until the whole shaft had doubled in length. He thrust the end into the water and turned it a few times. A few moments later, the water bubbled and boiled as an acorn-shaped submersible—big as a coach, made of oak, and held together with copper rings—ruptured the surface, right against the mouth of the cove.

Mr Sparrow spun a wheel on its side and a hatch opened in the waterproof tank. Sitting inside, Felix could just make out the figure of a man with a bag over his head, sitting bound and gagged. He moved to step onboard the submersible.

"Hold it," Mr Sparrow shouted. He kept his hand on the lighting pole. "One twist and the whole thing sinks. And I won't bother closing the door this time."

Felix stepped back a couple of paces. "Uncle Gregory! Uncle Gregory are you...? It's Felix, can you hear me? What is this? What have you done to him?"

Mr Sparrow's boat rocked from the disturbance caused by the acorn submersible. "I told you he was alive," he said. "Ms Underhay told me about this contraption your uncle uses for smuggling. A fully submersible chamber. Thankfully, it uses a common horological key. Your uncle uses it to store goods he can't move without fear of arousing suspicion. I doubt he ever expected to be kept inside of it himself."

"You're... You're disgusting," Felix said. "It's inhumane."

"It wouldn't have been necessary if he'd just given me the bracelet," Mr Sparrow said. "And it's not as if he can't breathe in there. There's a tube, see? Like a little chimney. It pokes up above the waves, just enough to let air in. If you didn't know to look for it, you'd never spot it."

"What is so special about this damn bracelet?" Felix asked. "It can't possibly be worth that much money."

"It's worth quite a lot," Mr Sparrow said. "My father had the bracelet made as a handfasting gift to my mother. He spent a fortune on it, safe in the knowledge he'd make more fortunes in their years together. The bracelet has haunted me my entire life. I was on board the coach when your parents attacked. I was only a boy at the time. Ten, maybe eleven years old. We were travelling through the woods from our house in the countryside to the harbour when we were set upon by two brigands. They held muskets to us and took everything we had. When they tried to take the bracelet my father resisted and was shot in the arm.

"His arm turned gangrenous and could not be saved. A surgeon had to remove it. My father never worked again. My mother was unable to cope with his change in temperament. We lost our money. Our home. I had to go to sea to earn a living. I hated every moment of it. I was born to smoke cigars in drawing rooms, not smoke fish in filthy holds. My family name held some sway in the C.T.C and I signed on as an officer. My first commission was on a merchant vessel shipping tea across the Atlantic, but the admiralty had other plans. They used our ship to launch surprise attacks on military targets."

"That's illegal," Felix said.

"The admiralty didn't care. One day, we raided an ailing Spanish ship. We broke into its hold and imagine my surprise to find sitting amongst it all," he pointed to the box in Felix's hand, "that very bracelet."

Felix's mind reeled. "What? How could...wait. My parents, the night they left Blackrabbit, they sold the bracelet to pay for their journey. The Spanish attacked the ship they travelled on and stole the bracelet. But that was years ago."

Mr Sparrow laughed. "It's probably changed hands a dozen times since then. I stole it before the rest of my crew spotted it. I wasn't about to let it slip through my hands—the thing that ruined my life. I determined then and there to make it pay. I would bring it back to Blackrabbit—back home—and sell it. I would use it to buy the nice house I always deserved and make a decent life for myself.

"This town used to be rife with fences but your friend Mr Knight put paid to them not so very long ago. So until I could find a buyer myself, I needed work. I heard about the lamplighter job, and I forced Admiral Boon to recommend me for it. I told her I'd go to the newspaper with what I knew about the illegal raids." His eyes had widened the whole time he spoke until they were pools of white. "Everything was going so well until the bracelet was stolen by your lout of a cousin, Tenner. And I had to beat its whereabouts out of him. And then your uncle, hah, your uncle refused to give it to me! He told me he'd hidden it in the Star. He even told me where, but he'd gotten rid of the only key.

"I thought about tearing the masthead from the building, gutting it, ripping out the metal chest and damn the consequences, but when you arrived with the key to the front door, I wondered if maybe, just maybe, your uncle had sent you the second key as well. When I saw you hand a key over to Vince Knight, I knew what it opened."

"You had Ms Underhay distract Vince, didn't you?" Suddenly it become all so clear to him.

Mr Sparrow tilted his head.

"There is no way you could have stolen the key from Vince otherwise," Felix said. "She knew what you were doing. She helped you."

"She did. But now all my plans for the future are gone. I can't stay in Port Knot any longer. I can't even stay on Blackrabbit. You're too close to that gorilla, Vince. Nowhere on this island is safe for me, now. I'm going to have to go to the mainland. Look at all the trouble the bracelet has caused, Felix! It's cursed. The longer either of us has it, the greater danger we're in. Now—give it over." He held his hand out.

"Let me get him out first."

"Don't make me do it." Mr Sparrow tightened his grip on the lighting pole.

"I have no guarantee you won't submerge him again once you have it," Felix said. "I can hardly run away, not with him in that condition. Let me get him out; then I'll give you the bracelet."

"But Mr Diamond, you have my word." Mr Sparrow

moved to turn the pole.

The deep waters lapped at the shore. Felix weighed the box in his hands.

"Don't," Mr Sparrow said.

"Don't what?"

"Don't throw it into the sea. I'm not so far gone as to dive in after it. I'll simply drown your uncle, then come ashore and batter you to death."

The look in his eye left no doubt in Felix's mind that he meant what he said. However, if he could coax Mr Sparrow into coming ashore, Felix could pull the baton from his coat and attack him with it. He could keep hitting until he was unconscious. But then what? Roll him into the sea and let him drown? Hardly. Felix was no killer. He could tie him up, help Uncle Gregory back to the Star, then get Vince? Yes, that would do it. That would make sense. Mr Sparrow needed to face justice for his crimes. It galled Felix to think of Mr Sparrow taking the bracelet and getting away with what he'd done. But *how* could he lure Mr Sparrow out of his boat? What could he possibly offer him? Felix's throat ran dry and his stomach heaved. Nothing. He had nothing to offer. He tossed the box over to Mr Sparrow.

Mr Sparrow caught it and immediately opened the box. "I honestly expected it to be empty." He took the bracelet out and checked it over.

"I thought about it," Felix said. "But you'd have to be incredibly stupid not to check the box before letting me go."

Mr Sparrow slipped the bracelet into his pocket and dropped the box into the sea. He raised his anchor and took up the oars. He left the lighting pole in place, sticking out of the water and still connected to some unseen mechanism. Oars in hand, he pulled his boat from the cove, to the open sea.

Felix dashed into the cramped and unlit submersible, almost slipping on the wet floor. "Hold tight, Uncle Gregory, I'm here, I'm here." He pulled off the hood from the figure tied to the chair. His heart sank to his feet. "Iron? I don't... How are you here?" He removed the cloth gag from Iron's mouth and untied his hands and legs. "What happened? Are you hurt? How did he get you?"

"He came to my workshop," Iron said. "He told me he'd changed his mind about the automation of the street lamps." He rubbed his wrists, still red from the bindings. "When I turned my back he hit me. There was someone else with him. Someone big."

"Ms Underhay, most likely," Felix said. "Oh, Iron, I'm so sorry, you shouldn't have been dragged into this. I never thought... I never meant..." He steadied himself against the curved wall of the submersible and gripped his chest. His heart thumped harder than ever before. His stomach churned like the worst winter squall, and he realised his hands had turned numb. He crouched, trying to control his trembling. He knew what was coming, and he knew how to control it, but his mind wouldn't let him. Iron was speaking, shouting, but Felix couldn't hear him properly.

Thoughts slipped out of reach, the lantern dropped from his grip, and he fell to his hands and knees. His breathing grew shorter and shorter. He tried desperately to reach for his lifeline, his refrain. "It is...it...it is the waves which break—not I. Not I." He repeated it over and over, he shouted it as loudly as he could, his voice echoing through the submersible. At last, his breathing steadied. He stood, aware the numbness in his hands came now from pressing them on the wet floor. "I'm... I'm sorry. I'm sorry...that shouldn't have happened. Not in front of you. Not now."

Iron held him as tightly as he could. "It's fine; don't worry. You..."

"No!" Felix said. "No, you're the one he took; you're the one who suffered. I have no right to..."

"You feel the way you feel," Iron said. "You are at the mercy of your mind and body as are we all."

Felix took Iron under one arm and helped him limp out of the submersible and onto the slippery rocks. In the low morning light, Mr Sparrow raised his sail and drifted off, away from Blackrabbit, forever.

The going back through the narrow smuggler's tunnels was difficult. Iron was soaking wet from the waist down, likely from when Mr Sparrow and Ms Underhay moved him from the boat to the submersible. He was also weak from his injury and stumbled as they walked. By the time they reached the cellar of the Star We Sail By, Iron had started to shiver uncontrollably. Felix called up through the hatch to Dahlia and Mr Tassiter for help. It took some doing, but they got him to a chair by the crackling fireplace.

"Where did he come from?" Mr Tassiter asked.

Ms Stock and some other customers gathered around.

"He must have been in the tunnels," one said.

"I thought the tunnels were meant to be a secret," said another.

"Get back," Felix said. "Give the man some air. And get his boots off." He went to fetch some water from a jug.

"His boots? Why?" Mr Tassiter worked at the buckles on Iron's shoes. He pulled one free, almost losing it to the fire.

Felix gave the water to Iron, who gulped it down. "His stockings too."

Mr Tassiter did as he was asked. "I don't see the need for all this fuss."

Felix took one of Iron's broad feet in his lap and dried it with a rag from the bar. He worked his thumbs into the sole, causing Iron to moan a little. "Wet stockings are no laughing matter," Felix said. "I've seen some awful things happen to feet kept wet for too long. Dahlia, could you please fetch some blankets from upstairs? Iron, did you lose consciousness at all?" Felix looked into Iron's eyes and made him watch his finger as he moved it from side to side. "Ship's cooks have to pitch in with the medical needs of the crew. I've treated a lot of head injuries in my time. I think you'll be fine." He held a damp rag to Iron's forehead. "This is my fault."

"I knew you'd say that." Iron clamped his hand around Felix's wrist. "The whole time I was tied up in there, in the tank I made for your uncle, I was thinking about how you'd blame yourself. But listen. Listen to me, Felix—you didn't do this to me. Jason Sparrow did."

"Did he... Did he mention Uncle Gregory?"

Iron shook his head. Felix's mind started to spin and his stomach heaved. He jumped when the front doors of the Star clattered open. A red-faced Vince barged in and demanded to know what had happened.

"I'm glad to see you," Felix said. "We need to pay a visit to Ms Underhay."

CHAPTER THIRTY-SIX

ON THE WAY to Ms Underhay's home, Felix filled Vince in on the goings-on at Chancewater.

"Should have known about the submersible," Vince said. "Sort of thing I used to know about."

"I don't think people are going to be lining up to tell you about things like that any longer," Felix said.

They had stopped off at the Watch House to pick up some reinforcements. Flowers, Sorcha, and Crabmeat trailed behind them. Vince had wanted to go alone, but Felix said they ought to have other Watchfolk present for safety, though the truth was he didn't trust Vince not to lose control.

Vince knew that Ms Underhay lived in a small house on the other side of Pudding Quarter. He banged on the front door so hard it popped a hinge and rattled open. They found Ms Underhay in her kitchen, stuffing some belongings into a case. In a flash, she threw the case at Vince and darted for the back door, but Vince bounded after her and caught her by the arm.

He dragged her back to the taupe-walled kitchen and all but threw her into a chair. "Know about you and Sparrow. Stabbed you in the back, he did."

Ms Underhay fixed her dark hair in place. "And it takes, what, four of you to arrest me? How many did it take to get Sparrow?"

Felix's posture shifted, involuntarily.

"Oh, you didn't get him, did you?" she asked. "What happened? Where is he?"

"He escaped," Felix said.

Ms Underhay slapped her thewy hands together. "Hah, good for him! Good. For. Him."

"It speaks well of you that you can be so happy for him," Felix said. "You know he isn't coming back for you though? He was never coming back for you."

Her smug expression flickered. "What are you talking about?"

Felix kicked the case on the floor. "You packed your belongings for nothing, Ms Underhay. Jason Sparrow's on his way to Cornwall. I watched him sail away."

Vince grunted. "Thought you were brighter than that."

Ms Underhay's lip curled into a snarl.

Sorcha laughed in Ms Underhay's face. "He took the bracelet with him, ye trusting amadán! I assume you were expecting a cut of the profits?"

Ms Underhay bristled under their scorn. "I never really expected him to honour the bargain. I can't blame him. I wasn't going to either. As soon as we had the bracelet, I planned to push him under the nearest horse and cart. But the important thing is he got the better of the Watch! And you most of all, Vince. My my." She shook her head and tutted, looking him up and down. "What they say is true. You *are* slipping. You *have* gone soft."

"Lucky for you," Vince said. "Else you'd be headed for the graveyard instead of the magistrates."

Felix clenched his teeth, his whole body tense. "Where is Uncle Gregory?"

"He was here," she said, nodding towards the back of

her house. "For a while. He refused to answer Sparrow once too often. Sparrow lost control and hit him over the head with that lighting pole of his."

A lump formed in Felix's throat. His eyes stung. "Where is he now?"

"I don't think you'll want to see him," she said. "Not in the state he's in."

FELIX AND THE Watch followed Ms Underhay to the docklands and out along a pier, waves lapping at its posts. At that time of year, the harbour was quiet with just a few ships docked for the night, bobbing and swaying on the morning tide.

Ms Underhay carried a Davy Light and took them to where she hung her lobster pots over the edge of the pier. She took one thick, grimy rope and heaved. Her foot slipped. "You could help, you know."

Vince took the end of the rope and pulled. Felix's chest tightened as though it were trying to crack its own ribs. Gulls circled overhead, and one even landed on a post, ready to make a play for whatever came out of the water. Vince and Ms Underhay both heaved, hand over hand, until something broke the water's surface. They pulled up onto the slippery pier a lobster pot as large as a travel trunk.

Felix turned away, certain he would vomit. Sorcha put her arm around his shoulders. Stuffed inside the pot was the bloated and lifeless body of his uncle Gregory.

"You're disgusting," Flowers said.

"Fish have to eat," Ms Underhay said with a shrug. "There's no sense in him going to waste. I was going to leave him there till he was just bones. It's easier to get rid of bones. Ground them up, burn them... Use them for glue, for paint... There's lots of things you can do with bones, you know."

Crabmeat approached the lobster pot and sniffed it until Vince shooed him away.

"How did you get him in there without anyone seeing?" Flowers asked.

Ms Underhay held her arms wide. "Look around you. There's hardly anybody about this time of morning and the nights are even quieter. A handful of packet ships coming and going, perhaps, but their schedules are far too tight for them to pay much notice to anything going on around them. And do you know what no people means? It means no lanterns. You can get away with anything in this town if you wait till after sundown." She looked Vince up and down. "But then I'm not telling you anything you don't already know, am I? Sparrow and I had no trouble. Of course, he was angry at Gregory for dying. Sparrow wanted to use him to get the bracelet."

Vince straightened up and puffed out his chest. "Sparrow roped you into this?"

"Oh yes," Ms Underhay said. "It had all been his idea. He knew Gregory and I were screwing. He came to me here at the pier one day and told me Gregory had something very valuable that belonged to him. He said he needed my help to get it. He'd been injured at sea. Something to do with his spleen or his kidneys—I don't know—I wasn't listening. He said if I helped him get it, he'd give me half what the bracelet was worth when he sold it."

Felix drew heavy breaths. "And that's all it took to betray the man you were...intimate with?"

"I've had better," Ms Underhay said. "And Sparrow assured me he could get us both a lot of money."

"What did you do?" Flowers asked.

"I went to the Star, in through the back door. I didn't want anyone to see me. Gregory came downstairs, and I told him what was going on. I told him the lamplighter was coming to get him."

"You betrayed both of them?" Felix asked.

"Gregory was more of a coward than people think. His family were scared of him, but I never understood why. Nonetheless, he saw Sparrow going about his duties at sunset and panicked. He threw everyone out of the bar and locked the place up tight. I told him I'd keep him safe, told him he should come to me when he was ready.

"Sparrow tells me Gregory wrote you a letter, Felix. He must have done it before he came to my house because when he did arrive, he found me and Sparrow waiting for him. We tied him up, made him tell us about the bracelet, about where he'd hidden it. We didn't have the key, which was a problem. Tearing the sailboat balcony apart wasn't really an option. Not without drawing an awful lot of atten-tion, and so we waited.

"Then you showed up," she pointed to Felix. "Spar-row read about the show in the Courant and told me to be at the Star that night. We saw our chance when Felix handed the key over to you, Vince. I kept you distracted while Sparrow, pretending to be drunk, staggered past and stole the key from your pocket. Straight after, Sparrow went outside to the privy and slipped out the back gate. After closing time, he climbed up the outside of the Star. All those pipes make it so easy. As long as they're not piping hot, of course.

"He was so scared when that mangy animal of yours barked he snapped the key in the lock. I laughed when he told me, I must say. He's terrified of dogs. Did you know? Bad luck you happened to have one with you."

"The curse of the bracelet strikes again," Felix said. "Why did you drag Iron into this?"

"Who? Oh, the clockworker? Is that his name? Sparrow said we needed some leverage. We'd both seen you two making eyes at each other the night of the show, so he seemed like our best option. We thought about taking your cousin, Dahlia, but honestly we weren't convinced you'd care if anything happened to her."

The skin on Felix's face tingled, and he knew he was blushing. He didn't like it, but she was right.

Vince grabbed her by the arm. "Coming with me to the magistrates. Flowers, get to the undertakers. Sorcha, wait here till they arrive. Guard...him." He nodded to the body of Uncle Gregory. "Felix. Need any...?"

Felix held up his hand. "All I need is to go home."

CHAPTER THIRTY-SEVEN

VINCE WALKED INTO his office to find Sorcha in his chair with her feet up on his desk. Crabmeat sat by her side, her hand resting on his head. Crabmeat wagged his tail and waddled over to greet him as he shook off his damp overcoat and hung it on a hook. He cast his tricorne onto a hatstand and warmed his hands by the little fireplace.

"I just got back from a meeting with the council," Sorcha said.

"Promoted you to Commander, did they?" Vince stood at his desk with his hands on his wide hips.

Sorcha frowned before realising what he meant. She swung her skinny legs down and got out of his chair.

"Bad news?" Vince asked.

"No, quite the opposite." She found another chair and dragged it to his desk. "They read the article in the Blackrabbit Courant about how Mr Sparrow and Ms Underhay were able to move the body of Gregory Diamond unseen through the streets. They came to the conclusion that had there been street lamps, someone might have spotted what they were up to. The council want to extend the lamps throughout the whole town."

Vince took over the petting of Crabmeat. "Don't look happy about it. What you wanted, isn't it?"

"It is, and I am happy."

"Tell your face."

She stuck her tongue out at him and crossed her arms, sinking back in her chair.

He sank heavily into his seat. "Talk."

Sorcha huffed and squirmed.

"Don't make me order you. Be wildly uncomfortable for both of us."

"It's Jason Sparrow," she said.

"Thought it might be."

"I should have seen it coming. I should have seen what kind of man he really was."

Vince stuck out his bottom lip. "Couldn't have. No one could."

"I was working side by side with him, and I hadn't a clue what he was really up to!" She jumped to her feet and paced around the little office. "How does that make me look? Like an incompetent eejit, that's what. I'm just so angry. I'm...I'm..."

"Disappointed," Vince said, "with yourself."

She stopped dead in her tracks. "You're right. Exactly. Ah, Vince, if I'd known—if I'd spotted the signs, then maybe Gregory Diamond would still be alive."

"Maybe." Vince leaned his forearms on his desk. "Maybe you could have stopped Sparrow. Maybe you could have saved Gregory Diamond. Maybe Sparrow would have killed you too. Maybe Sparrow would have panicked; killed Tenner. Killed Iron Huxham. No way to know." He looked at her and tried to smile. "Maybes will eat you alive, Sorcha. Need to find a way to keep them from your door."

She flopped into her chair and idly flicked through the papers on Vince's desk. "How do you do it?"

"Good drink first. Good screw after."

Sorcha couldn't help but laugh. "So vulgar. It's beyond me why I talk to you at all."

"Go out with friends," Vince said. "Iron. Felix. Whoever. Go see people your own age."

"Flowers is my age."

"Flowers is a watchman," Vince said, crossing his hands on his desk. "Important to have people outside the work. People with other experiences. Other perspectives. Stops you from wallowing. From being consumed by one way of life and tricked into thinking it's the only way."

"And who do you have outside the work? On Blackrabbit, I mean?"

Vince grunted. "Got a brother on Merryapple I can turn to, if need be. Got a bottle of whiskey in my top drawer that really understands me too." He stopped and took a little breath. "Did a good job, my girl. Lamps will make the town safer. Done something to be proud of, there. Something worth celebrating." Sorcha stood up and fixed a stray lock of hair into place behind her ear. "Maybe you're right. Oh, there's another one. Those maybes, they just creep up on you, don't they? Will you come out tonight for a drink? I'm thinking the Star We Sail By might be good? I'm sure Felix could use some support too."

Vince picked up a report from Flowers and started reading. "Don't need an old man around when you're trying to celebrate."

"I do need my friends around me though."

Vince tried not to smile. "Will try to stop by."

DAHLIA SAT ON the edge of the stage wrapped up in an obscene amount of shimmering blue taffeta. It lay about her in rolls, like a waterfall. "I can't believe he's really dead."

Felix stopped sweeping and leaned on the brush. "You said he was, all along."

"I know but I... To have it confirmed. It's different. Before, his being dead was an idea. Something to be held and observed, looked at and teased into various shapes. Now it's a fact and there's nothing more to be done with it. Gregory is dead." She gathered more of the material about her. It slipped from her bare, milky white shoulders. "I worry we'll be lost without him. Without the Star. The

Diamonds never stay anywhere too long—we get evicted or run out of our homes. But Gregory and the Star have always been there. No matter what happened to us all we could always come here. I know he had his rules, he didn't like us drinking here, gathering here, but if we needed a place to sleep—really, truly needed it—he welcomed us in. He couldn't conscience the notion of a Diamond without a roof over their head. Without that, without him, what will become of us? We could be scattered to the four winds."

Felix brushed up a pile of dirt into a pan. "There are plenty of people in this town who would celebrate if we were."

"All the more reason to fight against it."

"Fighting," Felix said. "The thing Diamonds do best."

Dahlia slapped her hands on the stage and leaned forward. "That's something you've never understood, Felix. You always thought we spent all of our time fighting amongst ourselves, and maybe we do argue, and maybe things do get out of hand from time to time, but the real fight is against everyone else. For all times the family has fallen out with one another, we've made up. For all the times we've stormed off, we always, always come back. Because we're family. It's always been the Diamonds versus the world. Even you. It took time, I admit, but here you are. Back again. And why? Because your uncle needed you. Because your family needed you. So stop acting as though you're above the rest of us. You're a Diamond. And like it or not, you always will be."

IRON ENTERED THE bakery and found Mrs Farriner chatting with Vince Knight.

"Well, you look in fine form today, Mr Huxham," she said. "Your usual?"

Iron nodded. "Commander Knight, good to see you. Mrs Farriner, I have some good news." He took his bread from her and handed over some coins. "As of this morning, I am now a Journeyman Cogsmith. And Mr Williams heard from someone who heard from someone who heard from the council that they're extending the street lamps to the whole town. Mr Williams admitted the lamps were a good idea and has decided to officially hand over the business to me. From next week, *Williams Clockworkings* will become *Huxham Horological.*"

"Oh, what wonderful news!" She hurried around from the counter and kissed Iron on the cheek. It meant a good deal more to him than he would have imagined. "I'm very proud of you. Is that a silly thing to say?"

"Not at all, Mrs Farriner. Not at all," Iron said, staring at the floor.

"Hope you'll be celebrating," Commander Knight said. "Big achievement. Should be very proud."

"Oh, ah, yes, yes, I suppose I should," Iron said. "I haven't really... I've only just found out, and my head is still in the clouds."

"Spoken to Sorcha today?"

"No, not yet. I want to tell her the good news."

"Said she'll be at the Star tonight. Tell her then. Assuming it's open."

"Oh, I will, yes. Thank you, Commander Knight."

Commander Knight gripped his tricorne cap, squeezing it and turning it. "Thought it might have been you, you know."

Iron blinked hard, over and over. "You thought what might have... You thought I had something to do with Gregory Diamond's murder?"

"Crossed my mind," Commander Knight said. "Knew

you didn't get on with him. Knew he stole from you. Knew you had a weapon like the one used on Tenner."

Iron thought back to the day Commander Knight and Flowers came to the workshop. "You mean the first lighting pole I made?"

Commander Knight nodded. "Took me a while to realise what caused the welts on Tenner's arm. Thought about it and realised it couldn't have been you. Pole you had rattled like a bag of spoons falling down the stairs. Tenner would have heard it a mile off. Sparrow had the only other one like it. Meant he had to be involved. Went to check his room at Ms Hornby's house."

"What did you find?"

"Nothing."

Mrs Farriner crossed her arms. "So how did you know he was definitely involved, then?"

"Because," Commander Knight said. "Found nothing. Clothes gone. Shoes gone. Belongings gone. Sparrow wasn't going back there." He put on his tricorne cap. "Been around awhile. Know what it looks like when someone's going on the run. Regret not figuring it out sooner. Might have spared Felix the fright of meeting Sparrow. Might have spared you the kidnapping."

Iron rubbed the back of his own head. "Don't worry, there was no harm done. Apart from a bruise and a bit of a scare."

"Speaking of which," Mrs Farriner said, with a knowing smile and a tilt of her head, "have you told your fancy man yet?"

Iron's cheeks grew hotter. "Not, ah, not yet, no. And he isn't my... I mean we haven't really spoken about it."

"Some things don't need to be said, lad." Commander Knight clasped his massive hand on Iron's shoulder as he made for the door. "Hester, good seeing you." He turned sideways to leave and shuffled off down the road.

CHAPTER THIRTY-EIGHT

CUSTOMERS FLOCKED INTO the Star that evening. Drawn by rumours of a grisly discovery at the pier, some had come to learn the lurid details surrounding Gregory Diamond's death, some had come to offer their condolences to Felix and Dahlia, but most had come expecting another show. Felix found himself pulled from pillar to post, serving drinks with Ms Hornby, clearing tables with Dahlia, preparing food in the kitchen, and fielding questions about when the next show would be happening.

"I've got a nephew who'd love to perform," said a tipsy Ms Stock. "'E asked me to let you know 'e's available whenever you need 'im." Her weather-beaten complexion had turned a deeper shade of red from the gin she'd been consuming all evening. "And did I tell you? 'E's letting me stay with 'im and 'is wife. Lovely couple, they are, absolutely lovely. Well, just between you and me, she likes a drink. Bit of an 'andful at times, she is, but you didn't 'ear it from me."

Felix nodded along. "What does he do, your nephew?"

"'E's a thingummy, you know. What's it called? Oh, it's on 'is lap, all stiff, and 'as a funny 'ead on it?"

Felix's head flinched as though a wasp had just barrelled past his eyes. "What? Oh, you mean he's a ventriloquist?"

"That's the one!" Ms Stock said. "A ventrilikissed. 'E's got this little wooden boy, and oh, it says the most awful things!" She tittered then, like a schoolgirl. "The bluest language you ever did 'ear. I don't know where 'e gets it from. Where would a puppet learn language like that, do you suppose?"

Felix bit the inside of his cheek. "I'm sure I don't know. But tell your nephew I may well be in touch."

When things had quietened down a little, Felix took a chair and joined Iron and Sorcha's table.

Sorcha reached over and held his forearm. "How are you doing?"

"About as well as can be expected," Felix said. "Staying busy helps."

"You're in luck tonight, so," Sorcha said. "Plenty to keep you distracted."

Just then, the front doors opened and two men dressed in slops and leather jerkins stalked in. The hairs on the back of Felix's neck stood on end.

"I've seen them somewhere before..." Iron said.

The two men dashed through the bar, wielding bludgeons they pulled from their overcoats. In a flash, one of them grabbed Dahlia by the arm. The other raised his club above his head, but before he could bring it down, Felix propelled himself at the man's waist, tackling him to the floor. The man quickly recovered and kicked Felix off, but not before Felix landed a solid punch to the man's pockmarked nose. It popped beneath his fist.

Dahlia stamped on her assailant's foot while Sorcha smashed a chair over his back. Dahlia pulled the bludgeon from his grip and whacked him on the shins, eliciting a howling scream from him.

"Should have gotten here earlier." Vince, in his

Watch uniform and cap, filled the doorway. His slobbering dog snarled by his side. He clicked his fingers, sending
the animal darting towards the attackers.

A couple of customers hastily finished their drinks
and slipped outside as soon as they could.

Vince marched over and grabbed the man with the
broken nose who was desperately trying to get away from
Crabmeat. With his other hand, Vince clutched the howling man by the shirt. He dragged them both out from the
bar, into the hallway, and threw them against the dingy
stairwell.

Felix dusted himself off. "Don't worry, everyone. Just
a minor misunderstanding. Please, stay and enjoy a free
drink. Ms Hornby, if you would?"

He joined Vince, Dahlia, and the attackers in the hallway. Iron hesitated by the hallway door, ready to stop anyone from coming through. Vince had both of the assailants
by the throat. In the low light, with his hefty overcoat and
his tricorne casting a deep shadow across his face, he was
every bit the monster Felix had always imagined him to be.
His hands, big as dinner plates, held fast to the men. Their
eyes wept and bulged, their faces turning a shade of purple.
Crabmeat stood and snarled the whole time. Finally, Vince

let the men drop to their knees on the floorboards. "Bad idea to do this sort of thing in a busy alehouse. Never know who might be in."

"Don't give them tips!" Felix said, running his hands through his own wavy hair. "And it's a playhouse!"

Vince glared at him before turning back to the men. "Explain."

The man with the broken nose found it hard to speak and kept his wide eyes firmly fixed on Crabmeat.

The other man piped up. "Here for her." He pointed to Dahlia. "How long did you think you were going to get away with not paying your debts?"

Vince put his hands on his hips. "Marwood sent you. Didn't think he'd stoop this low. Attacking an unarmed woman."

"It's just business," the man said.

Vince leaned down, causing the man to fall back on his heels. "Just business? Fine. Tell Marwood. Watch gets wind of anything like this happening again, his opium den gets shut down. By me. Personally. Understand?"

Dahlia dashed forward and kicked the man's leg. "That'll teach you."

Vince gently brushed her back, away from the man.

Crabmeat barked loudly.

The man was unable to stop his lips from quivering. "Wh-what about the money?"

Vince stared at Dahlia. "Has a point. Den is perfectly legal. Provided you a service. Money has to be paid. However... Think Dahlia is owed some compensation for tonight. Half should cover it."

"*Half?*" The man with the broken nose found his voice at last. Blood had soaked into his beard.

"Half," Vince said. "Marwood can take Dahlia to court for the rest of it."

Vince called for Sorcha to escort the men out of the bar. He sent Crabmeat along for extra protection. He said he thought about throwing them into the Watch House cells for the night but reasoned they'd make more of an impact on Marwood if they returned to him before they'd gotten a chance to clean up and compose themselves. "Courts will work out a payment plan," he told Dahlia. "Something fair for both of you and Marwood. Will make sure of it. Best I can do, under the circumstances. Now, anybody got any injuries?"

"Nothing. Just a couple of scratches," Felix said.

Dahlia hugged herself tightly. "Mr Marwood offered

to buy the Star for far less than it's worth. He said if I agreed, he'd clear my debt."

"The offer was an insult," Felix said. He held her arm lightly. "If you keep going there, you'll never pay him off."

She tapped his hand. "I know. I've been thinking about it a lot. I am going to stop."

Felix tilted his head.

"Well, I'm going to try to stop," Dahlia said with a shrug. "I'm only human."

Felix laughed and hugged her waist. "If there's anything I can do, just ask."

Iron approached her. "Can I get you anything? Are you sure they didn't injure you?"

She shook her head. "I've been meaning to apologise for the way I spoke to you that day in the Entry."

Iron dipped his chin into his chest. "Think nothing of it. You were under a great deal of pressure."

"You're much too nice to get involved with a Diamond," she said. "Are you certain he's worth it?" She poked Felix in the ribs, making him giggle and blush.

"I intend to find out," Iron said.

With the assailants gone, Vince ordered some drinks at the bar and carried a tray of them to Sorcha and Iron's table.

"Thirsty, are you?" Sorcha asked.

Vince set the tray down, pulled up a chair, and removed his overcoat and tricorne. "Always. Got them for you all though." He nodded to Dahlia, asking her to join them.

He plonked down onto the chair, causing it to creak, and handed out the drinks. Crabmeat sat by Sorcha's side. She took some sausage from her stew and fed it to him. Dahlia took a low stool and joined them at the round table. Vince gave her a drink too.

Iron sniffed his glass and wrinkled his nose. "I don't usually drink whiskey."

"Don't worry," Felix said, "this looks like the good stuff from the top shelf, not the watered-down muck that I...definitely don't usually serve here." He laughed and shrugged while Sorcha playfully shoved his shoulder. "What can I say, Uncle Gregory taught me everything I know about being a taverner."

Vince rolled up the sleeves of his topshirt, revealing inked forearms as thick as Felix's legs—on one a tattoo of a mermaid lying seductively on some rocks, on the other a merman in a similar repose. "Sorcha. Wanted to congratulate you on the lamps. Did a good job there. Proud of you. Iron, don't know you very well yet. Probably won't mean much coming from me. But well done on finishing your apprenticeship."

Iron smiled at him. "Thank you kindly, Commander Knight."

"Call him Vince," Sorcha said. "That's what you were going to say, isn't it?"

Vince nodded. "Felix. Faced some tough days recently. Did it with pride. Did it with dignity. Will have some tough days ahead. But you'll get through them too."

Felix set his hands on the table. Hearing those words coming from Vince, of all people, blindsided him. More so, because Felix could tell he really meant them.

Vince cleared his throat. "Feel like I owe you an apology. Both you and Iron. Should have found Sparrow before he got to you."

Iron sat up straighter and blinked over and over again. "Oh, it's not... I don't... I don't blame you if that's what you're thinking?"

"Nor do I," said Felix.

"Nobody knew what he was up to," Iron said. "He had us all fooled."

"Different for me," Vince said. "Not your responsibility to stop killers like Sparrow." He rubbed his own thigh. "Still new to this. Being a watchman."

"I've been with the watch longer than you," said Sorcha. "We've never operated like this before. It's new to everyone. We've all got a lot to learn, I'd say. And didn't you tell me not to blame myself earlier today? So you get to do it, but I don't?"

"Privilege of rank," Vince said with the tiniest of grins. His whole comportment changed when he smiled, and for the first time, Felix could understand what attracted Iron to him.

Felix held up his glass. "If you can forgive me for whacking you over the head with a baton, I can forgive you for not catching Jason Sparrow."

Iron, Sorcha, Dahlia, and Vince all clinked their glasses above the table.

"Wait," Sorcha said, "you did what?"

Felix finished his drink. "Didn't he tell you about it?"

"I'm certain I would have remembered."

Dahlia wiggled her shoulders. "Tell us every little detail!"

Vince drained his glass and stood, then put on his

overcoat. "Leave you to fill them in. Look after Crabmeat tonight, will you?"

"Sure you're only after getting here, where are you off to now?" Sorcha asked.

"Had a good drink," he said. "Off to the cherry house for the rest."

Sorcha laughed as he gave her a little salute and headed for the door.

Felix frowned. "What do you mean?"

"Never mind," Sorcha said with a giggle. "What's this about you hitting him over the head?"

The four of them sat and drank for the rest of the night, swapping stories. At times when it became busy enough for Felix to help Ms Hornby, he found himself watching the table of his new friends. Watching them laugh and tease one another. Most of all, he watched Iron. The way he waited politely for someone to speak to him, his broad, warm smile, the way his shoulders heaved when he laughed. Every now and then, Iron would catch him watching, and it would make Felix's heart flutter. The Star We Sail By had been the one place from his past that he'd never wanted to return to, but it might just be where he'd find his future.

CHAPTER THIRTY-NINE

IT DRIZZLED ON the morning of Gregory Diamond's funeral, enough to coat Felix's clothes with a fine mist. He and the Diamond clan had gathered at the little graveyard between the Star and the cliff edge. Dick Tassiter stood close to the graveside. Ms Hornby attended, though she kept her distance, choosing to stand by the low stone wall next to Iron, Vince, and Sorcha.

As far as Felix could tell, every Diamond who was on Blackrabbit—and not presently resident in the gaolhouse—attended. He recognised some aunts and uncles he hadn't seen since he was a boy in the company of few unfamiliar faces. The poor wretches they'd handfasted and dragged into the Diamond clutches, he assumed.

The family stood beneath the sprawling branches of the solitary yew tree while a veiled Aunt Alma, clad in a fuchsia gown patterned with eight long, embroidered tentacles descending from the bottom of her tangerine bodice and curling at the hem, recited a few words about the childhood she and Uncle Gregory had shared. About the importance of family. Of the strength of a blood bond. Felix paid no heed to her. It was no more than he expected from her. Instead of celebrating the life of her brother, she seized the opportunity of a captive audience to tighten her grip over the family as a whole. He felt sorry for the younger cousins, the children, the ones who would be wholly taken in by her rhetoric and swallowed up by the Diamond family lifestyle.

"No matter what differences he and I had," she said, "he was a guiding light for the Diamond family. A permanent fixture, or so it seemed to us. There's hardly one of us present who didn't rely on him at one time or another. The doors to the Star may have appeared closed to us, but they would open when we really needed them to. It is my fondest wish they remain open now that he has passed. It is, I believe, what he would have wanted."

The ceremony culminated in the placing of Gregory's gravestone. Like all the others, the stone was a sphere, a little planet orbiting the larger stone with the names of the Diamond family ancestors engraved upon it. Nobody knew for certain if the people named were actually buried there, but they represented the noble lineage to which the Blackrabbit Diamonds belonged. Gregory's stone read *In honour of Gregory Diamond. He was the star so many of us sailed by. April 1739 - December 1781.*

Dahlia might well have been the only one to shed a tear at the graveside. She had lived with him longer than anyone else. Felix put his arm around her shoulders and held her close. As the family began to disperse, Felix spoke up. "I would like to invite you all back to the Star. For one last drink to the memory of Uncle Gregory."

As the mourners filed across the field and lane towards the backyard of the Star, Felix crouched by the gravestone. He laid his hand upon the engraving. "I'm sorry I didn't find you sooner. I'm sorry I left the way I did. I never got the chance to say... I..." Waves of burning heat and bone-chilling coldness washed over him in equal measure. His breathing became laboured, and he dropped to his knees, eyes stinging with tears. "You were the closest thing I had to a father, and I never said I was sorry. And now I'll never have the chance."

Dahlia laid her hand on his shoulder. "He talked about you often," she said. "He used to give the rest of us a dressing down any time we made a mistake. *Why can't you make something of your life like your cousin Felix? Why don't you get proper work, like Felix?* He held you up as his greatest success. He was proud of you."

BEFORE THE FUNERAL, Felix had set out every glass and tankard in the bar. The mourners milled in through the back door and found the tables heaving. As the family took their seats, puzzled by the way Felix had chosen to prepare, Felix himself walked among them, pouring ale with one hand and gin with the other. Dahlia followed him with a bottle of whiskey and a bottle of rum.

By the closed front doors, the young bedworker, Rudyard, sat alone with a glass in his hand. Felix had invited him and, knowing full well Rudyard would have no desire to attend the funeral, told him he could help himself to anything from the bar. When everyone had their drink poured, Felix stood before the counter and raised his glass. "To Uncle Gregory."

The family all raised their drinks and joined in with the toast. When they were done, Felix threw his glass on the floor. It shattered into a thousand pieces. He reached behind the counter and withdrew a long crowbar. Some of the cousins jumped out of the their seats, ready to defend themselves. Felix took the crowbar and with every ounce of strength, he heaved it into the top of the bar. The bar split open and he tugged, tearing out huge chunks of wood. Dahlia produced a sledgehammer, borrowed from the cooperage across the road, and began whacking at the bar's supports. Within seconds, the pair of them had reduced it to kindling.

Felix took the crowbar to the empty shelves lining the wall, where the glasses and tankards had once been stored. "I hope you enjoyed those drinks," he said, "because they're the last we'll ever serve here. The Star We Sail By will never again be mistaken for an alehouse because it will simply no longer serve ale. Or rum, or whiskey, or gin, or any other kind of alcohol."

Dick Tassiter's saggy face dropped. He almost fell to his knees. "You can't do this to me, lad."

Aunt Alma had remained seated the entire time. She calmly pulled back her lace veil. "You've taken leave of your senses."

Felix ignored her. "If I'm going to be a Diamond—and I've recently been reminded that I have no choice in the matter—it will be on my own terms." He looked to Dahlia and smiled. "Upstairs will remain as a place for bedworkers to safely ply their trade. I won't be taking the so-called Diamond Cut, and neither will anyone else."

Rudyard, his legs crossed, cheered and held up his drink.

"The stage will be enlarged," Felix said, "and every night, the finest acts will perform, as well as those just starting out. I believe our Dahlia to have an exceptional voice, and I strongly encourage her to perform as often as she can. As often as she is able. And as often as she wishes. It will be a consistent way to earn money and pay off any outstanding debts. Should such a thing be necessary."

Dahlia, the sledgehammer over her shoulder, performed a short curtsy.

"Ms Hornby, of course, will be welcome here, if she

wishes to remain. And furthermore, to my cousins, I say this: the Star has played an important role in our lives. It isn't simply a place where our parents could dump us. It is an opportunity to see what life could be like. It offered us a way out. And so long as it remains in my hands, that's exactly what it shall always be.

"Uncle Gregory wanted the Star to be an anchor in the lives of the Diamond family, but he kept most of you at arm's length. For what might well be very good reasons, he didn't trust you, and so it pains me to say he was always doomed to fail. In his spirit, though, I make this offer. Should any of you need work—good, honest work—you will always find it here. Anyone willing to make an honest go at turning their lives around will find a place on the staff. However, I remind any of you who take me up on my offer with an eye toward causing trouble that I am on friendly terms with Vince Knight. Make of that what you will."

At the back of the room, Vince straightened his back, his face completely expressionless.

"Mr Tassiter, I'm very sorry for your loss. Perhaps I can put in a good word for you at the Salt Pocket or the Lion Lies Waiting?"

Dick's voice thinned to the point of breaking. "Won't

you reconsider?"

"The Star is mine," Felix said, "and I shall run it as I see fit."

Aunt Alma set down her glass, brushed her dress, and rose to her feet. Felix spread his weight, preparing for a verbal onslaught.

Instead she simply laid her hand on his shoulder, leaned down, and kissed him on the cheek. "You have some of the Diamond fire in you, after all," she said. "There's hope for you yet."

The cousins followed her out, with Clarity and Slate dawdling behind.

"I might just take you up on your offer," Clarity said. "And him too." She jabbed her thumb to Slate, who quickly nodded and looked to the door, afraid of being seen.

"You'd be very welcome to," Felix said.

The cousins slithered out the door to catch up with the rest of the family.

Tenner arrived back from the privy to find the rest of the family had left without him. He muttered under his breath, and he made for the front door.

"That's how little they think of you," Felix said to him

as he passed by.

Tenner paused and spun to stare Felix in the eye. "What did you say, Lucky?"

"It doesn't have to be like this," Felix said. "We used to get along when we were children."

"That was a long time ago. A lot has changed since then."

"There's no reason for you and me to fight," Felix said. "Whatever Aunt Alma says, we've never had reason to quarrel, have we?"

Tenner's jaw clicked as he ground his teeth. "Not directly."

"And indirectly?"

Tenner rocked on the balls of his feet. He turned this way and that, making for the door then changing his mind. "I thought we were going to be friends," he said. "When we were young, it was always you, me, and Dahlia. We did everything together. I thought I had a friend for life. Another brother. But then you left. You got out, and *I* was left behind. *I* had to pull your weight. They had plans for you, you know. Gregory, Alma, the others. They had plans for all of us. With you gone, I had to be the fighter. I had to be the one to take the lumps. And every time, every single time, someone landed a punch on me I'd think that was meant for Lucky. I'm nothing but Lucky's bleddy punching bag." He sniffed away a tear, angry at its very existence. "What makes you so damn special? What makes you think you had the right to turn your back on this family?" He gritted his teeth and sized up to Felix.

From the corner of his eye, Felix could see Vince clenching his fists, readying himself. "There's nothing special about me," Felix said, as calmly as he could. "I simply wanted more from my life. And you can have it too. I've been talking to Sorcha and Iron; the town needs more lamplighters. I suggested you."

Tenner's eyebrows squashed together. His hands fell open by his side.

"I had the chance of a different life, a better life, by going to sea. Now I get another chance with the Star," Felix said. "Dahlia has a chance with the stage, with her performances. Why shouldn't you have a chance as well? A chance to earn an honest living." He held up his hand for Tenner to shake. "Maybe this can be your way out."

Tenner stared at Felix's hand and then at the other people in the room. He leaned forward, as if to come closer to Felix, but instead, he turned and burst through the front door out into the road.

"He'll come round," Dahlia said. "Just give him some time."

Felix put his arm around Dahlia's waist and hugged her. "He's right, the three of us used to be inseparable. I'd forgotten that. He only lived here for a couple of years, but he felt like...like..."

"Like he belonged," Dahlia said. "Like he was the missing piece."

"Well, that was all frightfully tense," Rudyard said. "Mr Diamond, I look forward to getting back to the sailboat balcony."

"And I look forward to working with you," Felix said.

Rudyard gave him a friendly squeeze on the bum and winked at Iron on his way out.

Vince kicked some of the broken counter. "Hope you know what you're doing, lad."

Felix exhaled loudly. "I think I do. With no alcohol, Aunt Alma won't want to come here. The cousins won't want to either. They can't ply people with drink and rob them when they've had too much. They can't swindle people at cards without those looking glasses overhead. The Star is a playhouse. I'm just putting it back the way it always should have been."

"How can you afford to?" Sorcha asked. "I thought Gregory didn't leave any money?"

Felix looked around to make sure none of the family had returned. "Admiral Boon paid me a visit. She was concerned about what Jason Sparrow might have said to me. When I told her what he had revealed about... Well, never mind the details. Suffice it to say the admiral was keen for me not to tell the Blackrabbit Courant about it. So keen, in fact, she offered me quite a bit of money to keep it to myself."

"Isn't that blackmail?" Sorcha asked.

"No," Felix said. "It's business. And she did offer first. Besides, the greencoats can afford it."

Vince put his hands on his own hips. "Hope you like running a playhouse. Doubt you'll ever sail on a greencoat vessel again."

CHAPTER FORTY

THE SAILBOAT, STOLEN from the harbour, had seen better days but it had been the easiest to take. It rocked in the choppy waters of the Celtic Sea. Mr Jason Sparrow kept touching the gold cuff bracelet in his pocket over and over again. He would make for Mousehole, a tiny village on the Cornish coast. There he would find lodgings and rest before continuing on his journey east. He wanted to put as much distance between him and Vince as was reasonably possible.

The moon was barely a fingernail in the cloudy sky, attended by a lone star. In the pitch-black night, he had no other guidance, for there wasn't so much as a compass aboard, and his only illumination came from the Davy Light by his feet. He cursed himself for not thinking to bring any equipment, but then he hadn't planned very far ahead.

He knew he needed to get away from the island but hadn't thought much about what would happen with Felix Diamond. He expected Felix to cooperate; he was too much of a dullard not to. Which was just as well because had Felix brought Vince and the Watch with him, there was nothing Jason could have done. The Watch would have rescued the captive horologist, Jason would have been apprehended, and then both he and Ms Underhay would spent the rest of their lives in Blackrabbit Gaol-house.

Had Felix not realised Jason was the one who'd abducted his uncle Gregory, then Jason would have been happy to wait for a better chance to steal the bracelet. But that flash of recognition in Felix's eyes had escalated things. Jason had been forced to act—and forced to act quickly.

Once he'd left the Star, he'd rushed back to Ms Hornby's house to pack up his belongings. A quick word with Ms Underhay had led to them abducting Iron

Huxham, the horologist. Jason had seen him and Felix together the night of the show and reasoned Felix's affection towards him would be useful leverage. Ms Underhay had helped get Mr Huxham into the boat but refused to go any further. Jason had hoped to knock her into the sea at some point on the way around to Chancewater. She, instead, insisted on returning to her home for some belongings and would meet Jason back at the harbour where they would book passage on a vessel headed for the Americas. Clearly, she thought he wouldn't risk the open sea in the little stolen boat. How little she knew him.

As he wrapped his cloak tightly around himself to protect against the bitter night air, he wondered what would become of Ms Underhay. She would be arrested for her part in what had happened, he assumed. Perhaps she would try to blame it all on him, pretend as though she were just an innocent caught up in his schemes. It's what he would do in her shoes. He never planned to share so much as a single farthing with her.

The wind picked up, whipping the tattered old sails. Jason fought to hold the line. He should have been able to see a lighthouse by now but ahead lay nothing but unbroken darkness. The waves threw the little boat about, splashing over the sides and soaking his boots. He was moving more quickly than he realised. On and on the boat went, its sails heavy, and above him, the sole star his only guide. He touched the bracelet in his pocket once again. It would all be worth it when he sold the thing and started his new life.

With a thunderclap of splintering wood, he lurched forward, smacking his head against the mast before being thrown face first into the ice-cold sea. He gasped for air, kicked his legs, and reached upwards. A mighty wave caught him and flung him against sharp rocks, black as the night.

The bracelet slipped from his pocket, and he tried to grasp it in the inky wash. But he couldn't. Of course he couldn't. Lit by the sinking Davy Light, the bracelet whirled and spun away into the void. As he sank beneath the waves, for the final time, his lungs filling with saltwater, his only thought was of that damn bracelet. Of it gently landing on the soft sea bed. Of it basking in the glow of the lantern until the air inside ran out. Of it sleeping in the cold and lonely dark, slowly being buried by sand and by time.

WHEN THEY WERE alone, Felix bolted the door and invited Iron to join him on the sailboat balcony where he'd laid a little table and two chairs. All around the balcony, striker-lanterns burned. The early evening air was chilly but bearable.

"What's this?" Iron asked.

"It's been a long day," Felix said. "I thought you might be hungry." He pulled out a chair for Iron.

"I am famished, now you mention it," Iron said.

From underneath the table, Felix produced a blanket which he draped around Iron's shoulders. "Don't move," he said. "I'll be back in a moment." He kissed the top of Iron's head and hurried into the lift.

It shook and rattled the whole way down to the green-tiled kitchen. There he had left a pot of beef dripping simmering on the stove. He dropped into it a number of French bread rolls which he'd hollowed out to make bowls and filled with a mixture of shredded lobster, onion, parsley, and egg yolk. When the rolls had crisped, he scooped them out and plated them up.

Upon his return to the balcony, he found Iron tinkering with the star in Atlas's outstretched hands. "Here we go," Felix said.

Iron took his seat once more and gleefully tucked into his dinner. He sat back with his mouthful and groaned. "Amazing. Simply amazing. I hope you'll be serving this in the newly refurbished playhouse."

Felix laughed and took a forkful of lobster.

Iron cleared his throat. "If I may ask, how, ah, how are you coping?"

Felix tore a little of the bread bowl with his fingers. "I can't stop thinking about Uncle Gregory in that lobster pot. Oh. I didn't even..." He held up a forkful of lobster meat on the end of his fork. "Is this ghoulish? I honestly didn't make the connection until just now."

Iron smiled his kindest smile. "It's fine. Your head must be awash with the events of the past few days. It will take time to sort through it all."

Felix set his fork down again and sighed, inadvertently whistling through the gap between his front teeth. "When I close my eyes, he's all I can see. I can't stop thinking about him scribbling his letter to me, fearing for his life. A part of me keeps thinking I should feel guilty. I should feel that if only I'd stayed and never gone to sea in the first place this would never have happened. But I know that's nonsense. I couldn't have stayed. If I hadn't left ten years ago, it would have been nine years ago, or eight. I firmly believed my life wasn't supposed to happen within these walls. And now look." He held his arms wide and smiled. "Shows how much I know."

Iron stretched over and took his hand, rubbing it with his thumb. "We never really know how our lives will go. What would you have done with the bracelet? Sold it? It would have made your life a lot easier."

Felix licked his own lips. "I thought about taking it back to my parents."

"Whatever for? I thought they wanted nothing to do with you?"

"I know but I thought... I don't know. I thought bringing the bracelet back to them would...heal the rift, somehow?"

Iron smiled his perfect smile. "Break the curse, you mean."

"I suppose. It's silly."

"Are you still going to go back to see them?"

Felix considered it for a moment. "No," he said. "They don't want anything to do with me. There is little sense in pursuing that notion."

"I'm glad," Iron said. "I would miss you greatly. Not that I would have had much time to. Sorcha and I shall be working together a lot in the coming months. We have so many street lamps to make, and test, and approve. It's rather a lot of work, when I think about it. Not to mention the extra work I shall have as a journeyman..." He started blinking heavily and nibbling on his thumbnail.

Felix took his hand and held it. "Calm down...deep breaths...you'll be fine. Do you remember my refrain?"

They repeated the line together. "*It is the waves which break—not I.*"

"It does help, actually," Iron said. "Whoever would have believed it? Oh, look, I want to show you something."

He led Felix to the bow of the sailboat. There he reached over to the glass star, opened a hatch, and turned a key. Slowly, a flame flickered to life. He closed the hatch and with a great creaking, the glass star jerked to one side, then sluggishly started to turn, casting a shoal of light across Felix and Iron, and on the street below.

Despite the chill air, Felix's insides warmed. "I haven't

seen it shine since I was a child." He held up his hand, watching the coloured light swim across it—red, green, blue, purple, yellow—like a school of tiny glowing fish. "I want to apologise for falling to pieces in Chancewater. You needed me, and I let you down. I made the situation even worse."

Iron leaned his elbow on the balcony gunwale. He gazed out across the road. "There are people in this world who think that who we are in moments of weakness—the parts of ourselves we show at our lowest ebb—reveals who we really are. But if a clock falls and shatters into a pile of cogs, and springs, and pinions, that doesn't mean that's all it's ever been. Clocks can be repaired. And so can we."

With Iron's beautiful face illuminated by the star's cascading rainbow, Felix drew in close, kissing him. They embraced, hands grasping and arms squeezing.

Felix rubbed Iron's hand. "I worry about what will happen should Ms Underhay ever return."

"I doubt you'll have to worry about her," Iron said. "The magistrates sent her to the gaolhouse for a long time."

"If only the same could be said for her accomplice."

"Yes, what a legacy Mr Jason Sparrow has left behind.

The town's inaugural lamplighter. A thief, a kidnapper, and a murderer."

"And all because of one gold bracelet." Felix pulled Iron in close again. "It's almost enough to make one believe in curses."

ACKNOWLEDGEMENTS

I'd like to thank my amazing husband, Mark, for putting up with me disappearing into my own head for hours at a time, and my brilliant and supportive family and friends. Thanks as well to my beta readers, Tony Teehan and Christian Smith for their feedback: it's more useful and more appreciated than you'll ever know.

Special thanks go to my tireless and eagle-eyed editor, BJ Toth. My thanks also to my publisher, Raevyn McCann. And of course, thank you to Jaycee DeLorenzo @ Sweet & Spicy Designs for the gorgeous cover.

About Glenn Quigley

Glenn Quigley is an author and artist originally from Tallaght in Dublin, Ireland, and now living in Lisburn, Northern Ireland with his husband.

His first novel, *The Moth and Moon*, was published by NineStar Press in 2018. When not writing, he paints portraits in watercolours and pastels. He maintains a website of his latest work at www.glennquigley.com.

He has four novels to date—*The Moth and Moon, The Lion Lies Waiting, We Cry The Sea*, and *These Young Wolves: The Knights of Blackrabbit, Book One*—and a short story, *Use as Wallpaper*. His novella, *The Great Santa Showdown*, was included in the anthology: *2023 Top Ten Gay Romance*.

In 2022, he created a series of portraits based on characters from his *Moth and Moon* trilogy which were displayed in Kallio Library, Finland, and at a gay event in Estonia.

Email
glennquigley@gmail.com

Facebook
www.facebook.com/glennquigleyauthor

Twitter
@glennquigley

Bluesky

glennquigley.bsky.social

Instagram

@glennquigleyauthor

Moth and Moon Series
The Moth and Moon
The Lion Lies Waiting
We Cry the Sea

The Knights of Blackrabbit Series
These Young Wolves

Use as Wallpaper

Connect with NineStar Press

WWW.NINESTARPRESS.COM

WWW.FACEBOOK.COM/NINESTARPRESS

WWW.FACEBOOK.COM/GROUPS/NINESTARNICHE

WWW.TWITTER.COM/NINESTARPRESS

WWW.INSTAGRAM.COM/NINESTARPRESS

Milton Keynes UK
Ingram Content Group UK Ltd.
UKHW032020110224
437614UK00009BA/74

9 781648 907425